Heartseeker

Heartseeker

✳

MELINDA BEATTY

G. P. Putnam's Sons

G. P. Putnam's Sons
an imprint of Penguin Random House LLC
375 Hudson Street
New York, NY 10014

Library of Congress Cataloging-in-Publication Data
Names: Beatty, Melinda, author.
Title: Heartseeker / Melinda Beatty.
Description: New York, NY : G. P. Putnam's Sons Books for Young Readers, 2018.
Summary: "When the King hears that Only Fallow can see lies and only tells the truth, he
summons her, and she must learn to navigate the dangerous, political world of the King's court"
—Provided by publisher.
Identifiers: LCCN 2017041588 | ISBN 9781524740009 (hardback)
Subjects: | CYAC: Fantasy. | Courts and courtiers—Fiction. | Kings, queens, rulers, etc.—Fiction.
| Ability—Fiction. | Honesty—Fiction. | BISAC: JUVENILE FICTION / Fantasy & Magic. |
JUVENILE FICTION / Action & Adventure / General. | JUVENILE FICTION / Royalty.
Classification: LCC PZ7.1.B4342 He 2018 | DDC [Fic]—dc23
LC record available at https://lccn.loc.gov/2017041588

Printed in the United States of America.
ISBN 9781524740009
1 3 5 7 9 10 8 6 4 2

Design by Eileen Savage. Text set in Maxime Std.

⇥✳⇤

To the ladies who Order me around—
I love you all to Manayunk and back.

1

Call out, call out, you loud jays, you honey-throated sparrows!
Sing out the summer as it pours into the valleys,
Into the Hush, the Rill, the Lannock, and the Blue.
Cry warmth for the Sandkin plains,
For the Mollier vines.
Lift up your voices for gentle Dorvan tides
And cool Folque stone.
You sons and daughters of Orstral,
Join the chorus of the coming of the long light!

—Jylla Burris, poet, *Songs of Orstral*

Lies are beautiful.

But when we're small, "You mustn't lie" is near the first thing we're taught. I didn't understand Mama's and Papa's serious faces when they finger-wagged my brothers and said that lying about wrongdoing was even worse than doing the wrong itself. But then, no stern looks ever passed my way on the subject—of lies, that is. I knew from little that lies carried their own punishment and their own reward. Mama could always count on me to answer questions like "Who tracked in all this mud?"

or "Who broke the leg off the best dinner chair?" It wasn't that I *wanted* to tell her, but the truth always seemed to pour out before I could even think about fudging the story. Besides, saying anything other than the truth always ended with a dull thump behind my eyes. Not everyone could gasp like I could over the twinkling sparks or the colors that ringed bright halos round the liar, making the lie itself prettier than a summer sunset over the orchard. But I'd have given it all up in order to be able to tell one of my own.

I wasn't sure it was natural. The rector at sanctuary had always made plain his thoughts about unnaturalness. "Mother All sees you," he'd intone from the lectern, "and knows your heart. Seek out those things that are contrary to Her laws and push them far from you, lest you be corrupted by them." I knew well enough what corruption was. It was a blemish on the apple— the brown, mushy blight under the skin that spreads, making the fruit fit for nothing. So I kept my secret close, buried under my own skin, like the seeds at the apple's heart. But as my non says, "Seeds ain't ever content to stay seeds. Seeds grow roots to take what they need from the dirt so they can see the sunlight."

When I'd just about seen seven harvests, Jonquin came in from the orchard bruised, bloody, and covered in earth and the stink of rotten fruit. Mama was at the stove, apron still wrapped round the brown day dress that she wore at the bakery. My brother's entrance surprised her so much that she dropped the ladle into the soup. It was usually Ether who could be counted upon to wander in covered in Mother knows what. But Jon—the

Jon me and Ether got told we needed to be more like—wasn't one to come to dinner in such a state.

"What in the name of All happened to you?"

"Was climbing," he muttered, swallowing his words as if they'd had a bitter taste. "Fell out of Grandfather."

Ether was warned half a hundred times before breakfast not to venture too high into the tallest tree in the orchard, but long-legged Jon, who was thirteen and sure-footed as a squirrel, wouldn't be so clumsy. I couldn't help wondering what he was hiding with his eyes cast straight down to the floor.

A lapis-blue shimmer rippled around him, like the haze of a hot summer's day across an empty field. Ether told whoppers so often, he shone like a blacksmith's forge. He hadn't even got any shame left about it. But Jon did. And, oh, wasn't it *lovely*? I was so taken, I laughed out loud, dropping the pea pod I was shucking back into the basket between my knees. "Tell us another, Jon!"

Both my mother's and brother's head turned sharpish at me. They didn't half look alike, framed by the same ashen hair and peering with the same blue-gray eyes, though Mama's face was beset with puzzlement while Jon's was near murderous. I bit my tongue inside my mouth, trying to punish it for flapping when it should have been still. I wished I could've shrunk down to the size of a pea and dropped right into my own basket.

Mama gave him the hard eye, and her hands bunched on her hips in two tight circles. "Jonquin Fallow, have you been brawling? You think I don't know what it looks like when a boy falls out of a tree?" She caught him by the jaw, turning his face toward the kitchen window, revealing several fist-sized bruises on his cheek. "I'd expect this sort of nonsense from your brother, not you!"

Jon opened his mouth as if he was going to deny the whole thing, then thought better of it.

"It won't happen again," he growled, wiping a smear of bloody dirt from the corner of his mouth. Blue flared out from behind him, daring me to look.

"Who was it?" Mama pressed.

Jon pressed his lips together, firm and thin, but his stubborn was no match for Mama's. "Lutha and Mandrake Bonniway," he answered at last.

"Those nasty whelps ain't no concern of yours. You go letting your pride get bigger than your sense, and a beating'll be the least of your worries." Mama picked a few bits of twig from his unruly hair, her face gentler now. "You're better than that, Jon."

My brother's face screwed up, and he cast his eyes at the floor, wrestling with shame.

Mama's nose wrinkled. "Ach, you smell like the bottom of the cider press. Go clean yourself up for dinner. We'll speak on this later."

Jon's shoulders, too narrow to be a man's but too broad to be a boy's, slumped in relief at having been dismissed to the washroom. The washroom was new—a spoil of our recent fortune.

It was only a bit of good luck that the Bird in'th Hand tavern had started selling Papa's Scrump—a strong, smooth cider— when the Master Brewer of Bellskeep came through on his way to Mollier's Hold in the south. He made a great fuss over it, took four barrels back with him, and, not three months later, returned with a royal warrant to supply the palace. Pasture that had been wild last season was now mown and either lined with new apple tree cuttings or purple with new lavender, which gave the Scrump its color and flavor.

But with the new coin came new troubles.

Having water that came into the house was a blessing to our backs, which got bent hauling bucket after bucket in from the well, but it didn't do much to wash away the envy of our hallsmates. Presston was a simple place with simple folk—we all got on pretty much the same. When the warrant came, Mama and Papa urgently schooled us on modesty about our recent wealth. They knew what was coming, though it was a nasty surprise for me, Ether, and Jon. We never spoke a word about the washroom, the feather beds, or the clothes that weren't threadbare anymore, but we didn't have to. Everyone in town already knew.

For Jon and Ether, it was nothing short of a joy to have a wealth of fawning new friends. But, unlucky for me, I could see through the compliments not meant, the invitations given just 'cause of our coin. I began to prefer my own company to the false fondness of my hallsmates. They thought me proud or vain, but small as I was, being avoided felt better than lied to.

Then came the whispers that weren't really meant to be quiet. The shoves in the play yard that were harder than they needed be. It all told me one thing—they thought I was too big for my britches.

I snuck a peek at Mama, who was looking toward the washroom. I wondered if maybe I could make an escape and dodge any uncomfortable questions, but all too quick, she turned her eye on me. I froze like a rabbit faced with a hound.

"And you, little miss," she said sternly. "If you come across your brother tussling with those boys in the orchard again, I expect to be told straightaway, are we clear?"

She thinks I saw it, I realized. "Yes'm," I said quickly.

She turned back to the stove, muttering her frustrations under the bubbling of the pots. I slid from my chair, put the basket on the floor, and crept into the stone room with its giant copper basins. Jon stood with his back to me, waiting for one to fill, but already he was hard at work, scrubbing his ears with a wet cloth. Blood from a cut on his temple clotted in his sandy hair. "Go away, Only."

I sat on the wooden stool that Papa had made so I could reach the washing basin. From there, I could see the bruise darkening on one of his cheekbones. "What'd Lutha and Drake do this time?"

A hard look came over my brother's dirty face. "They think they can just steal from us like it's nothing, but they'd never have done it before King Alphonse and his warrant. Lutha said we have fruit to spare now that we're rich."

"We ain't rich!" I exclaimed. The words were familiar—it felt like I didn't go one day at halls without someone raising my dander with a taunt of "cat that got the cream" or "jinglepockets."

Jon didn't look at me as he held the cool cloth to the bruise. "Well, you know that and I know that, but all anyone else knows is that Father makes Scrump for the king now, so we must be. And that means we got ideas above our station."

I thought for a moment. "Why did you lie to Mama? About falling out of Grandfather?"

"And that's another thing," he hissed, moving closer to my face. "Why would you fink me out like that? Where were you hiding? Up a tree?"

My heart sank. I never could bear his displeasure—not my Jon. If I couldn't tell *him*, who *could* I tell? "I wasn't there, Jon, honest. It was just so . . . pretty."

"What do you mean, 'pretty'? What was pretty?"

"The lie you told. I could see it. Like a shimmer of blue, all round you."

His face twisted in confusion. "Only, you can't *see* a lie."

"But I did, I *did* see it!" I protested. "Tell another one and I'll prove it!"

"Don't be stupid," Jon grumbled, stripping off his dirty tunic. "Just leave me alone so I can wash."

Mama was right. The rotted fruit flesh that was starting to dry on his clothes smelled to high All. "If you didn't fall out of Grandfather, how . . . ?"

"They pelted me with rotten apples from the ground after I lost the fight." My brother hung his head. "Just get out, all right?"

Tears stinging my eyes, I slunk out the door feeling mad *for* Jon, who didn't deserve to be abused by the neighborhood boys, as well as *at* him for not believing me.

Peeved, I stomped out of the washroom only to run straight into Non.

Non's steady hands had brought me into the world and showed me the working of it. They taught me how to hold a knife, a spoon, and an apple peeler. They soothed my skinned knees and other small hurts with balms she made from the herb garden.

Everyone in town knew that Non was the one to go to for wisdom that'd bring peace to a troubled mind or an upset stomach. There was scarcely a soul in town that hadn't had some help from her healing hands—hands that now gripped my shoulders while her twinkling, crinkled eyes fixed on me like she'd never seen me before.

"It's a bad habit, mind," she began, her voice hushed, "but I couldn't help but sneak a listen at what you were jawing about with our Jon."

I crossed my arms in a temper. "Jon was just trying to stick up for the orchard. Those Bonniways deserved anything they got."

"Psht," Non snorted, waving her hand. "Boys'll always use their fists when they ought to use their words instead. What interests me more," she said, bringing her wrinkled face close to mine, "is what you had to say about lies."

Non shuffled me through the kitchen and toward the stable door that led to the garden. Mama turned her head as we passed. "Mam, where are you going with Only? I aim to put food on the table soon."

"Won't take but a minute, lovey," Non replied, giving my mother a gentle smile. "'Tain't nothing important, just pulling rosemary to go with the stew."

The same blue shimmer that had covered Jon shot faintly round Non, but her soft eyes turned to me, sharp and gray with warning. I heard my mother's voice exclaiming, "I've got plenty rosemary, Mam!" as Non hurried me out into the twilight.

The air was heavy with the scent of damp good earth and late-summer lavender. The faint sound of a fiddle drifted up the hill, along with bits of laughter and song. It was the first year Papa was to have the help of the Ordish with the harvest, and my heart was powerful curious. I'd seen the river folk's barges pass by before, but it was another thing to have them just at the bottom of the hill with all their strange ways and little magics that could fool the eye or move the elements.

Non twigged the shine in my eyes. "Sounds lively, don't it? They're good folk, the Ordish. And they're hard workers, too."

"Papa says we're not to go near," I groused. There's nothing like being told not to do a thing to make you want to do it something fierce, but neither me, Ether, nor Jon wanted to be the whelp to have to clean the mash from the presses at the end of the season as part of our correction.

"And you must mind your papa," Non declared. "It takes a while to know the hearts of strangers. But I reckon we'll find them nowt too different from ours." She chucked me under the chin. "And it's matters of the heart we come out here to jaw on."

We walked toward the small plot a little ways from the house where she grew her herbs. I knew well enough never to pluck anything from the soil without Non watching, as not everything there was friendly. Black currant grew next to nightberry, mint next to snakewort, and summer lemon next to daggeroot. It wouldn't take much to make a terrible, sickening mistake.

9

Non took a deep breath of the fragrant air as she sat on the stone bench beside the laurel bush and patted the empty space beside her.

"You know, Pip," she said after a moment, "you know that you're a good girl, don't you?"

I nodded. "Yes, Non."

She yanked a small sprig of rosemary and crushed it between her fingers. The savory smell made me think of the thick, delicious stew on the stove. My stomach grumbled, and I couldn't help but wonder why were we out here instead of sitting round the table.

"Your papa built that," she said finally, pointing at the handsome stone wall.

"I remember, Non. It was just this spring."

She chuckled and tapped the side of her head. "You think old Non's had a funny turn, I reckon, but I know what I'm about. What I'm trying to tell you is that lies are a bit like walls." Non pointed to the end of the garden. "What's on the other side of that one?"

Surely even Non wasn't so forgetful. "The lavender fields," I answered, puzzled.

"Good girl. How do you know?"

I folded my arms. "I just *know*!"

"Ah, but if you *didn't* know, how could you tell?"

I jumped off the bench and marched over to the wall. Jamming my feet into the uneven stones, I climbed to the top. The fields of sweet purple blossoms stretched down to the edge of the river in the distance. "I can *see*, Non!"

My grandmother rose slowly from the bench and joined me by the side of the wall, lifted me down, and covered my eyes with her hands. "What if you couldn't see over the wall? How would you know then?"

"Non!"

She took her hands from my eyes and grasped my shoulders. "Child, you mind me, do you hear? I've heard more odd complaints from folk over the years than you can imagine. Usually more'n once. But one thing I've never heard of is someone who can do what you said you could do, so I need you to answer me."

I never knew there was such a thing as something Non didn't know. What did that make *me*? *I shouldn't have opened my mouth to Jon!* A few fearful tears spilled down my cheeks, but Non wiped them away with her thumbs. "See here, no tears, no tears, Pip. You're a Fallow of the orchard. You're as tough as a green apple in summer. Now, once again, if you didn't know what was on the other side of the wall, how could you go about finding out?"

For a moment, I thought and breathed deep, trying to put aside the worry in my heart. Then it came to me.

"I can smell the lavender!"

I looked at Non eagerly, hoping for praise at my cleverness. She was smiling, but there was a sadness in it. Though I was heavy, she picked me up and rested me on her hip. We stared out over the darkening fields together.

"A lie," she began quietly, "is just a wall round the truth. Could be that it's built strong like your papa's wall, or it could be built out of something that'll collapse the minute you shake it. But no matter what it's made of, the truth is *always* going to want to get out, whether it has to climb over, break through, or leak out the cracks."

"What does that mean, Non?"

She didn't meet my eye, but her lined face looked more serious than I'd ever seen it. "The Ordish have got their auguries. Some can work the wind in the sails or the water beneath their keels. I heard tell of some who can even read the heavens, but those things ain't too common among landwalkers. You hear stories sometimes, down south where there's been more folk that marry into river clans or out of 'em. There'll be a whelp come up that can do some little magics—glamours and the like. Nothin' of particular use. But you . . ." She trailed off, her eyebrows making a worried V on her forehead.

Just the mention of magics put the fear of All up my spine. It never occurred to me that my little talent might be an *augury*. The words made me think terrible thoughts. Would Mama and Papa put me out of the house if they found out? Would my brothers hate me? Would I even be allowed to attend halls if someone found out my secret?

The cry of the fiddle drifted into the garden again, clear as a night heron.

"Mam! Only! Come to table!"

Non started at Mama's voice from the house. She looked at me as if she'd forgotten I was there and smiled a sad smile. "Psht! Look at us, mooning over the fields like a couple of daydreamers when there's a good stew on the go. Come on, you heard your mam."

"But, Non . . ."

Non held up her finger. "We'll have no more tonight. Let me sit with it for a while. But let's keep this between us for now, eh?"

She stood and offered me her hand to make our way back to the house, which looked warm and welcoming with light spilling out the windows. The halo it made round her stirred something in me.

"Ain't we forgetting something, Non?"

She cocked her head, puzzled. "What's that, Pip?"

"Rosemary."

Non chuckled. "I plum near forgot." She stooped to tear a few sprigs from the earth and put a warm arm round my shoulders.

"You'll keep me right, Pip. You'll keep me right."

2

Winter brings the frost
Summer brings the rose
Sure and fast as Mother's love
Your inmost heart she knows.

—Children's sanctuary rhyme

Lies *are* beautiful, but it sure as sugar wasn't something I was planning to share with anyone else—Rector Wither in particular.

Truth is, I paid far more attention to Non's sermonizing than I ever did to the white-haired man who stood behind the lectern every Matins. Her word on my little "wile," as she called it, was more absolute than the testaments. As I grew to understand that folk sometimes had more than one reason for acting the way they do, more colors appeared round the liars for me to puzzle out. But one commandment remained above all—silence is golden. And by the Mother, I kept that one close to my heart, but it never bothered me more than when I was sat in the solemn quiet of sanctuary.

In summer, contemplation of Her love and mercy was done while staring at the backs of other folk's heads and sweating like a pig, sandwiched on the hard bench between Mama and Jon. The sun hadn't even broke the sky, but it was already hotter than six of the seven hells and Rector Wither's homily was as flat as the buzz of the locusts outside. Even the flames in the sanctuary lanterns seemed listless. My skirts were ruched up in the back, and my legs stuck to the bench. I snuck a look at Daisy Loler, Liss Tunnock, and Bete Markey, whose parents let them sit together by one of the big, open windows. No doubt, if I asked Mama and Papa, I'd be allowed to join them, but Bete and Daisy made it clear long ago at halls with their cold backs and poisonous whispers that they didn't want anything to do with me. I shifted on the bench, trying to chase away the old hurt, but I only succeeded in doing myself a new one when my legs came away with a sweaty rip.

"Be still, Only," whispered Mama.

I puffed some air up into the hair matted to my forehead. I didn't know how she managed to look so unrumpled, every strand of her sandy hair in place and her long neck untroubled by beads of sweat. The air around us was soupy enough for frog spawn. Jon gave me a gentle poke in the ribs. In his hand, he had one of the orchard's wooden markers—head of the king on one side and an apple on the other. Flexing his knuckles, the marker began a tidy roll over each of his fingers before disappearing into his palm and then reappearing at his pinky to start the journey again. It was an old trick—one he'd used at my bedside when I was small and frighted of the dark. Though I wasn't so small anymore, watching the slow roll of the marker still made me feel as calm and dopey as the hens Papa stroked between the eyes before they went to the stump. Over and over it rolled, and lower and lower drooped my eyelids. I forgot about my discomfort and watched till my head dropped against Jon's shoulder, starting awake when the whole sanctuary murmured, "Thanks for All."

Jon smirked at me. His little bit of token trickery had let me miss the rest of the homily, which I didn't mind one bit. After eleven harvest seasons, I could practically recite the Tale of the Five Seeds right along with him. The rest of the sanctuary was stirring, too, eager to get on with the morning's chores before Matins luncheon. The rector reached down to pick up the pile of tithe baskets at his feet. The sounds of folk freeing purses from belts and pockets filled the sanctuary.

"Now is the time when we tithe to give thanks for all that we have by the work of our own hands," droned Rector Wither. "And as you give, so shall you receive the Mother's blessings upon you. Your tithe shall work among those in need and in the service of Mother All. And while we reach into our purses, let us also reach out to our neighbors to pass the Mother's Peace."

I wish I could've slept through the Peace, too.

If there's one thing I've learned, it's that people have got a lie for almost every occasion. Big lies, small lies, lies told from shame or envy, lies meant to hurt and lies meant in kindness—I saw them all. Thanks to Non's good counsel, I'd come to know a dishonest lie wasn't always the mark of a bad character, but it still didn't feel any good when they were told me by my neighbors. The Peace was meant as a time of goodwill, but I, better than anyone, knew it wasn't always the case.

As Mama and Papa reached for their purses, Jon and me turned to greet the folk on the bench behind and found ourselves face-to-face with the Bonniways.

The years since Lutha and Mandrake showed their faces in our orchard hadn't done much to improve their dispositions. Those years had made them bigger and meaner than a bear with a toothache. Jon, slim and strong as he was, would no doubt come off much worse in a tussle with the burly twins than he'd done as a boy. But we were sat in sanctuary with the Mother's watchful eye on us, so there wasn't much chance of fisticuffs.

Jon did the neighborly thing and put out his hand to Drake. "Peace of the Mother be with you."

The big fellow blinked his heavily lidded eyes and returned the handshake. "I hope it'll be with you, too, Master Fallow."

Jon's face went purple as the wreath of ill will that ringed Mandrake as he squeezed my brother's hand so hard, I could almost hear the bones crunch. Jon clenched his teeth in the shape of a smile and bore it best he could, but no sooner had Drake released his iron grip than Lutha took over.

"I hope your harvest is bountiful this week," he said, grinning, the same ugly bruise color spreading round him.

"Kind of you to say," gritted Jon, false politeness spreading over him the color of the sky before a funnel cloud.

All round me the sanctuary was lighting up with colors that had become as familiar to me as my own face. Mistress Ward was exaggerating in light pinks to Mama about the size of the shortwolf she'd seen in her garden. Master Fullham was covered in kindly sparks complimenting the cut of Master Roth's coat, which he clearly did not care for. Old Mistress Moor was nodding as Ether lied in shameful blues about his good marks in halls.

Maybe if I were sat with Liss, Bete, and Daisy, I wouldn't notice so much.

It was a relief when the baskets made their way to the front and everyone ceased their chatter for the sending-out.

"Go forth into this harvest week grateful. Grateful for the small seeds that multiply to feed many. Grateful for the trees that blossom and produce fruit—enough for our own needs *and* to share with those who are less fortunate. May the Mother make seeds of us all, so we may grow, nourished by Her love and the love of one another. Thanks be to All. Go in peace."

In cooler weather, folks like to linger and jaw inside; but today the benches cleared quickly, everyone anxious for the fresher air outdoors. Usually, I would be the first through the threshold into the sanctuary yard, but I found myself staring at the three girls on the other side of the sanctuary.

"Move, you lump!" Ether's voice cut in on my thinking.

"Mind your mouth, Ether," Mama snapped. She gave me a gentle shove toward the end of the bench. "Come on, sweetling, let's not dawdle."

We shuffled out, Ether giving me a sharp pinch as he shoved by. Mama was quickly waylaid by Rora Blessed, who wanted advice about a new filly, when I caught sight of Liss walking down the aisle toward us. From my desk at halls, I admired her shining yellow hair and often thought how pleasant it would be to sit in the orchard, braiding butterweed into it and whispering secrets to each other. Her family had taken over the mill only six months before, and she seemed better disposed to me than most. With Daisy and Bete nowhere to be seen, I thought to put on a brave face.

"Good Matins, Liss," I said as she passed by.

A shy smile touched her lips. "Good Matins, Only."

I hadn't thought much beyond hello, so I stumbled over my tongue a bit. "Is . . . is your family beginning the harvest tomorrow?"

"We are. I hope it's not as hot as it is today or I might melt clean away in the field!"

Boldened, I leapt. "Well, if your mama's agreeable, maybe you could come for a swim in the river after supper?"

There was an ugly, barking laugh. "Only if you don't mind a watering hole full of river rats!"

Bete appeared behind us, her pointed face in a sneer. "Everyone knows Master Fallow would rather keep company with the Ordish than honest folk."

A flush of shame burned my ears. "Our estate's a big one," I said. "We need help with the harvest."

Daisy sidled up between us and took Liss's arm. "Your estate's as big as your head, Only Fallow. Everyone knows about your royal warrant. You don't have to keep bringing it up."

"I *didn't* bring it up!" I half shouted, causing a number of folk to turn heads our way.

"Come on, Liss," declared Bete, taking her other arm. "There's enough hot air in here without her adding more."

Liss looked at me, helpless. "Maybe . . . maybe another day?"

Blinking back tears, I looked down at the creaky wood floor so I didn't need to see the kind and regretful shower of sparks above her head that meant she'd not be swimming with me anytime soon.

Out in the sanctuary yard, the sun was just beginning to peak over the valley to burn off the morning dew. Ether was playing some rough-and-tumble game with the elder boys in the broad sunlight while Papa and Jon stood under the big oak with a good many other folk who wanted to get away from the early heat of the day. I tried hard not to see Daisy, Liss, and Bete laughing and weaving poppy chains in the grass.

"They ain't worth your worry, Pip," Jon said as I joined them under the tree.

"Who says I'm worried?" I replied, trying to blink the red out of my eyes.

Jon leaned back against the tree, wiping the sweat from his neck that was dripping into the collar of his best blue tunic. "Some folk are just looking for an excuse to boost their notion of themselves by setting others apart. If it weren't the warrant, they'd find something else to harp on."

"Bete was on about the Ordish," I grumbled. "Said we don't keep company with decent folk."

Jon's face got thunderous. "'Decent folk'? That's rich, coming from a hopped-up little whelp like her. I didn't see *her* papa helping rebuild old Master Gabe's barn after the fire. Or *her* mama taking dinner to Mistress Lorey after she lost her son. It's funny how some folk define *decent*."

I leaned my head against the rough bark of the tree. "Mama always said folks would come round. Why haven't they come round?"

A bellow interrupted us from across the yard. "Good Matins to you, Master Fallow!"

My brother and I groaned softly, as we both knew all too well who was coming our way. Even Papa's eyes fluttered shut for wishing himself anywhere but there, but he turned with a friendly countenance.

"And to you, Master Anslo." Not many folk cared for the shopkeeper with his big mouth and loud notions on everything, from the state of the sanctuary walk to the color of Mistress Halefont's new frock. But Papa was a powerful gracious person, so he shook Anslo's thick hand all the same.

The big man drew a forearm across his sweaty forehead, flattening the few strands of hair he'd left against his scalp. "I'd give just about All to be sat on one of our northern neighbors' ice floes this morning!"

"It's certain shaping up to be a scorcher," Papa answered.

Anslo hooked his fat thumbs through the buttonholes in his coat. "Speaking of Thorvald, Mistress Buch was telling me her cousin was just back from Bellskeep, and the talk's all about the match between the crown princess and that great walrus Eydisson. Can you believe it? A Thorvald on the throne? Can't abide 'em, myself. That growling tongue of theirs makes 'em sound more beast than man. At least they ain't Ordish, though." A mean look crept into his beady eyes as he gave a disdainful sniff. "Suppose you've got them in for harvest again this year?"

There was a quiet rumble in Jonquin's throat, but Papa smiled mildly at Anslo.

"You know there ain't enough help in this valley to bring in our harvest, master. The Ordish are good workers. And they've always done right by me."

"They certainly ain't interested in doing right by the king," the shopkeeper grumbled. "Ain't a one of 'em pay a single coin in tax. You'd think with all their whelps being took to the capital by His Majesty's ransomers, they'd change their tune. They don't even value their own issue like proper folk!"

I tugged at Jon's sleeve. "What's he on about?"

But I got no answer. Jon's face was a-twist with temper, all of it directed at Anslo.

Papa's back stiffened, but he schooled his face polite and careful. "I believe they feel those losses deeply, master, though I'm not one to question the king."

Anslo raised a bushy brow and folded his arms. "Oh, come now. They ain't like *us*. And surely you heard about all the grain stores being set alight up north. Their work, no doubt. Not to mention all them savage auguries!"

Though I was still trying to puzzle out what Anslo meant with the talk of ransomers, I willed myself to be still at the mention of augury. I was all too mindful what the shopkeeper would say of me if he knew what I could see.

Anslo wasn't finished. "I don't know why you croppers give

those folk a stopping place in the valley every harvest. I'll tell you one thing—those dirty river rats better not come round my shop!"

"They don't need anything *you're* selling!"

Papa and Anslo turned to Jon, who suddenly looked very dangerous—his eyes hooded beneath his brows, casting a shadow on his face.

"I don't need lip from a lad without a hair on his chin," Anslo said, puffing out his chest so that it strained against the buttons of his waistcoat.

Papa laid a hand on Jon's shoulder. "What my boy is trying to say, master, is that the Ordish get most of their sustenance from the river. They'll have no need to trouble you."

Anslo grunted. "You see that they don't. That warrant of yours might make you feel high and mighty, but believe you me, Presston ain't going to tolerate any Ordish devilry or graft."

"Graft like putting your thumb on the scales to squeeze a few extra pennies out of folks?" Jon shot back hotly.

By then, near half the congregation had a pair of ears on the feud. Everyone knew Anslo was heavy-handed, but those hands were tied up in a lot of businesses in town. The shopkeeper himself went as red as a ripe apple. "Insolent whelp! I ought to show you the back of my hand!"

Papa stepped between them. "If you do, master, I assure you you'll see the back of mine."

I'd never seen him raise a hand to anyone, but his broad shoulders and strong arms meant he didn't have to. Folks always told me I looked like Papa, with his dark auburn hair and sharp blue eyes, but chances were I'd never look half so fierce.

Undeterred, the shopkeeper took a step toward him, his voice low and wicked. "Someday, Ellis, you and your wetcollar friends are going to get put in your place." Stepping back, he spat at Papa's feet, turned on his heel, and marched down the path toward the sanctuary gate. Whispers broke out all round and eyes darted between us and the retreating back of the shopkeeper. Papa watched him go, arms tense beneath his coat sleeves, before turning a hard eye back to Jonquin.

"That was foolish, Jon."

My brother was still staring arrows at Anslo's bald head. "He's a crooked old crank," Jon announced loudly. "And he said they don't care about losing their whelps!"

Papa grabbed Jon's arm and spoke in a hush. "Anslo might be a crooked old crank with not a care in the world but for himself, but he's not alone in his thinking on the Ordish," Papa said, waving a hand at the yard.

It didn't take but a few peeks around the sanctuary yard to note the number of unfriendly faces and shaking heads pointed our way. Papa lowered his voice even further so those still ear-wigging might not hear. "A lot of folk are all too ready to believe the rumors that trickle down from the north. Of course, the Ordish've got some bad apples. Who doesn't?" He pointed a finger at the empty space full of bad will Anslo had left behind him. "It ain't as if you've got to look very far to find 'em in Presston."

I'd got my mouth open to question him on the Ordish whelps when Mama, Non, and Ether finally pushed their way through to find us.

"What's going on, Ellis?" Mama demanded as she swept in

with her fine cobalt gown and a high flush on her cheeks. "I heard there were some cross words between you and Master Anslo out here. And in front of the sanctuary! What were you thinking?"

"Did he stomp off all sore?" asked Ether gleefully. "Hatter Leyward threw some flour bombs in his shop once, and sweet All, did Anslo's head turn bright red when he came out to chase after him!"

Papa frowned. "Come on, the sun's getting high and there're chores to be done before luncheon." He offered Mama his arm and began leading her out of the yard, Ether following behind, hoping for a tale of a good scrap. Jon didn't seem to want to move. I took his hand.

"It was good of you, speaking for them like that." I'd always watched the barges float into the valley with a mix of wonder and disquiet. You couldn't help hear the things that got said or know the story of Kester's Weir, but all I ever saw in the fields or over the garden wall were folk who sang while they worked and danced while they played. And then there was the matter of the ransomers. What did *that* mean? As for their auguries . . . it wasn't as if I could cast stones in that direction. I was glad Jon had stood nose to nose with Anslo. I wondered if he would speak for me if I was discovered.

"They don't know them," Jon declared. "How do they dislike them if they don't even know them?"

My curiosity leapt up. We weren't allowed near the Ordish encampments. "How do you know them, Jon?"

My brother's ears turned pink. "I . . . know 'em well enough to know that there's nothing to dislike." He pulled away to follow

Mama and Papa. "We ought to be after them. There's chores to do." And before I could question him further, he was out the gate and off down the path, leaving me standing under the tree with the rest of the sanctuary stragglers.

"That boy's got a briar in his britches." Non appeared at my elbow, staring after Jonquin.

At least Non wouldn't hush me. "Non, what'd Master Anslo mean about the king and ransomers?"

It wasn't often she was lost for words, but Non's mouth screwed up tight as if she wasn't sure she should let them out. "It's shameful, that's what it is. I don't know what's got into that old fool on the throne."

My mouth fell open. I never heard anyone speak ill of the king—certainly not in my house, where everything we had came by the king's hand. I cast a nervous glance round the yard.

"Pssh, ain't no one listening," Non scoffed. "A good scrap, they got ears for. An old woman spouting off and suddenly they all go hard of hearing."

I spoke in a hush, nonetheless. "What does the king *do*?"

"There ain't really an easy way to say it, Pip. The Ordish don't want nothing to do with his law or his taxes, so he's gotta show he's boss some other way. Sends in ransomers to take the whelps, then drags the poor things up to Bellskeep to serve as indentures until their kin can pay to free 'em."

The idea was so horrible, it took a moment for it to sink in. "The king . . . *steals* children?"

"For about five years now." Non grimaced, leaning up against the tree. "I know your pa's certainly lost some sleep over it."

"It's not *Papa* who's taking the whelps."

"No, but . . . y'see, Pip . . . the warrant . . ."

What she wasn't saying was suddenly louder than what she was. "We're *helping* him!" I burst out. "Our coin is going to help him pay the ransomers!"

"Our coin would go to the king in tax, warrant or no, child, and he'll use it for what he pleases. At least, by giving the river folk harvest work, we're giving something back to the folks who are most wronged."

I bristled. "We just . . . shouldn't pay! Keep back the share that goes to the folk doing ill."

"Things ain't always black and white, Pip," Non replied. "What good would that do? Your papa'd go to a debtors' farm and we'd lose the warrant. Maybe the king would grant it to some other orchard. Maybe that landholder wouldn't be as keen on hiring the Ordish. Why, whole clan's worth of wages would be lost! Where does that leave everyone? Worse off, that's where!"

"But . . ."

"I ain't saying I think it's rosy, Pip, and it sure as eggs ain't just, but it is what it is."

I looked round at all the folk from Presston, dressed in their sanctuary best, feeling the Mother's blessing on them once more. "Does everybody know about it?"

"Most folk do, I reckon."

"And nobody minds?" I cried, outraged.

Non took my hands. "Look at you, Pip, wanting to move mountains! You can see more than most, but you can't see what's in their hearts. Maybe some of 'em are just as sore about it as you."

I didn't think many of the folk headwagging at Papa were terribly sore about it. Non must've read the thoughts right off my face.

"Sometimes we gotta be content to change what we got charge over, child. We don't make choices—our choices make us. And we should make our little corner of the world as right as it can be." She chucked me under the chin like she used to when I was wee. "You'd be surprised how far a bit of good can spread."

There was a burst of musical laughter as Liss, Bete, and Daisy embraced and waved to one another in parting.

"Shame it can't spread to them," I grumbled.

Non took my arm. "You know those three's notion of you don't change who you are, right, Pip?"

"And who am I, then?" I asked glumly. "Apart from unnatural."

"You're Only Fallow, that's who you are," Non declared. "You got a strong back and an open heart. You like to climb trees in your bloomers and you come home with dirt under your fingernails. And if those whelps can't look at you without green-colored glasses, then you're better off without 'em."

Grateful, I put my head on her shoulder as we walked. "Mama'd probably like if I didn't climb trees in my bloomers."

"I'd probably like to spend my days with a dozen handsome young bucks feeding me apple tart, but that ain't gonna happen either."

Ignoring the upturned eyebrows of the other folk on the road, Non and I giggled our way back to the orchard in the early-morning sun.

3

My brothers and me didn't waste any time shucking off our sanctuary threads when we got home. My soaked shift now felt mighty comfortable with the breeze blowing in from my window, and I decided then and there I'd not be putting on my tunic to attend to the chickens. It was *our* garden, and no one would be any wiser to my undress.

I slipped past Mama in the kitchen quick as a wink. The heavy dew on the grass washed over my bare feet as I made my way to the hen roost, swinging the egg basket by my side. Inside the snug brown shed, I could hear the cackle and fuss of a gaggle of chickens upset over something or other, though it doesn't take a whole lot to upset chickens. I hurried my steps, anxious for the hens to quiet. Angry chickens don't lay eggs.

Over the squawking inside, I could hear voices, bickering.

"They're already raising enough stink to wake up the house!"

"Stop being a baby. Just a couple more—they'll never miss them."

I rounded the corner and burst into the small coop. The hens, already in an uproar, began to complain even louder. Standing before me, caught red-handed, were two Ordish whelps.

Both of them were barefoot and dressed in traditional red tunics. The girl's frightened eyes were ringed in kohl, as is the way with river girls who've seen their first moon. The boy was a little shorter than me and just as startled. The three of us stared at one another for a split second before the two of them turned and bolted out the other side of the roost, a small pail filled with eggs swinging in the boy's grip.

Anger roared through me and I quick forgot the horror of my jaw with Non in the sanctuary yard. I dropped the empty egg basket and set off after them.

They crashed through the hedge with me close at their heels. They streaked through the ditch that brought water to the lavender fields and still I followed. We were approaching the river encampment when the girl glanced backward, her dark braided hair streaming behind her and fear on her face.

"STOP!" I hollered.

My shout distracted the boy for a moment and he, too, turned to look at me, long enough not to notice the hulking figure of a man who stepped out from behind a nearby tree. By the time he turned back, it was too late. He collided with the man at full speed, by some miracle not spilling a single egg from the pail. The man caught him round the waist in an iron grasp, a morning's spent searching for unruly whelps writ all over his face. The girl stopped in her tracks and moved to dodge round him, but he was too fast for her. A meaty hand fastened round her collar.

"Where've the two of you been? I sent you to fetch water forty minutes ago!" His voice was deep and menacing, promising punishment. He glanced down at the pail still in the boy's hand. "That don't look like water to me, Rowan. Does this look like water to you, Lark?"

"No, Pa," the girl mumbled, misery putting lines round her mouth.

"This looks like thieving to me, is what it looks like, you little wretches! Are you trying to make all them stories they tell true?"

Though I didn't mean to, I let out a squeak, suddenly very aware that I was far from the house and not properly dressed. The man's anger was frightening, even though it wasn't directed at me. His head swiveled round, and his eyes, the same green as the children's, widened. His grip on the two loosened, but they made no move to escape.

The man, who just a moment before had looked like a terrifying beast, seemed to lose half his height as he turned to face me. He swept the broad-brimmed hat from his head and held it to his chest. "Good met, Miss Fallow."

It took me a moment to realize that he was talking to me. Usually, if I met the workers down by the pressing sheds, they tousled my hair and called me titch or poppet.

"Good met, Master . . . ?"

"Bula, miss. Master Bula Fairweather." He glared at the two children that stood on either side of him, their heads bent in shame. "And these are my whelps, Rowan and Lark. It seems they have something that belongs to you."

Bula delivered a swift swat to the backside of the boy, who quickly held out the pail to me. Bula's face reddened. "If you could see fit, lady, not to mention this to your pa . . ."

I don't know what made me do it. Maybe I recognized the same fear in their eyes that gripped my heart since Non told me of my unnaturalness—the fear of punishment, of being found out. Maybe it's 'cause I could imagine their father's face pale with grief if either were taken from him. But I spoke up.

"No, sir, I gave them the eggs."

I recognized the dull thud behind my eyes that accompanied a lie, but I pushed on nonetheless. "Our hens laid so well last night, and . . . well, they were passing by and I thought maybe they might like to bring them back for breakfast."

Bright spots of light began to prick my vision. Bula's mouth hung agape. "But . . . why were you chasing them?"

Rowan and Lark turned back to me, eyes pleading for a good answer.

"I forgot . . . ," I stammered, through the mounting pain in my head, "I forgot my mother wanted to ask if . . . if you were camped well. I mean, if there was anything you needed before harvest begins tomorrow. I thought maybe they could take the message for me."

The angry flush began to fade from Bula's cheeks. "No, thank you, miss. We're quite comfortable. Thank you . . . for the eggs." He narrowed his eyes at Rowan and Lark. "After breakfast, perhaps I can give you two a lesson in following direction."

"Yes, Pa," exclaimed Lark.

"We'll take these to Auntie Maven and go straight to the river, Pa," added Rowan.

"Mind that you do," Bula warned. The three of them turned back toward the camp, and Bula donned his hat, touching the brim in my direction. "Goodly bye, Miss Fallow."

"And to you, Master Fairweather," I answered, feeling sick with the throbbing in my temples. I squeezed my eyes shut, willing it away, and when I opened them I could see the Ordish disappearing down toward the river. As Bula and Rowan vanished behind the line of slender trees, Lark hung back. Making sure no one was watching, she gave me a quick wave before joining them, leaving me standing in the middle of the field alone.

4

Once, long ago, there were some Ordish whelps play-ing on the Bellskeep shore. The son of the king rode by on his fine horse and one of the whelps let fly with a pebble. The prince and his escort stopped, and without warn-ing, the prince thrust his sword through the child's belly. Unfortunately for the prince, the whelp's father came bar-reling toward the heir to the throne and opened him neck to navel. There was soon fighting in the streets between the royal guard and the Ordish, but in the days following, every barge in the kingdom converged on the capital, tip-ping the scales in the river folk's favor. The city of Bellskeep was left burning as the clans sailed off to the south.

The king, mad with grief over his lost son, ordered the very course of the river diverted so the river folk could never return. Most thought it a fever dream, but before long, a call for laborers went out across Orstral for the king's great project. It's said to have cost three thousand men their lives to build it, but Kester's Weir, an enormous wall of stone and mortar named for the fallen prince, blocked off the branch of the River Hush that ran through Bellskeep. As

for the muddy, snaking hole that the waters left behind,
the king had plans for that as well.

He would rebuild the city to be an impenetrable
fortress.

—The story of Kester's Weir, unattributed

I wasn't sure I could make it up the hill. The pain in my head made my stomach turn, and the syrupy air in the fields wasn't helping. As I picked my way through the rows of flowers, I thought about Lark and Rowan. Was saving their hides worth such a misery?

I managed to make it back to the hedge, pushing my way painfully through the grasping branches and into the safety of the yard. The egg basket I'd left outside the roost was missing, and I could hear Mama inside, shushing the birds. I groaned. If she was doing the chore she'd asked me to do, there wasn't much chance she'd be in a good humor. All I wanted to do was find a place on the cool stone floor and lie facedown. I hoped to escape her attention by making my way quietly across the lawn, but the minute I put my hand to the stable door, there was a loud creak and her head popped out of the roost.

"Only Fallow!"

Her bellow went through me like a lightning strike and I winced. Slowly, I closed the stable door and turned, putting on my best, most sorry face. "Yes, Mama."

She stormed from the roost with a basket full of eggs. The hens *had* laid well. At least that part hadn't been a lie. Mama fixed me with the look she usually used on Ether if he'd broken something.

"Just where were you, young miss? And in such a state?" She picked a few stray twigs from the hedge out of my hair. "Gone from the garden and in just a shift! Chores unfinished! I got Ether and Jonquin out searching for you! What have you got to say for yourself?"

I looked up at her wretchedly. The only answer I could muster was to be sick on her shoes.

I WAS EXCUSED from the rest of my chores.

Non offered to look after me down in the cool of the cellar. Mama still wasn't best pleased, but she used a wet cloth to wipe down my burning cheeks in the washroom. "Don't think this is over," she warned. "But right now, you rest. We'll talk later."

My brothers, both hot and tousled, shot me dirty looks as they disappeared outside to finish their tasks. Non took me by the hand.

"Come on now, let's get you comfortable."

She led me down the steps to the cellar, where she'd set up a pallet. On the hottest nights, the whole family would sometimes sleep down there on folding beds. It always seemed strange to go to sleep under bits of dried meat or next to bushels of fruit, but the dark cellar was a welcome escape from the heat upstairs. Only Non didn't join us on account of her snoring, which Papa said could wake the three days' dead.

I slipped under an old sheet on the rough canvas. Non brought me a cup of ginger water, cool, sweet, and spicy, to settle my stomach. As I laid my head on the down pillow, I sighed with relief and closed my eyes. I wanted to drift off, but Non's stare was burning a hole in me, so I opened them again.

"You got a story to tell, missus. Had your mam in a worry. The rest of us, too."

My aching head couldn't take another lie. "It was the Ordish, Non. Two of them, in the roost, taking eggs."

Non puffed up like the barn cat when a stray dog wandered into its path. "Why didn't you tell anyone? Did they hurt you?"

I shook my head, even though it complained. "No, I chased after them. But—"

"Chased after them?" exclaimed Non. "Child, you ain't got the common sense Mother All gave to a horsefly! You went running after two Ordish in your underthings? Has the heat tainted your wits?"

"They were whelps!" I pleaded. "I was so wild at them for stealing, I didn't think. But then . . ." I bit the inside of my lip. "Their papa caught them. He was dreadful sore, and I kept thinking about the ransomers, so I told him I gave them the eggs."

Non went real quiet until she finally said, "And that's when you got to feeling peculiar?"

My head throbbed again just remembering. "Every time I say something not true, it hurts till I can hardly stand it."

She frowned. "That started a few years ago, didn't it, right round your birthing day? Has it gotten worse since then?"

I nodded miserably. Non crossed her arms and leaned back in her chair, staring at the wall. "Seems like it's growing right along with you, like a bad knee that troubles you more the older you get."

I rested my cheek against the cool pillow. "It ain't gonna get much worse than this, is it? What's it even good for?"

Non rested her chin in her hands. "Don't rightly know. Show me the way of it again—I'll do some fibbing and you tell me what you see." Her eyes narrowed. Then she straightened up with a half smile on her face.

"Once," she said slyly, "when I was a girl, I wrestled with a dragon."

A quick volley of twinkling lights burst out around her, and I couldn't help but grin. "Tall tales and kindnesses look like a bunch of candles flickering out."

"Pst, that was an easy one," she scoffed. "Try this. When I was a girl of sixteen, my best friend and I were sweet on the same young man. It pained me to do it, but I told her she should be the one to ask him to dance at the harvest festival."

A blue shimmer began to ring her round. I frowned. "Did you do something shameful, Non?"

"You ain't got any kind of right mind when you're sixteen. I did tell her to ask him, but then I ran and asked him myself before she had a chance. Then I told her that *he* asked *me*." She shook her head. "Only reason that I ain't more sorry is because the young man was your grandpap."

I went warm inside, imagining Non as a lovesick whelp. "Those were pretty easy ones. You only had one thing in mind while telling 'em. It's when there's more than—"

"If you keep your head down, Pip, I don't reckon there's any danger in your little talent," she interrupted.

The warm feeling turned cold as winter as the dim cellar lit with green and twinkling white—the telltale marks of both fear and charity. My grandmother's face told me all I needed to know—after all these years, my little trick had her worried.

"Non . . ."

Suddenly, upstairs, there was a rap on the front door.

Non and I glanced at each other, perplexed. Friends and neighbors always used the stable door in back. Non said the only time you should come through the front door is if you're being carried—coming home from the midwife's as a babe, being hoisted after a hand-fasting, or being borne to the burying yard for a sending-off. Since no one'd been born, married, or died, the knock meant business.

"Wonder who that could be?" Non mused. "Everyone in town's doing morning chores." She eased herself out of her chair and headed for the cellar steps. "Won't be a tick."

As Non disappeared up the creaky stairs, I stared at a bundle of dried lavender hanging from the rafters above my head. Its faint sweetness drifted down like the orchard itself was trying to soothe my troubles.

"Only?" Non called from the top step. "Child, I do believe it's for you."

No soul had ever come to the door in search of me. "Who is it?"

She held out my dressing gown to me and jerked her head in the direction of the great room. "See for yourself."

I shrugged on the dressing gown and padded across the kitchen, then poked my head round the corner.

What I saw made me jump straight back. Sitting on the gathering bench and looking a bit lost were Lark and Rowan. I turned to Non in amazement. *What are they doing here?* I mouthed. Non, who'd begun to peel potatoes for luncheon at the sink, shrugged her shoulders and shooed me into the great room with her free hand.

I took a deep breath and stepped around the corner. The two children had been swinging their legs and casting curious looks round the room, but when I appeared, they both leapt off the bench and stood stick straight. Both of them had unruly, dark brown hair with colorful strands of thread-woven braids throughout, sun-kissed skin, and the same uncanny silver-green eyes their papa had. Their red tunics swished as they rocked back and forth, all aflutter. The three of us stared at one another, just as we had in the coop, until the boy finally elbowed his sister. She stepped forward.

"Good met, miss."

"Good met," I started suspiciously. "What do you want?"

"Um, you see, my brother and me, we . . . just wanted to say . . . to say . . ." She broke off, biting her lip and worrying the end of her braid.

"To say sorry," the boy piped up. "And thank you. For not ratting us to Pa." He had a mischief smile, just like Ether. And just like Ether, it made me sore to see it.

I puffed up just like Non, forgetting for a minute how small I was. "You were thieving from us!"

"I know, I know," Lark said hurriedly, "and it was dreadful poor thanks for the work your pa gives us. This here . . ." She thrust her hand out toward me. "This is to beg your pardon."

In her palm was a doll. Its head was made from reeds woven cunning like around a dried walnut and fastened tight at the neck with a string of small, olive-colored beads. Its legs and feet were carved from branches. But the most interesting part was in the middle—the belly was a cage of carefully bent willow with an acorn rattling at its bars. It was a marvelous little thing, and for a minute, I forgot I was angry.

"What is it?" I asked in wonder.

"It's Jack of the Green," Rowan replied, as if any fool would know.

"It's the prettiest doll I ever seen," I said, reaching out to trace the lines of the willow. Lark quickly thrust it into my hands.

"The Jack ain't a *doll*," exclaimed Rowan. "He's a spirit who lives in the forest. Likes to play tricks. Sometimes he'll take the antlers of a deer and give 'em to a rabbit. And then he'll take the rabbit's long floppy ears and stick them on a snake."

I knew the Ordish didn't go to sanctuary. Unlike Master Anslo, Mama said that their beliefs didn't do no one any harm, but Jack of the Green certainly didn't sound like the friendliest of spirits. I ran my thumb over the beads at his neck. "Does he do . . . anything else?"

Lark rolled her eyes at Rowan. "Don't listen to Ro. He likes all the stupid stories about the Jack." She pointed to the acorn. "What he *really* does is watch over things waiting to grow. Mothers bury one in the ground when we come to a new place so he'll watch over the whelps while we're there." Her words pricked at my heart, and she scratched the back of her neck nervously. "Anyways, we don't often come crosses with someone who wants to save our hides, so we made him for you. Some of the craftier folk make real fancy ones of bone or metal, but . . . I like the wood ones best. They feel more like the Jack's right there with you." She poked a careful finger into the Jack's belly. "Besides, with the metal ones, you can't do this."

As her finger touched the acorn, it burst into a tiny flame. I gasped and almost dropped it in surprise.

"Don't fret—it's just a glamour," she said quickly. "Have you never seen one before?"

I shook my head dumbly. I'd always heard of Ordish magics, but having one done right in front of my eyes was stupefying, but I held my nerve. *Don't be chickenhearted!* I chided myself. *You're more than a little acquainted with augury!* I turned the Jack over, watching the burning nut roll this way and that, merrily aflame without so much as singeing my fingers.

"W-will it stay like that? It won't set anything on fire, will it?"

The girl smiled and folded her arms. "Pssht, no. Glamours ain't real. But it should stay lit for a good long while."

For the first time since I set eyes on them, I was afraid. Was this why folks were so rattled when the Ordish floated into the valley? The whelp had just cast an augury in my house without a care—as easy as tripping over your own feet. As if it weren't something dangerous for her or her family. As if she didn't care what people like Master Anslo would say if he knew.

Wouldn't that be nice? a little voice in the back of my head whispered.

While I wasn't sure how I felt about the augury, or a spirit that liked to tinker with animals, I *was* sure that the two Ordish had been kinder to me than anyone at halls had in years. I wasn't about to overlook a gift of two whelps who might want to befriend me. My green-apple side decided to take a chance.

"Thank you. I like him very much."

Lark and Rowan beamed. "D'ya think your pa would let you come down for campfire tonight?" Rowan blurted out. "It would be awfully fine to have you. Older Harven's strung a new fiddle and there'll be dancing!"

"Oh . . . I . . . ," I stammered, "I don't know . . ."

"I don't think her folks would want her to come down for campfire, Rowan," scolded Lark. "It ain't . . ." She dropped her eyes to the ground. "Well, it ain't seemly for a landsman's girl."

"Seemly don't keep her brothers away," complained Rowan. "Auntie Maven says Master Jonquin's sweet on Mauralee. She says last season she saw them behind—"

"Rowan, mind your mouth!" Lark hissed. She looked at me and bit her lip. "Sorry, he don't always know when to stop talking."

So that's how Jonquin knew the Ordish! How come I didn't guess he had a sweetheart on the river? More to the point, I wondered how Mama and Papa would feel to know that Jon—the Jon that could do no wrong—was stealing away during the harvest to frolic with river folk.

Despite being shook by news of Jon's secret flame, I felt like I had a burning acorn right in the heart of me that was cracking its shell to let out an adventurous sprout. "I'll come," I said. I didn't stop to think how foolish it would be to disobey my parents twice in one day, or how I couldn't possibly explain myself if I were caught. But I knew I'd go just the same.

The children exchanged surprised looks and grinned at me. "We'll look for you, then—by the big oak just after the first star," Rowan said as he and Lark made to leave the way they'd come in. I reached out to grab his hand.

"No, not that way. None of our friends use the front door."

There came a light in Lark's eyes, warmer than the flame in the Jack. "You're a good 'un, Only," she said as the two of them bounded out the door.

The latch on the gate had barely clicked when Non cleared her throat.

"So."

I turned to her, eyes pleading. "Non, I know you heard all of it, but please don't tell Mama and Papa. Lark and Rowan seem so pleasant and they don't care that I'm . . . I'm . . ."

"A lady of a house," Non finished, regarding me with a raised brow. "With a warrant from the king."

Even with her smile that meant all fun, I wasn't sure if I understood her meaning. "Does that mean I can go?"

"I reckon you're old enough to look after yourself."

Unable to believe my luck, I threw my arms around her waist and hugged her. "Thank you, Non!"

"Not too fast, child," she chided, tapping my head lightly

with the dripping spoon. "I'll not tell your mam and pap, but if they come looking for you, you'll have to lie in your own bed, you understand?"

"I understand." To tell the truth, I wasn't hardly listening to her—my imagination was too busy conjuring up fantasies of laughter and wild dancing beneath the half-moon.

Non recognized the faraway look in my eyes. "And just so we're clear, little dreamer, this don't mean that I'll have with all manner of rule breaking from now on . . . but those two whelps seem like they'll have a care of you. And more'n likely, your brothers won't be far off neither. Especially if Mistress Mauralee's about this season."

I rolled the acorn round the Jack's belly. "Non, you don't suppose any of their folk might know anything about . . . what I got, do you?"

I might have imagined it, but Non didn't seem to want to meet my eye as she gave the potatoes a rough tumble in the pot. "I don't reckon it's wise to go asking around, no matter how kind they seem. You'll no doubt see all manner of strange and wonderful things tonight, but you keep yourself to yourself, you hear? Sometimes auguries can call like to like, so you stay canny."

"All this time, I've never told another living soul," I protested. "I ain't going to start now."

"I know you won't, Pip, I know. It's just that magics aren't so predictable." She smiled and shook her head. "The Ordish are interesting folk. You must've made quite an impression for them to give you that. Can I have a gander?"

The acorn spit and guttered as I handed over the Jack. She traced the bowed wooden bars of its cage, studying it. After a moment, she broke into a soft, singsong voice.

> Bonny Jack, Merry Jack
> In'th bush and briar.
> Wise Jack, Wily Jack
> Crack the seed with fire.
> Crack with water, crack with ice,
> Crack with weight of earth
> For only in the breaking
> Are seedlings fin'ly birthed.

"What's that, Non?"

She waved her hand before handing the Jack back to me. "Just a Ordish children's rhyme. Now, you go stow that someplace safe and secret in your room." She gave me a gentle shove toward the hallway. "Then have more of a rest until luncheon. You'll need some spirit in you tonight."

I sprinted to my room. I ducked under my bed and pulled out the small wooden chest Papa had made me for my nameday the year before. Inside were my birthday Allcloth, feathers from an applejay, a few smooth pebbles I'd found by the river, a purple snail shell, and a bunch of dried lavender. I tucked the Jack with its tiny, harmless flame under the Allcloth, closed the lid, and slid it back as far as it could go into the darkness underneath the pallet.

Non came with my pillow and my sheet, so I made myself comfortable as she tucked it all around me.

"Sleep well, Pip," she whispered, kissing my forehead. She made to leave my room, but stopped at the threshold. "You remember now, stay canny."

"I will," I murmured.

As Non's footsteps faded up the hallway, I drifted off to sleep dreaming of seeds, fire, and fiddles.

5

Dusk couldn't come fast enough.

But first, I had to take what was coming to me. A week
of taking care of the roost before harvest chores, Mama told
me. And I had to beg pardon from my brothers before dinner.
I knew I was getting off light. If Ether or Jonquin had skipped
out on their chores and ran out into the countryside in their
underthings, they'd have been in ten times the pickle. They knew
it, too, so I doubted my apology was going to make either of them
any happier.

As the six of us took our seats round the table, Papa folded
his hands. "Before we sup, I believe Only has something she'd
like to say."

Mama and Papa believed we shouldn't break bread together
if there was anger around the table, so whoever needed to beg
pardon always did it right before we ate. Ether had it down to an

art form—he had to stand up before dinner practically every day. It's probably why he looked so pleased when I pushed my chair out and cleared my throat.

"Mama, Papa, Non," I began, looking at each of them in turn, "I beg your pardon for leaving my chores this morning, for being dressed improper, and for worrying you."

"You're pardoned," they all said together. Non's mouth quirked up at the corners.

I turned to my brothers. "Ether and Jonquin, I beg your pardon for making you run round looking for me."

"You're pardoned," Jonquin replied stiffly.

"You're pardoned, I guess," grumbled Ether.

"That's that, then." Mama folded her hands and began our thanks. "Thanks for forgiveness."

"Thanks for the harvest," said Papa.

"Thanks for family," said Non, looking at me.

"Thanks for no halls," said Ether, sighing, no doubt looking forward to a week in the fields instead of the classroom.

"Thanks for friends," said Jon.

"Thanks for Mistress Mauralee," I whispered under my breath.

"What was that, Only?" asked Papa.

"Thanks for our—*ouch!*—apple trees." I rubbed the spot on my leg where Jon had jabbed me with his fork, his eyes wide as saucers.

"Thanks for All," we concluded together.

Out of the corner of my eye, I saw Jonquin giving me the

evils. As the knives and forks clanked against serving bowls, I turned and met his stare head on.

You're in a heap of trouble, his eyes told me.

Not as much as you'll be in, mine told him back, *so mind how you go.*

GLOAMING FELL ON the valley and my heart fluttered, bird light, under my quilt as I listened through the door to the sounds of the house bedding down. The light deepened from rosy red to purple on the gauzy curtains while the water trickled in the washroom, bed-shoed feet whispered against the stone floors, and finally, the latch clanked on Mama and Papa's bedchamber.

I crept from beneath my sheet and began to dress. I wasn't sure what a body wore to a campfire, so I chose my deep blue overlet to cover my shift and a soft pair of field moccasins. Just as I'd checked my face in the glass, the latch of my own door flipped up. For a second, I thought I was caught before I'd even begun, but on the other side stood Non and my brothers in the shadows of the dark hall.

Non's face was serious as she looked at us all in turn. "I know you two have been at this for well nigh on three years now—"

"Three years?" I gaped, turning to Jon and Ether. "It's been three years and you've never thought to take me?"

"You were too green," Jon whispered haughtily, probably still sore about my vexing him at dinner.

"You still *are* too green," Ether complained, appealing to Non. "Why's she coming?"

"Because she's been invited by those that wants to see her, that's why. And less of that tongue with me, whelp," said Non. "I ain't asking you to be her shepherds, but keep half an eye peeled, you hear?" She leaned against the wall, her arms folded. "The only reason I have owt to do with this is 'cause I think it does good to see there's more to the world than what's behind your own garden gate. Don't give me reason to change my mind."

My brothers shuffled their feet and mumbled, "Yes'm," under their breaths. Satisfied that was as much of a promise as she was like to get, Non shooed us out like a line of wayward chicks. I followed Ether and Jon to the room they shared on the other side of the kitchen, where a chair was already pressed up to the wall underneath the window. Without speaking, each of the boys climbed over the frame and dropped into the grass outside. Ether gave me his hands and guided me down as Jonquin strode across the yard, looking as if he'd like to put as much space as possible between himself and the pair of us. In fact, he was already halfway across the field by the time we reached the gate.

"Since when have you started keeping company with Ordish?" Ether asked, pulling a foxreed to tuck between his teeth.

"Since this morning," I answered saltily. "Why's Jon in such a humor?"

Ether shrugged. "Just antsy, I s'pose—"

"To see Mauralee?"

The reed was spat on the ground. "How in the name of the Mother d'you know about Maura?"

"Lark Fairweather told me," I replied, pleased to feel my new friend's name roll off my tongue.

Ether eyed me with something bordering on respect. "Well, Jon's been sweet on her for the last two seasons. Harvest ain't long, so he tries to spend all the time he can. Probably doesn't want to play lookout for poky little sisters."

I bristled. "I don't need looking out for. I can take care of myself!"

Ether grunted. "Sure you can, Only. Look, if you get into bother, I'll be about, but don't make a fuss and shame us. I'll be with Fen Piven, the boatswain's whelp. Anyone'll know him." He squinted into the gloom ahead of us. "That who you're looking for?"

As promised, standing by the trunk of the oak were Lark and Rowan, waving at me. The smile that broke over my face at the sight of them must have lit up half the field, in spite of the flutter of fear in my guts. I waved back.

"We'll meet back here when the Maiden is overhead, so keep one eye on the sky," Ether said, breaking from me on the path. "Don't be tardy."

I glanced up. The constellation wasn't even visible on the horizon yet, so I knew we had several hours before we'd need to make our way back.

As Ether disappeared down one of the far rows of lavender, I made haste to where Lark and Rowan were waiting.

"Good met, Only!" Lark chirped, embracing me like a sister. It was so familiar, I almost forgot to embrace back. None of my acquaintances had ever greeted me so. As she let me go, Rowan immediately swooped in to kiss both of my cheeks. I barely had time to be surprised before both of them took hold of my hands and pulled me toward the camp.

"I'm glad you came," said Lark, grinning. "D'your mam and pa know you're here?"

"No," I confessed. "But my non does. She can be a little bendier when it comes to rules."

"Mistress Beulah ain't been down yet this season," remarked Rowan. "Last year she came with a paste for that sting I got from a muck wasp, remember, Lark?"

I near tripped over my own feet. "Wait, you know Non?"

"Sure as tides. Comes every season to jaw with Auntie Maven on healing and the like."

"Am I the only one of my kin that hasn't been haunting your camp the last few years?" I cried indignantly.

"Oh, don't take it so," Lark reassured me. "You're here now, ain't you? Come, come to the fire."

I'd never been allowed down to the site during harvest, so it was a bit of a jolt to see the big, bare space by the river full of noise, fire, and a sea of riotous red. Ordish barges lined the bank—nearly forty in all, each almost as big as two houses lashed together. A small tent city had sprouted on the shore, in a dizzying array of colors. In some, sleeping rolls were spread on the ground. Others had open sides where delicious smells of cooking drifted into the night air. In the middle of it all roared an enormous bonfire, whose heat I could feel even standing a ways off. In its dancing light, I could see bare-chested young boys and men trying see who could stand closest to the flames the longest, before running to take a howling leap into the river. Lark heaved the same sigh Mama did when she was faced with my brothers' foolishness. "Flame-baiting," she said. "Rowan tried last year. He lost his eyebrows."

Rowan gave his sister a punch on the shoulder. "They grew back!"

"After two months!" Lark snorted. "Oh, I'm sorry, Ro, I don't mean to shame you, specially not before Only, but you did look awful rich without 'em!"

"Auntie Maven's our cunning woman. She had to make me a salve and all," grumbled Rowan, rubbing his grown-back brows.

"Cunning woman?"

Rowan's hand darted into a nearby tent and emerged with three sticks, all dripping with strips of succulent pork. He handed one to me. "You know, medicines. Birthing. Seeing. Lore. Things like that. Like what your non does."

I'd never heard of cunning women before. "Is that what you call them?" I said, testing the hot morsel with the tip of my tongue. "My non does the herbs and the birthing, and she can talk the hind legs off a donkey, but I don't know about . . . seeing?"

"Reading the stars? Tea leaves? Divining?"

"Mistress Beulah don't practice augury, Ro—she's a land-walker," said Lark, with the air of an older sibling that I knew all too well, but my heart did a leap in my chest at the word and I wondered for a second if I should have come after all.

But I didn't have time to dwell on it, as Lark and Rowan pulled me onto the gangplank of the nearest barge and the three of us scrambled up to the roof. My legs felt wobbly as the vessel beneath us bobbed up and down in the current, so Rowan kept a steady hand on my elbow until we sat by the dovecote. The pigeons inside ruffled their feathers, but seemed used to sharing space with two-legged folk.

"Ain't you ever been on a boat before?" Rowan asked, tearing a piece of meat from the stick. He shot me a quick look as I settled myself. "You ain't afraid of the water or anything?"

"Course not! You don't grow up on a riverbank without knowing how to swim." The gentle sway of the boat in the current was hypnotic. "It's nice, this. Like being rocked in a cradle. What's it like living on one?"

"Hot, in the summer. That's why we set up the tents outside," replied Lark. She patted the roof. "We share the *Briar* with Pa's kin—his brother's and sister's families. Fifteen of us!"

"The *Briar*?"

"It's the name of the barge," explained Rowan, pointing toward the bow. I leaned careful over the lip of the roof to see curling script spelling out the word *Briar* on the side of the vessel. Beautiful painted thorny roses wove in and out of the lettering. "They all got names." He pointed down the line. "*The Greenling, Firefloat, White Lady's Bane* . . . but everyone knows *Briar*'s the queen of the river." He puffed up like a partridge and Lark laughed.

"It's true enough," she agreed. "She can outsail the king's skiffs any day."

Rowan snorted in a temper. "The king can go hang."

Lark aimed a not-so-gentle punch at her brother's arm. "Don't speak so in front of Only!" she hissed.

"It's all right," I said quickly, my stomach filling with stones.

"I know why you ain't got much love for the king. Non told me about . . . you know, the ransomers."

Lark's gaze fluttered down to the river. "Our mate Echo Gladbrook got took down near Whiteburn Watch last season."

Rowan put his chin in his hands. "Linden Varley's oldest boy's been in Bellskeep for two years now. He'll have enough after this harvest to go north and fetch him."

What could I even say to folk who'd lost so much? "Just so's you know, I think it's dead rotten. I wish more'd speak up for you."

Lark shrugged. "Not many folks figure we're good for much but pulling in the harvest. Not that your pa ain't been kind to us, mind," she added quick like. "But not everyone in the kingdom feels as warm when they see barges on the river."

River rats. Sodden thieves. Wetcollars.

Our chat was interrupted by the cry of two fiddles that struck up round the fire. The crowd roared and hands were grabbed to begin a wild reel. I gasped as glamours erupted round the heads of the dancers in the form of wildflowers or twinkling fireflies. As the dancers began to whirl, I couldn't help notice a handsome young pair in the middle, their heads wreathed in glowing nightmoths. The girl, whose dark hair glinted orange in the firelight, beamed at her fair-haired partner as if he were the last word in wonderful.

Though I knew Jon would be at the campfire, it was like I'd never seen him before. He looked happy—the kind of happy I saw on Papa's face when he and Mama sat side by side on the garden bench on an evening. As I watched them turn in each other's arms, I suddenly realized why it was my Jon hadn't shared a joy so dear to him. It was the same reason I never told no one of my gift—he wasn't sure what he'd got to lose if he did. Rowan followed my gaze and nudged me in the ribs.

"Though some feel pretty warm indeed."

I blushed, hoping my friends couldn't tell in the dark. I hoped the Ordish looked on my brother kindly and not like some arrogant son of the land, come to take their daughter away. But it seemed no one cared for anything but the giddy tune that moved the dancers round the fire. And my brother's face, split from ear to ear in a grin, quieted my worries.

A whistle like a chicktail's sounded from the bank near the bow. Lark and Rowan cocked their heads to listen as it sounded a second time. "It's late for birds, ain't it?" I asked, confused.

A head suddenly popped up over the lip of the roof. It belonged to a merry-looking young man with dimpled cheeks and soft brown eyes. His dark curly hair exploded out of a dusty brown cap, which he doffed in our direction. "Good met, whelps."

"Toly!" Rowan cried, leaping to his feet and setting the barge swaying as he crossed to meet the newcomer. "Is it finished? Tell me it's finished."

The young man laughed. "Would I have come for you if it wasn't?"

Rowan turned round to Lark and me. "He's finished it, Lark! Let's go see!"

Lark bit her lip, torn. "Dunno, Ro—might not be so interesting for Only."

Toly looked past Lark, noticing me for the first time. It may have been my imagination, but I could have sworn I saw a flicker of something like disappointment cross his face. I scooted closer to the dovecote.

"Oh," he said, recovering himself brightly. "But you've got a mate, I see."

"Toly, this is Only, Master Fallow's girl," Lark told him. She turned to me. "Toly's finished a runner. Want to go and have a gander?"

"What's a runner?"

"A little boat," she explained. "The older whelps race them, and Toly reckons his'll be the fastest there is. Don't suppose you'd like to see?"

I did want to see. I wanted to see everything. The grin on Jon's face and the flash of silver beads in the hair of the dancers. The rigging in the sails and the magics. The thought of following Toly down the river made me nervous for some reason, but I wasn't going to look white-feathered in front of my new mates. I grabbed for Lark's hand and stood up, ignoring the wobble in my knees. Rowan'd already scrambled over the roof and his feet made two puffs of dust as they hit the dirt of the towpath. Lark helped me down the way we came up. Toly put on his too-bright smile once more. "This way, then!"

As the four of us skirted round the whirling bodies by the fire and crossed into the darkness beyond, the young man's eyes flicked back to me once more, filling me with disquiet.

Just the breeze off the river, I told myself. *Just night and water.*

6

Lantern swinging, Toly led us on a path that followed
the curve of the river, away from the bonfire at the center of the
camp. But lights from inside the barges spilled onto the ground
along the towpath, allowing me to peek inside. Through the
windows I saw small, perfect kitchens, tight rows of bunks, and
even large sitting areas, strung with hammocks and filled with
colorful pillows.

"Don't it feel awful crowded?" I asked Lark as we passed by.

Lark shrugged. "It's just the way of things. In the summer,
we camp a lot or some of us sleep on the roof. In the winter, it's
snug. We take turns with the chores—cooking, cleaning, fishing,
tending the little ones and the pigeons."

"You can't use magic to do that?"

"*Chores?*" she said, laughing. "Tides, that'd be a fine thing.
My uncle's got it in him to make a pot boil from cold and our

cousin Fern can call a decent breeze, but bewitching a rod to beat the carpets, *that* would be of use."

"Oh, beg your pardon! The way folks go on about your auguries, I thought they were . . . bigger."

"Most land folk do. The way they all scatter when we float by, you'd think we could turn them into toads or set the river alight."

My feet stopped carrying me forward a second. "You . . . can't do that . . . right?"

Lark laughed as we left the barges behind us on the path and headed into the willow grove that bordered the orchards. "If I could, Ro would have been sitting on a log croaking years ago!"

Ahead of us, Toly pointed to a spot downstream. "There she is." Rowan rushed ahead to get the first look.

The runner sat on the bank, gleaming in the light of the lantern. Its oars were painted red and polished till they shone, looking fine. The words *The Hare* proudly rounded the bow next to a beautiful carving of the animal itself.

"It's the green on the grass, Toly!" Rowan exclaimed, running his hands over the shining, curved wood. He looked up at the young man, excited. "Will you help me make my own next season?"

"Surely as the days get short in the winter." Toly grinned, patting Rowan's shoulder. Rowan beamed, but what I saw rooted me to the riverbank. Though the sun had long since disappeared and the night was dark around us, I could easily make out a blackness around Toly—it rolled and wobbled around the outlines of his body. It was bigger by far than the ugly guile of the Bonniways and boded nothing but ill. I shrank back behind Lark.

He looked from side to side, then turned to Rowan. "Fancy a quick go? See how fast she is? I promised the first trip to Ise"—he craned his neck for any sign of his sweetheart—"but she don't have to know, does she?"

The darkness around him spread so far, it almost covered Rowan, who still sported a hungry grin, unable to take his eyes off the runner.

Stay canny, Non'd warned me. Fat lot of good canny was going to do me with Toly spinning some dark and sinister tale to All knows what ends. We needed to be shot of the riverbank and the runner. I thought quick to anything that might get us back to the safety of the fire.

"But, Rowan," I broke out, "the dancing's just started. You and Lark need to come show me how it's done."

Toly gave a light chuckle. "Don't worry, poppet, I'll have him back in a blink."

"Can you take me after?" asked Lark, bouncing on her toes. "And then Only?"

Toly's smile began to falter. "I can come back for you, love, but . . ." He swallowed hard. "I wouldn't feel proper about taking Master Fallow's girl out on the river. It can be tricky sometimes and I won't risk it. You understand, don't you, poppet?" He tried to look sympathetic, but the darkness of his lie had begun to shadow his face.

"Oh," said Lark, disappointed. "Well, if you can't take Only, I won't go neither." She linked her arm through mine. "I'll go another time. You can go, though, Ro. We'll watch from here."

"Be a shame for you girls to miss the dancing." Toly's pitch crept a little higher. "Why don't you go on, and we'll meet you after?" He put his hand firmly on Rowan's shoulder and made to steer him into the runner. "Tell Ise to save a turn for me, eh?"

Rowan reached across the stern to step in. I didn't have no more time for canny.

"Wait!" The shout surprised all of us, but me most of all. I didn't even recognize my voice.

Toly turned, no longer looking open or honest, but angry. The dark round him was drifting in tendrils now, some taller than the young willow on the bank. "I'm sorry I can't take you, but there's no sense spoiling a boy's fun, now is there?"

"It's all right," Lark said, grasping my hand. "They'll just go upstream a bit and then make a run back, fast as they can."

"No! It's not that," I stammered. "He just . . . shouldn't go."

"Why not?" Rowan sulked.

"No good will come to you," I blurted. Anger at this man, who meant harm to my new friend, made me brave despite the danger the three of us were in. "I just got a feeling that . . ."

I got no further before the familiar wave of pain caught me between the eyes and I yelped like a dog with a trod-on tail and buried my face in my hands.

Lark grasped me by the shoulders. "Only? Only, what is it?"

"Oh, Mother's breath, I've not got time for this," swore Toly. When I finally looked up, blinking through the discomfort, his hand had darted to his boot and come up with a long, pointed dagger he notched under Rowan's ear. The blackness around him vanished in an instant, the lie dissolving like smoke along with his low-country accent. "You just *had* to bring the landsman's daughter."

"Toly?" Rowan squeaked.

The young man tightened his grip on Rowan's upper arm. "Quiet, boy. No squawking." He narrowed his eyes at Lark and me and jerked his head at the runner. "You two. Get in. Now."

"What are you doing?" Lark cried, reaching her hand out to comfort Rowan, who was utterly frozen with fear. Toly slapped it away.

"You heard me, get in," the man growled. "I don't need to let a little blood from your brother, do I?" To make his point, he pressed the blade tighter against Rowan's skin.

Lark didn't hesitate to step over the end of the stern, shooting Toly a murderous look. "This runner ain't built for more than three. All of us together'll scuttle it."

Toly grinned a grin that wasn't a grin at all, but just a way of showing off his teeth. "Won't need to carry more'n three for long—the bank's not so far. Can't have any of you running back to warn folk, can I? I've done well from this clan and I'm not quite ready to leave it yet."

Despite having a deadly blade pressed to his throat, Rowan let out a roar of outrage. "You're a ransomer! You took Thorne Varley and Echo Gladbrook!" He tried to elbow Toly in the gut, but a quick flick of the blade opened up a small red path under his ear that trickled down his neck and into his collar. Rowan cried out and tears sprung to Lark's eyes.

I quick put my foot into the well of the runner. "We're

coming, ain't we?" I sat down careful in the bow beside Lark, who was wringing her hands in her lap. My hand stole round hers for comfort. Toly shoved Rowan in after us and rested his foot on the stern, peering at me shrewdly. He pointed his knife.

"You had a little spell just then. What was that about?"

"It's got nothing to do with you!" I shouted, and was made to regret it directly. My temples gave an almighty *THUD* and I couldn't help but mewl into my hands.

"Oh, doesn't it?" he purred thoughtfully. I peeped from between my fingers at him, saw him staring at me like a thief in a countinghouse. "This evening might be the gold coin at the bottom of my ale after all."

"Oh! Beg your pardon!" A woman's voice rang out of the darkness. "Didn't know there were already folks here!"

Toly dropped the dagger in the stern in surprise. In the guttering light of the lantern, I could make out the figures of Jonquin and Mauralee.

"Making friends, Only?" said my brother with a grin.

I wanted to scream, to run to him, but I was stuck fast in Toly's cruel eyes, which clouded over at the sound of voices behind him. Those eyes told us pretty clear that if we made a sound, he'd be more than happy to practice carving on us. Then his cheerful mask fell into place and he was once more wreathed in his loathsome lie.

"Good eve, Mauralee, Master Fallow," he replied, not turning toward them, but instead watching the three of us, hawk-like. "Just finished *The Hare*. Thought these three might like to have a go in her."

Mauralee put her hands on her hips, her hair glistening in the lantern light. "Don't be soft, Toly! There'll be too many of you. I reckon Lark and Rowan have had a lungful of river water or two in their lives. One or two more won't do any harm, but leave Jon's sister."

Jonquin stretched out an arm. "Come here, Only. We'll let the other two go first just in case of leaks."

I stood to exit the boat, but Toly barked at me, "Sit down, whelp!"

Bewilderment crossed Jon's face while Maura's creased with annoyance. "What spirit's flown up your tailpipe? Don't be a fool, just let her—"

She broke off, staring across the water to the far bank of the river that ran close to the kingsroad. Lark and I turned, too, in time to see a lantern raised out of the blackness, once, twice, three times. Then again—one, two, three.

Maura's eyes grew wide and furious. "You gutless eel," she growled, starting forward. "This clan took you in when you had nothing. This is how you pay us? By stealing our children for the king?"

"What?" Jonquin growled, advancing on Toly.

Caught, Toly tensed, ready for Jon's charge. Lark squeezed my hand tight, ready for the moment to leap when he made his move, but it wasn't the move anyone was expecting. With a quick twist of his heel, Toly put all of his weight to the stern of the tiny boat, launching it out into the embrace of the river. Me and Lark were flung forward on top of Rowan as the craft tipped from one side to the other, dark water sloshing over our feet. But

Toly, who'd landed in the stern, grabbed one of the shining oars and kept us true, pushing us farther into the current with every powerful stroke.

"Only!" Jon's cry split the air as his boots crashed into the water. As I struggled back to my seat in the bow, I could see Maura racing up the towpath toward the camp, shouting for all she was worth. My brother got as far as waist deep before it was clear there was no catching us under his own power.

"Sit down and stop fidgeting, rats!" growled Toly. "You'll turn us over!"

"The White Lady take you!" shouted Rowan, making a lunge for the oar, but quick as a wink, Toly's ugly blade was in his hand again, this time pointed straight at Rowan's heart.

"I'll admit, I'd get less coin for two than three, but I won't lose any sleep over it," the kingsman hissed. "Now, you settle yourself before I send you to the bottom of the river."

Lark yanked the back of Rowan's tunic, pulling him down on his backside with a thud, as far away from Toly's knife as he could get. Pressed against her shoulder, I couldn't stop shaking, the merriment of the evening replaced with poisoned fear. Shouts of alarm could be heard echoing through the hot night, but the opposite shore with its mysterious lanterns loomed closer every second. Panic rose up to choke me, and I whimpered into the red fabric of Lark's sleeve.

She looked at me, brave and ferocious in the moonlight. "This ain't any place for you, Only," she whispered. "The woes of the river belong to the river. You belong to the land."

"What?"

She smiled, sad as winter. "You tell Pa we'll be just fine, you hear?"

And before I had the chance to ask her what she meant, she gave me an almighty shove. Toly's angry bellow was lost as I hit the river, too surprised to cry out. Water rushed into my ears and nose, and my tiptoes kicked desperately, trying to find the bottom. But we were in the heart of the cut, nowhere near the gentle shallows I'd always been allowed to paddle in. I broke the surface, gasping like a fish and turned around, not able to tell left from right. The current's strong fingers grabbed at my feet, trying to pull me back under, but I kicked against it for all I was worth.

I caught sight of the runner, which had stopped its swift progress toward the far bank. Toly struggled with the oar, trying to turn the tiny boat upstream after me. If I thought he was scary while he was lying, he was nothing short of terrifying as he attacked the water with every stroke, teeth clenched in rage.

"Swim, Only!" Lark shrieked.

I struck out hard as I could, straight across, just like Papa'd always taught us, in case we ever ventured too far into the river. *Don't bother trying to get back to the spot you came from, just get to shore. You always got feet to walk back home.* I didn't look round, but the steady swish of Toly's paddle sang at my back, even over my own thrashing. I kicked harder, as if one of the imaginary giant pikes Non'd tried to scare us with when we were small were snapping at my heels. My arms and legs screamed for mercy, the weight of my clothes pulling me down, even as I clawed my way toward the bank. I hoped I'd not have to make a choice between drowning or giving myself over to Toly's tender care.

The light of the first torch broke the bank, followed by six or seven others. Furious shouts of "Kingsman!" and "Traitor!" flew like bolts over the water while figures scrambled to untie runners lashed to the backs of the barges. The dreaded sound of the oar behind me stopped, and I risked a glance between kicks. The sight was almost more than I could bear. One of Toly's arms was wrapped round Rowan once more, the terrible dagger threatening the soft skin of his throat, while the other held out the paddle to Lark. He may have lost me as a prize, but he wasn't ready to go empty-handed.

"Row!" he barked. "And don't think I won't know if you're not doing your best."

Lark didn't hesitate to do as she was bid. She snatched the oar from the kingsman's hand and set to the far shore, her eyes never leaving the angry, frightened face of her brother.

"Lark!" I wailed, water filling my mouth. It poured down my throat, sloshing over into my windpipe. I coughed, but more followed as I tried to stay afloat. My next shout was more of a gurgle as my head ducked below the surface. Every summer, you'd hear of a whelp or two lost to the river. Their names were spoken like warnings. Would they speak that way of me? *Don't wade out too far! Remember what happened to Only Fallow.*

But I wasn't to be a lesson for this hot season. A sharp tug to the collar of my overlet yanked my head back up into the night air. A pair of strong arms slid round my middle, and legs that weren't mine tangled in my skirts, pushing us closer to the bank where a crowd of tense Ordish faces were gathered by lantern light. The blessed pebbles of the bank finally scraped at my calves, and a forest of hands dragged me onto dry land, clearing a path for me and my rescuer. I took two great handfuls of grass and earth to anchor me as I emptied the river from my lungs, being thumped on the back all the while by a wet and gasping Jonquin.

"Pip? Look at me, sweetling. He didn't hurt you, did he?"

I choked up some more muddy water, so pleased to be sucking down air again, I didn't care what manner of filth was running out of my nose and mouth. "No," I croaked. "But he's got Lark and Rowan!"

Maura appeared at Jonquin's elbow, out of breath. "There's a clan meet coming together. A few folk have got runners after them, but . . ." She broke off, putting a gentle hand to my heaving back. "I heard just about all there is to hear about you, Only Fallow. I'm sorry we've gotta meet like this. Are you well?"

I nodded weakly, resting my head against Jon's knee. I didn't want to move an inch, but the fright and cool breeze from the water set me to shivering in my sodden clothes. And worse than that, I thought to the greedy look in Toly's eye when he'd wondered after the pain in my temples. *This evening might be the gold coin at the bottom of my ale after all.* Surely he didn't have any idea about my . . . what had Lark and Rowan called it? My *cunning.* I ticked myself off for being foolish—how could a rat like Toly have the first clue about something neither me nor Non understood properly?

"Why don't you take her up to our tent?" Maura urged. "Get

some warmth back in her bones—and yours. I'm sure there'll be some who'll want to speak with her."

The face of Master Fairweather came unbidden into my head. I could think of ten things I'd surely rather do than have to face the man whose whelps had just been stolen. Lark and Rowan, who'd given me the Jack, a rich helping of kindness . . . and my freedom.

"Come on, Pip," coaxed Jon, his strong hands sliding under my arms, like they had in the river. "Let's do as Maura bids."

I stood on legs still made of butter from my escape, letting Jon lead me back toward the light of the camp. But all the while, my heart stretched farther away as the runner with my two new friends disappeared into the darkness, bound for unknown shores.

7

The inside of the tent was warmer than the cool night air outside. Jon pulled the flap of material closed behind us, muffling the noise of the frantic camp outside. Although I was a little glad of the quiet, sweat began to mix with the river water and trickle down my body in the close heat. My brother moved round as if he belonged there, stoking several oil lanterns to flame. On a low round table, one of them sat beneath a stand with an iron kettle on top. I stood like a lemon in the corner as he opened one of several dozen drawers in a large sideboard that ran the entire length of the back wall of the tent. Gathering ingredients from one drawer and then another, he lifted the lid of the kettle and cast them into its belly. Satisfied, he replaced the lid and turned to me.

"Sweet All, Pip, sit down before you keel over," he chided, guiding me to a pile of thick pillows that smelt of sage and dust.

My tongue was still tied up with worry, so I just hugged

my knees tight to my body and watched him bustle around the Ordish tent like it was his own. *This ain't a passing fancy,* I thought suddenly, more than a little jealous. *It's like he's chosen a different family.* But I could still feel his grip where he dragged me from the belly of the river, so I tried to squash those tiny, unhelpful thoughts best I could.

The hiss of the boiling kettle filled the tent as Jon came to sit beside me, his own wet clothes clinging to his skin. There was a darkness in his eyes I'd never thought to see there.

"I'd like to show his entrails the light of day," he murmured, low and frightening.

I recoiled in horror. "Mother All says that killing's the gravest sin there is."

Jon had nothing to say to that, but the lantern light deepened the shadows on his tight-clenched jaw.

I didn't care to think on what he was thinking of doing to the kingsman. "So . . . who was he? Toly, I mean?"

"He showed up 'bout two years ago. Said he was from a clan up north and he'd had a row with his pa. Happens some-times. Living as they do, sometimes there are things that can't be helped. People start again, join new clans." The kettle's thin whistle interrupted him and he rose to quiet it. Tin cups appeared from one of the drawers and he tipped the liquid out of the vessel, steam curling round his wrist like a cat's tail. "They're a lot like Papa—think everyone's worthy of a chance. Even if it turns out it ain't deserved."

He brought me my cup, which I took gratefully and inhaled. The warm mint, goldleaf, and chamomile quieted my soul as I took a cautious sip. We two sat quietly for a spell, each grateful for the other's wet shoulder to lean on. But I'd had too much inside to keep in for long.

"Will they catch them, do you think?"

Jon shook his head grimly. "Ransomers know what they're about. Those whelps will be half a mile away when the rest of the runners hit the shore. By the time they manage to find someone to loan them a cart and get to the crossing at Lochery . . ." He trailed off, his fist curling round the handle of an imaginary dagger. "I reckon Mother All might have looked the other way."

A rush of cool air swept into the tent, making the lanterns gutter and spit. Jon and I sprang to our feet as Bula appeared, his face knotted and anguished. I thought for a second he would shout or bluster, but instead, he crumpled, falling to his knees with a silent sob.

Just that morning, I'd known little of the Ordish, save for the old tales and what I saw season to season—and somehow, between sunrise and sunset, I'd got tangled up in the best and worst of their lives.

Jon covered the space in two strides to kneel beside the heart-stricken man. The same little jealous thorn pricked at me, and again, I swatted it away, ashamed. Instead of begrudging my brother's closeness with the river folk, I wanted to share it. Thinking of the acorn, silently burning inside my nameday box, I stepped closer. Bula's head jerked up, and I froze. His quivering lips parted.

"He . . . they didn't come to any hurt, did they?"

"No, master," I croaked. "Lark did as she was bid. She kept

them safe." A lump began to creep up my throat. "She kept *me* safe, master. And I wish . . . I wish I had a way to thank her."

Tears that felt muddy as the river pricked my eyes. One of Bula's calloused hands stole round my wrist.

"Ain't none of this is your doing, child, you hear?" The Ordish man's voice was thick with sorrow and his eyes rimmed with red. "No one bears the blame for this but that skunkspawn Pawlin, or whatever his true name is."

The tent flap opened once again. Maura's face was flushed and urgent. "The meet's ready. Ma and Barrow are just rounding up the last folk now." She reached in to grasp her clansman's shoulder. "A few of the runners are back," she said softly. "I'm sorry, Bula, they didn't find anything but a few spent lanterns."

The man's long, dark hair fell before his face. "Didn't expect they'd find much. We never do, do we?"

Maura and my brother exchanged pained glances over Bula's head. "Only shouldn't be put through no more tonight, but since you were there, Jon, you wouldn't mind speaking, would you?" she asked.

"Of course not. But if it's all the same, I'm going to take her and Ether home. The Maiden's nearly overhead anyhow."

Bula sat back on his heels. "He didn't do you no harm, did he?"

"No, sir," I said, and sniffled.

"I'm sorry you were caught up in this. I know it's much to ask in one day, but—"

"Our father would want to know," Jon interrupted. "Maybe he could help. I'm sure if we—"

Bula cut him off. "We like to keep our business our own, you understand? We don't want to make trouble."

Make trouble? Fire burned hot in my belly. It wasn't fair the Ordish had no one to share their troubles with. No one to stand up when their children went missing. No one to speak for them. While I sat comfortable at supper with my family, they knew that, at any moment, there might be an empty seat at their table.

Jonquin opened his mouth to protest, but Maura laid a hand on his arm in quiet counsel. The girl pushed aside the tent flap and he reluctantly ducked out, holding it open for me.

"Master Bula?" I said.

The man's eyes were fixed in the corner, on nothing in particular. "Aye?"

"She told me, before she pushed me out of the runner"—I swallowed hard—"she told me to tell you that they'd be fine."

Bula laughed—more of a bark with no mirth in it. "Fine. Aye, or whatever passes for it in that blasted city." An expression of pain, sharp enough to cut yourself on, gnarled his face. "Go on now, child. Back to your bed."

Not able to spend another moment drowning in the man's despair, I stepped out into the night, where Jonquin and Mauralee were close in conference. Jon kissed her on the cheek and took hold of my hand. The two of us began the walk toward the big oak where we knew Ether would be waiting. Sure enough, as we came close, he and his moon-shadow leapt up to join us, taking in our soaking wet clothes with a look of surprise.

"Great All, are you two all right? The lads just said there was a kingsman in the camp and . . ."

I waved him off. "We're fine."

"It don't need going over right now, Eth," Jon added sternly.

Ether's face dropped—he was being deprived of a second good story in one day. He kicked a stone on the path through the field. "I was just asking."

"You two've known all this time. What the king does."

My brothers looked at each other and then back to me. "They don't like to speak on it," Ether said.

"The woes of the river belong to the river. The woes of the land belong to the land," quoted Jon. "S'what Maura's pa says, anyway."

"That's just what Lark said, before she . . ." The river threatened to rise up in my eyes again. "Don't the Mother teach that we should take up our neighbor's troubles on our own backs? Ain't the Ordish our neighbors?"

"It ain't as simple as all that," Ether answered.

Jon had fallen behind us a bit and he muttered something under his breath. Ether's head swung round to hear him better. "What'd you say, Jon?"

"I said, it *should* be."

The way he said it meant the end of the conversation, so the three of us threaded through the rows of fragrant blossoms in silence. Taking care not to let the hinges on the gate squeak, we slipped back into the garden and Ether made for their open window.

Jon wrapped me in a hard, unexpected embrace. "I thought I'd lost you, Pip, when Toly pushed that boat away."

"Will he get them back?" I whispered.

My brother rested his chin on the top of my head. "A few years of hard work, then maybe he'll be able to scrape together the ransom for both of them."

Years. Lark and Rowan would spend a few *years* in Bellskeep. As prisoners. No, worse, as *slaves*.

Jon released me, our wet clothes peeling apart. "I've got to go back. Are you well enough?"

"He didn't hurt me, Jon." It was the best I could do without telling a lie. I pointed in the direction of the herbery. "I'm going to speak with Non. She'll want to know I'm home safe."

My brother nodded and stole off into the darkness, back toward the camp.

The herbery was attached to the house, but had its own entrance for those from the town who came looking for Non's advice or remedies. She kept a small set of rooms off the main workspace—a library and a place for her simple cot, which she claimed she preferred over the fancy feather mattresses that we got after the warrant.

I lifted the latch and let myself in. The smell of crushed herbs wrapped me up, green and familiar. Despite the wee hour of the morning, Non sat at her workbench, a book open, spectacles balanced on the end of her nose, blinking in the light of a single, flickering candle. She turned, a wide grin on her face that died as she took me in.

"So, did you . . . Sweet Mother, child, what happened?"

Every tear I'd held in during the night finally got its chance to escape. A sob tore out of my throat as I ran to my grandmother and let her wrap her strong arms around me while I cried and cried.

The woes of the river belonged to the river. The woes of the land belonged to the land. But my woes were all my own.

EVEN THE BLACKBIRD had stopped its nighttime symphony by the time I'd managed to tell my whole tale. Wrapped in a warm quilt, wearing one of Non's old nightdresses and sipping on another cup of goldleaf tea, some of the fear had drained away, but the sadness remained.

"That rotten, stinking kingsman'll have the Mother to answer to one day." Non shook her head. "Those poor folk, having to fret for their children like that. Maven'll be frantic, I reckon, her niece and nephew gone like that."

In all the furor of the evening, I'd near forgot about Non's visits. "Why didn't you tell me you spent time with the Ordish?"

My grandmother had the courtesy to look guilty. "Found out about that, did you? Well, like I said, they're interesting folk. I've had to be a little slippery about it, though. You know how people round here are."

The small, pesky flea of Toly's strange interest in me still gnawed on the edge of my thoughts, daring me to scratch at it. I knew if I said it plainly, Non might look for a way to dance round my questions—she'd got good at it, knowing all about my wile. I'd have to go round the long way to get any answers.

"Lark and Rowan called you a cunning woman."

Non settled back in her chair. "Well, now, that's a bit of flattery."

"They said you were the same as their auntie. She does medicine, birthing, lore, things like that."

"Aye, that's about the way of it. I ain't got the first notion about reading the heavens, mind you."

I stared at the dregs of my tea. "This morning, when I asked you if they might know about . . ." I took a deep, steadying breath. "In all the years you been jawing with the cunning woman of the Fairweather clan, you ain't never thought to ask about my magic?"

Non took a gulp of tea and sloshed it round in her cheek. Somewhere outside, an owl hooted mournfully. She was looking to decide something and I couldn't tell what.

"You *have* asked!" I burst out. "Why in All's name haven't you told me?"

"A few seasons back," she answered finally. "It weren't the most comforting tale, I'll tell you that. Maybe it's best left for morning."

I grabbed her hand, spilling some tea out of her cup. "No! If you know what this is, I want to know, too. I want to know now!"

"All right, child!" spluttered Non, wiping the small puddle of tea off her worktable with the edge of her sleeve. "I wouldn't put too much stock in it, mind. It's an old bit of lore, passed down through too many mouths to count."

"Oh, Non, just come to the matter of it!"

"I'm gettin' there, whelp," she said with a sigh. "The river folk call it the 'Tale of the Heartseeker.' So, before the Great Weir, there was an Ordish girl that got left behind in Bellskeep. Name of Makeen."

"Like the waterbird?" Flocks of makeen wintered on the river below the fields. Their black feathers and bright red beaks always looked fine against the snow.

"Aye, like the waterbird. Any rate, she went begging to the palace kitchens for work, and an old cook took her in as a scullery girl. Called her Mayquin, as the folks in the capital like to pronounce it. Mayquin turned out to be pretty handy round the kitchens, but it wasn't 'cause she was quick at peeling potatoes. Can you guess what else she could do?"

I knew the answer though I hardly dared say it, even in a small voice. "She could see lies?"

"She could," replied Non grimly. "But couldn't tell 'em to save her life—the pain it caused was too great. The cook soon cottoned on and would always have the girl by her side when she haggled with merchants. Folk wondered how the old bat never got cheated, but the two of 'em kept it real quiet. Course, a palace is a bit like Presston. You can't sneeze in the cellar without having someone in the attic knowing about it. Word got upstairs about the girl in the kitchen, and she was brought before the queen who ruled in them days and made to stand beside the throne while three of the royal advisors came forward to be questioned. The man in the middle had a fearful darkness round him and Mayquin said as much. As you can imagine, the fella was hauled away hollering and vowing his innocence. Turns out he was plotting against the queen's life."

"What happened to Mayquin?"

"She'd hoped to return to her clan when they came back to Bellskeep, but the queen didn't really want to give up her prize, so Mayquin never did get to go back to the river. She spent her life in service to the crown—to the queen, her son that came after her, and her granddaughter after that."

A part of me felt hollowed out. "So, she was a slave. Just like all the Ordish whelps in Bellskeep."

"I told you it weren't terrible comforting."

"Do you think . . . do you think it's a tale a lot of river folk know?" I asked, trying not to sound as afeared as I felt.

"I couldn't say, Pip. Maven knows hundreds of tales. I can't imagine anyone asks to hear *that* one very often." The lines on her face deepened as she leaned closer to me in the candlelight. "You ain't wrong, though. I should have told you sooner. I just didn't want to put that kind of worry in your head. Like I told you, it's an old tale—might not even be true. But it's all the more reason to stay canny, you hear?"

I shrunk farther in the cocoon of the quilt.

"You look half dead, Pip," Non declared, shooing me from the table. "Go on, you bed down on the cot. I ain't tired just yet."

Non's cot smelled of her—lavender, mint, and a hint of the charcoal she used in some of her compounds. I knew I should feel safe as I settled my small, weary weight, still swaddled in her best quilt, but even the quiet of the herbery and Non's faint humming couldn't steal away the shivers underneath. I thought of Lark and Rowan, wondering if they were laying their sorry heads down in a jostling ransomer's cart and hurting for home. I thought of Bula and the empty bunks in the Fairweather barge. I thought of Jonquin and his place among the Ordish.

But worst and most darkly, I thought of Toly's hungry eyes and the glint of moonlight on his blade.

8

It's a long way down the Baltway
It's green all down the Blue
But I'll sail right through the summer
If it brings me back to you.
Oh, the tides may rise and fall, my love,
But Mama Deep runs true,
I'll see you down in the winter bay
When she brings me back to you.

—"The River Reel," Ordish folk song

It would have been easy to lose myself in the bustle of the harvest. I *wanted* to lose myself—in the sharp vinegar of the pressing barn. In the dusty purple haze of scythes in the lavender fields. In the cool, dim fermenting cellars. In the floury-sweet warmth of the kitchens, where I spent most of my time peeling fruit and pinching crusts. But none of those places offered me a place to hide from the kingsman and his black cloud of lies.

I jumped at the slightest sound, convinced I could see Toly's wild mop of curls round every corner. I broke dishes, dropped pots, and tripped over my own feet. Exasperated at picking up the shards of one of her serving dishes after a long day spent in the kitchens, Mama huffed and puffed. "Honestly, child, what's got into you? You'd think we had a spook in the house for all your blundering!"

My heart only grew heavier when the sun sank behind the hills and I could hear the Ordish round their evening fires, not so free or merry as before. Jon and Ether both tried to coax me back. Even Non tried to get me to sit with her and Maven Fairweather for a spell, but I wasn't to be moved. I didn't want to remind everyone of their loss. Every time I was even tempted to the river, the memory of Toly was always waiting for me. *Well, ain't that just a gold coin at the bottom of my ale.*

On the day after the harvest ended, I sat with Ether at the edge of the field, watching the now-familiar tents collapsed, rolled into bundles, and stowed neatly on the roofs of the barges. He pointed them all out to me, even listing off the families that called them home—*The Red Darling* belonged to the Dells, the *Fair Man's Folly* to the Reeves, *King's Sorrow* and *The Raven's Roost* to the Cutteryjoys. As far as I could see round the bend in the river, the Ordish were preparing to move on, two less than they'd been when they'd come.

Ether lounged on the ground beside me, knotting stems of autumn grass together. "Wouldn't it be grand to go with them? To see the south where they winter?"

If I squinted, I could almost see Lark and Rowan peering round the side of the big oak where we met. "S'pose it would," I muttered.

"And the sea, of course. Fen Piven says if you throw a pebble in at high tide during the full moon and make a wish, it'll come true."

I closed my eyes and tried to imagine the sea. I'd seen drawings, in the books at halls, of the white-headed waves throwing themselves against the sand. Maybe it would be worth it to dig my toes into the sand of the southern shore. I could make a thousand wishes to bring my friends back—enough wishes to build a seawall. After all, what had I got to look forward to? Another year of halls and the familiar, cold glances of my hallsmates.

But, I thought, *at least I ain't Jon, having to watch Maura's barge sailing away down the cut.* As melancholy as I felt, I couldn't imagine how my brother felt every season, peering after *The South Wind* until it was just a speck in the distance.

A shrill whistle sounded from up the hill and the steady *clip-clop* of hooves began to close in. It was time. Ether and I scrambled to our feet and raced to join our family.

Papa had gone to the lenders the day before to collect the coin. When I asked why the Ordish preferred them to the markers the orchard workers got, Papa looked sheepish. "Lending houses often don't trust the river folk—won't give them the coin the markers are worth."

I fell in line beside Non as we all made our way down through the now-bare lavender fields, the two chests containing the wages swaying on the back of Mama's horse, Waymer. When I was small, I'd always looked forward to the parting—partly for the song and partly for the spectacle of dozens of barges at full sail downstream. But this year, I had only a lump of sadness in me. Even though it gave me heartache, I wished the riverbank crowded and lively a little while longer.

Out of the corner of my eye, I watched Jonquin turn to make upstream to where *The South Wind* was moored. Papa was jawing to Mama over some bit of business or another, but I saw their eyes flick toward my brother's retreat. I wondered for a second if Papa was going to call to him, but Mama spoke to him quiet like.

"Let him go, Ellis. Let him say what needs to be said."

I tugged on Non's sleeve. "Jon's just going to say good-bye to Mauralee, ain't he?" I whispered.

"Your pap and mam . . . they found out about Maura. They ain't keen on their oldest boy courtin' an Ordish girl."

My mouth fell open. "What? Why?"

"I tried to talk some sense to 'em, but Jon's almost a man now and he's gonna have more responsibilities. Only a year or two before he'll think about taking a wife."

"But . . . you said Papa was helping them by giving them work. He doesn't believe all the nonsense that folk say of them!"

"There's a difference between not believing the nonsense and having an Ordish daughter-in-law, Pip. The warrant—"

"All take the warrant!"

Papa pulled Waymer's harness and the old horse came to a stop. Both he and Mama twisted round.

"This ain't none of your concern, Only," Mama said, folding her arms over her bosom. "And don't think we don't know about your little adventure, either."

If her tone was meant to hobble me, it didn't. "Mauralee's the green on the grass! She's strong and good and she—"

"It ain't what she is, Pip—it's who she is," Papa explained, with no little shame on his face. "Jon should've known better before throwing his heart into the river. Better he makes a break now than—"

"Than in a few years when you make him marry a girl he doesn't care for? One that the king likes better?"

I knew the moment the words flew from my mouth, I ought've swallowed 'em down instead. Mama grabbed me hard by the arm.

"Only Fallow, don't you ever speak so to your pa or me again, d'you hear? You got a lot to learn about the world, but I can tell you two things—it ain't fair and it sure don't follow your rules." She let go, and I rubbed the spot where her fingers dug in. "I know you don't mean ill, but this ain't a matter for discussion. You take my meaning?"

I took her meaning. Why'd Papa even bother defending the Ordish to the likes of Master Anslo if he didn't believe them to be worthy of Jonquin's love? Meanwhile, our apples and our Scrump became coins in the king's coffers. Coins he could use to take more Larks and more Rowans from sorrowful parents. I scowled, glaring daggers at my own parents' backs, and we continued on our way down the hill.

As our slow procession came to the campsite, the river hummed with activity. Barges swayed as last-moment bits were stowed and children clambered up on the roofs, chasing one another from bow to stern. Men and women at the tillers shouted orders for the short masts to be unfolded to make use of the breeze that kicked up along the water. Short, fat red sails unfurled as the vessels began tugging at their tethers, eager to be under way. The site by the river was just empty dust once more, and there were bees in my belly.

Bula was waiting for us as I knew he would be. I'd seen him in the fields since the night by the river, working twice as hard as some of the folk around him. As if every swing of the scythe, every piece of fruit dropped in a bucket were a moment he didn't have to remember how bad he was hurting. I wished Papa could have known all of it as he hailed the Ordishman cheerfully and began to unstrap the two chests from Waymer.

It's not fair, buzzed the bees, *none of this is fair.* Not the way the king treated the Ordish. Not that Jon couldn't be with Mauralee. Not that I'd lost the only two friends I'd got. And definitely not that Toly was still out there somewhere, knowing more about me than he ought.

Jonquin appeared round the river bend. He joined Mama, Papa, Ether, and me, his jaw set hard and his eyes ringed red. I wanted to tell him that it was okay to cry when your heart was floating away from you, but he just stood there looking so serious, I didn't think he'd really care to hear such a thing.

Bula closed the chests, satisfied that all was in order, and clasped Papa's hand. "Another good season. We thank you, Master Fallow."

"And I you, Master Fairweather," Papa answered. "Wind to your backs and safe sailing. We'll look for you next season."

Bula gave a curt nod, his gaze darting to me as I stepped forward, to the surprise of my family.

"Master, I was given this, but I think maybe it should go with you."

Out of the pocket of my apron, I pulled the Jack. I'd stared at the acorn every night since Lark put it in my hands, trying to take some comfort in its tiny, dancing flames. Though it pained me more than I could say to give it up, I thought Bula might be more in need of its cheer.

I wondered for a second if I'd done wrong—it looked like the man might burst into tears on the spot. He took the Jack from my hands and traced its willow ribs, feeling the magic lingering in it. After a long silence, he handed it back.

"It's kind of you to offer, child, but my girl made this for you." His voice hitched. "Perhaps he's why you're standing here among your kin today. Keep him close. Let him watch over you for the next turn of the wheel."

Gruff and proud, the man laid his hand on my cheek as he sang the first notes of the parting song in his rich baritone.

Look to the river,
When the fruit's on the vine,
When the land is ripe.
We'll come again,
We'll come again.

He raised his arm and the chorus of hundreds of voices sprang from the barges on the river. The sound of it near melted my spine with beauty. Bula and the remaining Fairweathers boarded the *Briar*, and one of Lark and Rowan's many cousins pulled up the mooring pegs, shoving her from the bank and leaping to catch her as she went.

> *Look to the river,*
> *When the days are long,*
> *When the hands are many.*
> *We'll work again,*
> *We'll work again.*

Mama, Papa, Ether, and I waved as the line began to drift past us. Merry voices still sang out from decks, roofs, and windows as sails snapped to, propelling the great boats with the current. From far up near the front, where we could barely tell one barge from another, I could still see the lone figure of Bula standing on the roof of the *Briar*, looking back toward the shore.

> *Look to the river*
> *When we take our leave,*
> *When round the sun we go once more.*
> *We'll meet again,*
> *We'll meet again.*

IT WASN'T UNTIL early the next morning, when Mama went to rouse the boys, that we realized Jonquin was gone.

I'd heard Mama screaming before. Like when Ether brought home a bowl of slugs. Or when the cat brought in a meadow gliss to lay at her feet. But when I woke up to the commotion, I knew instantly that it wasn't either of those things.

I leapt out of bed and flung open my door. Papa and Non were already hurrying down the hall toward the boys' room, where Mama's shouts were becoming more frantic.

"Did you hear me? Where is your brother?"

I peeked into the room round Papa's sturdy frame in the doorway. A bleary-eyed Ether was still under his quilt, blinking at Mama as if she'd just fallen out of the sky. Jonquin's bed was made, showing no signs of having had a Jonquin in it the night before.

"I don't know," Ether started, trying to banish the night from his tongue. "He was in his bed when I fell asleep. Maybe he got up early?"

Mama's voice shook. "I've had to fight the both of you every morning of your lives to rise for halls. Your brother does not get up early." She turned to Papa and Non. "I've looked everywhere. The stables, the henhouse—"

"Now, don't fret, love," Papa said. "Maybe he just needed some thinking space. Yestereve wasn't easy on him. I'll rouse some of the boys at the pressing barn and we'll find him."

Non's face was wrinkled up like a bag of knitting. I could tell she didn't believe Jon's disappearance had anything to do with thinking space any more than I did. "You do that, Ellis. Ceilie, why don't you head down to the river and see if he might be having a bit of a mope. I'll make sure these two whelps get off to halls on time."

Only after the kitchen door banged to and my parents'

worried voices retreated into the garden did Non turn the full force of her gaze onto my brother, who was still sitting in his bed, looking bewildered.

"Now, tell me true, boy. You got no idea where your brother's gone?"

Ether shook his head while stretching. "Honest, he was in bed after Mama came in to put out the lantern."

Non gave me a sideways glance to see whether Ether was fibbing or not. I shook my head. "Did he say anything? Anything at all?"

"No. He was mighty sore. I asked him if he wanted to speak on it, but he told me to shut my mouth. Didn't feel like getting a thumping, so I let him be." He frowned at the open window and the curtains swaying in the morning breeze. "You don't suppose he's run off, do you?"

"I don't really want to suppose anything just yet. He didn't speak to you, did he, Pip?"

"I didn't see him after the parting," I answered. A house without Jonquin didn't bear thinking about. A house that Jonquin left without even saying good-bye was well-nigh unbearable.

There was a ticklish feeling between my ears. Like a dream I couldn't remember trying to find daylight. In the dead of night, had I heard a voice? Had it told me to shush and sleep again as my head rolled to the side?

I ran for my room.

"Pip?" Non called from the hall. "What's the matter?"

I jammed my hand underneath my pillow and it came up

against a piece of crinkled paper that I pulled out into the daylight. On the front was my name written in Jon's neat script and on the back:

> *Ether told me you stood up to Mama and Papa.*
> *I don't have the words to tell you what that means*
> *to me and Maura. By the time you read this, the*
> *Fairweather clan'll be on their way down to Farrier's*
> *Bay, and me with them. Look to the river when the*
> *wheel of the year turns and we'll come again. Stay*
> *strong, Pip, and keep making trouble.*
>
> *Wind to your back,*
> *your loving brother, Jon*

NON HAD TO fetch some applejack from the icehouse to calm Mama. Papa always had the distillery make a small batch, but never sold it like he did the Scrump. He always said it was too strong and only good for getting over a shock or getting into a fight. I hoped Mama and Papa weren't thinking of getting into a fight, because there'd been enough trouble for one morning.

Papa talked to one of the waggoners who'd done the first early-morning run to Lochery. Jon had gone with him, saying he had some errands in town to finish before halls, but hadn't showed up for the return trip. What he did after, we just had to guess, because Papa couldn't very well ask at the waystation without a lot of folk finding out Jonquin Fallow had run away from home. Even worse, Jonquin Fallow had run away from home to join the Ordish.

Me and Ether sat in the great room in our halls clothes, listening to Mama's rage blow itself out like a late-summer storm. So far, we counted five plates and two glasses that had met their end against the wall. Even Non seemed inclined to stay out of her way until it looked like her and Papa's hand-fasting bowl was about to be the next casualty.

"Now that's enough, Ceilie," barked Non. "Tearing the kitchen apart ain't going to bring Jon back any quicker. Take a slug of jack and becalm yourself before you do something regretful."

Mama's angry breaths began to give way to hitching sobs, and we heard a chair groan across the stone floor as she sank down in it. "That's more like it, my love," said Non. We peeked around the corner and saw her rubbing Mama's back as she wept with her head down on the table, a small glass of jack by her elbow.

"I didn't think he'd really *do* it," Ether whispered to me.

"You mean . . . he *told* you he was going to go?"

"No, nothing like that. He just said the Ordish had the right idea, not having to answer to anyone. Keeping to themselves and doing what they pleased. And when he talked about Maura, I thought it was just a fancy. Didn't know he was proper smitten." He scowled. "Sure didn't think he'd leave. If he don't come back, that means the orchard's *my* responsibility."

"Of course he'll come back," I insisted. "He's got to. Besides, why wouldn't you want to care for the orchard?"

Ether leaned back in a sulk. "You wouldn't understand, Only. You're the youngest. No one expects anything of you." He glanced toward the kitchen. "I don't *want* to be an orchardman. The Pivens told me that the shipwrights at Dorvan Bay are always looking for prentices. Was going to try to talk to Papa about it, but I sure can't *now*."

"How can you think of your own hide?" I hissed. "Jon's *gone*."

"Don't I know it! You know what folk at halls will say if this gets out?" he growled back. "Not that it'll matter to you anyhow, since you've got no friends."

Before I could stop it, a whole harvest's worth of hurt exploded out of me, my hand leaving a stinging path across Ether's cheek.

The look of shock on his face turned into a sneer. I only had a second to brace before he tackled me round the waist, slamming us both to the ground. I'd been fighting Ether since I was a wee thing, so I knew just where to jam my fingers—under his left arm, as hard as I could—so he'd untwist his vicious grip on my hair. Before I could land another blow, he was jerked upward, Mama's strong arm clasped cross his chest. Non yanked me back none too gently before I could kick Ether in the shins.

"Great All, what's gotten into the two of you?" shouted Mama. "If you think this is the time for whatever nonsense this is, you got another thing coming."

"She began it," Ether bellowed, straining against Mama's grip. "She laid hands on me for nothing!"

"It wasn't for nothing!"

"That's enough!"

Some of the fight went out of the both of us to hear Non's do-what-I-say-or-else voice. At times, I imagined Mother All might look like Non when she was riled, and I wasn't keen to cross either one. Her grip on my arm loosed. "That's something like better. Now, it don't matter to me who began it, because the two of you are too old to be settling your troubles this way."

Both of us muttered hasty beg-pardons under our breaths, but it was just the fastest way to be out of each other's sight. Mama dragged Ether out the stable door into the garden while I let Non lead me to my room.

"Non—" I started, but she held up her hand until she'd latched the door. I shrank back under the look she gave me—the one that made me feel about three inches tall. "I'm sorry."

"I know this ain't easy on you, child, 'specially after what you been through. But it ain't easy on anyone else either."

"Yes'm," I whispered. I peeped up at Non. "What's gonna happen? Is Papa going after Jon?"

"It's a long way down to Farrier's Bay. If he joined them before the river gets wide and they can hit full sail, he'll already be a fair ways off." She sighed heavy. "Might be better to give him a trip round the sun to think on what he's done."

A whole year without Jonquin? My poor heart could barely fathom it. "But . . . he'll come back . . . won't he?"

Non sat down heavily on my bed. "Jon's of an age to want to make his own way. We'll just have to see whether that way leads him back or not."

9

The wheel of the year turned the orchards gold, and the house was a little quieter. A little sadder, too.

Mama finally moved the empty chair from round the table to a spot in the great room because she couldn't bear to look at it come suppertime. Ether and I split up Jon's chores without much complaining, even though it roused us both out of bed earlier than we cared for. All of us spent so much time trying to get used to the new kind of normal, I hardly had time to think about my own heavy heart.

So that's why, when the inquisitor showed up, we were all taken by surprise.

Most of my classmates had left off questioning me after the first week of Jon's disappearance. I found out the only way to answer their questions without being untrue was to either tell them I wasn't supposed to talk about it or that it was none of their business. Both of those things were true, but neither made me any more popular. I pined for Lark and Rowan, whispering my hopes for their safety to Mother All at my desk at halls and to the Jack in the dark of my bed at night.

The morning Master Iordan arrived, Mistress Averil rapped on her desk to call us all to attention. "Young masters and misses, we have the honor of a distinguished visitor in our study today." The halls mistress's plump cheeks were pink with pride, and her hands trembled as she motioned to the door. Standing in it was a tall, gangly man in gray robes so fine, they looked more fit for a palace than a country study. Behind him stood a serious, brown-haired boy in a faded blue-and-silver jerkin, his face as covered in freckles as a field with lightning bugs. Mistress Averil and Master Iordan didn't feel he warranted introduction, but he looked as out of place in our study as his master.

Though the iron stove in the corner of the room had been lit near a week to keep out the autumn chill, a shiver went through me, head to toe. Mistress Averil didn't seem to feel the blast of cold air our visitor brought in with him. "Master Iordan is one of the inquisitors at the royal lyceum in Bellskeep," she continued, hardly able to contain her excitement. "He was passing through on an errand and graciously agreed to visit with us. Please welcome him."

"Welcome, Master Iordan," the study said all together.

The inquisitor gave a thin-lipped smile that stood the hairs on my arms on end. "I thank you, mistress. It's always a pleasure to visit the study halls from which the next students of the lyceum often come."

Mistress Averil pinked further, and her grin stretched from ear to ear. She was a kind soul from a family of merchants near the capital, and her dearest wish was to have a student selected for the lyceum. Every year, she pestered us to "strive for more and bring honor to your families!" She hadn't caught on that, in the country, leaving your family a hand short on the estate so you could study dusty old books in Bellskeep wasn't anyone's idea of honorable.

Master Iordan strode to the front of the hall, leaving the boy behind. He leaned his bony frame against the headmistress's desk, crossed his arms, and looked down his beaky nose at the class. "Let us see what Presston's finest minds have to offer."

He began calling on students in the study, from the tiny whelps to the elders, who'd soon end their days in the study hall and be prenticed or begin work on estates. I knew somewhere toward the back of the room, Ether was hoping hard the inquisitor wouldn't call on him. Master Iordan nodded lightly in approval as he listened to recitations of numbers, poems, and passages from the testaments.

My fingers tapped at my desk, and my legs wiggled beneath my skirts. The ill ease the beaky scholar brought with him felt familiar, like the first moment I'd met Toly. He hadn't belonged to the Fairweather clan any more than Master Iordan belonged in our hallsroom. The kingsman had wanted money. What was the inquisitor there for? I snuck a glance at the boy, who'd been abandoned in the doorway by Master Iordan. He didn't look at any of us, but instead, stared straight ahead like he was used to pretending he wasn't there.

"Only?"

Mistress Averil's voice brought me back to myself. To my embarrassment, the entire study was staring in my direction.

"Sorry, mistress?"

She pursed her lips in annoyance. "Master Iordan has asked you a question, Only."

My head snapped front to where the inquisitor was studying me with great interest. "Beg your pardon, master."

"Stand up, child," he said, not unkindly. Nervous as a cat, I pushed back my chair, my ears burning at the attention. "What's your name?"

"Only Fallow, sir."

"Oh, a Fallow of the orchard? Where the Scrump is made?" he asked.

Whispers and tittering broke out among my studymates, stoking the fire under my skin higher. I heard the harsh mutter of my brother's voice telling Hatter Leyward to shut his face. "Yes, sir," I managed.

"It's become a popular cup in the capital. If it isn't too much trouble, after your studies are concluded for the day, I should very much like to see where it's brewed."

And that's when it happened. Dark fingers of purple and brown shot through the disturbed space around him, and the terror of the night by the river with Toly came together in one heavy, painful ball at the pit of my stomach. The inquisitor wasn't just passing through for a pint of Scrump.

"The tables, please, Miss Fallow, beginning with twos."

The inquisitor certainly wasn't just passing through to hear me recite my multiples.

"Two by one is two. Two by two is four. Two by three . . ."

The inquisitor was there for me.

THE ROAD BACK from halls never seemed so long.

More than anything, I wanted to run straight home, leaving Master Iordan, the liveried boy, and Ether behind in a cloud of dust, but I put one foot in front of the other, forcing myself into step with my brother and the lanky man at his side.

As we crested the hill, the inquisitor pointed to the familiar, stubbly lavender fields and the orchard beyond. "These lands," he said. "They all belong to your family?"

There was something in the tone of his question that made me anxious, but Ether answered, unconcerned by the tall stranger. "Yes, master. Down past the bend in the river."

"I've had occasion to taste the brew from your estate. It's quite fine."

Ether all but skipped like a pup being praised. "Thank you, master. Our family's proud of it."

I risked a glance behind me at the boy following silently in our footsteps. His cheeks were still a little plump with baby tallow, but he was likely of the same years as Ether. I couldn't help notice how he kept his eyes fixed on the back of his master's neck. Probably so he didn't have to look at me.

"The king values those that take pride in their work, young

master." Iordan stared over my brother's head to find me in Ether's shadow. "And what about you, miss? Are you proud of your family's accomplishments?"

"Yes, sir." The answer was a lump of fat as it fell off my tongue. I knew what I had seen in the classroom, and the stranger from the capital was up to no good, in spite of his mild smile and quiet voice.

Our gate came into sight and I sped up, hoping to get through it and as far away from Iordan as possible, but my heart sank. Papa was in the front garden, patching a hole in the wall. He stood up straighter than usual when he saw the four of us.

"Papa!" called Ether as we came near. "Papa, this is Master Iordan. He's an inquisitor at the lyceum in Bellskeep. He's passing through and wanted to see where we brewed the Scrump."

"Well met, Master Iordan," Papa said, extending his big hand to shake Iordan's more delicate, pale one. It was satisfying to see the inquisitor wince under Papa's grip. "It's an honor to have you with us. Ether, go fetch the inquisitor a pint from the cellar."

"Oh," Iordan said hastily, "just a half for me, thank you kindly. I have not much stomach for strong drink."

Papa noticed the boy, standing in the inquisitor's shadow. "And one for your man?"

I could have sworn I saw the corners of the young fellow's mouth curve upward with Papa's offer, but Iordan shook his head. "That's kind of you, but no. Just the half, thank you."

Ether dropped his satchel inside the gate and disappeared round the corner of the house. I looked after him in envy, wishing Papa had sent me instead. I had to content myself by hiding behind my father's back, but even there, the inquisitor was still watching me. He smiled politely at Papa.

"You manage these lands yourself, Master Fallow?"

"I do as much as I can, master. I have a staff of brewers and orchardmen that live on-site. Overseers, too. My wife manages the bakery and the stables. There's a clan of . . ." Papa stopped, frowning. "Well, I know how folks in the capital feel toward the Ordish, but none of the estates down this way would be able to bring in the harvest without them."

Iordan's nose wrinkled. "No explanations needed, master. We make what friends we must when a task needs doing." He glanced idly around the yard. "Is it just you, your wife, and your two children here?"

Papa fidgeted in discomfort. "Yes, sir, at the moment."

"You have an elder son, do you not, Master Fallow?"

Papa bristled, sensing danger. "I do, sir."

Master Iordan continued calmly, as if he couldn't feel Papa's vexation. "You're teaching him the ways of the estate?"

"I am, sir. He'll be a fine overseer someday."

The inquisitor glanced over Papa's shoulder and then at me. "I should like to meet the next orchardman of Presston! Child, run and fetch your brother, will you?"

The smirk on Iordan's face was near unbearable. The dark purple veins of his deception curled toward me, and I tried not to flinch as they began to twist round my ankles. There was no answer I could make that wouldn't give either me or Jonquin away. All I could do was stand and gawp like a fish caught on a hook.

The inquisitor cocked his head. "Did you hear me, child? Don't you know where your brother is?"

Papa quickly answered in my place. "Our eldest has gone down south for a spell, master. My wife's got a sister there in the horse trade." I'd heard him tell the lie half a dozen times, but I still couldn't keep my eyes from the hazy ring of green and blue that made round him. It spread out, meeting the tendrils of the inquisitor's lie in a fog of muddy brown. "Thought it might do him some good to learn a few things from a business mind like hers. He'll be back with us come harvesttime next year."

"I beg your pardon, master, but I was asking your young mistress here," Iordan said in a polite way that wasn't meant to be polite. "Now, miss, do you know where your brother is?"

I noticed the liveried boy peering at me side-eyed from behind his master's back. He'd not said a single word yet, but his presence was almost more infuriating than his master's. He was the audience and I was playing my part on whatever stage the inquisitor had put me upon.

I tried to ignore him. "Like Papa said, sir, he's gone south."

The thin eyebrow of the inquisitor arched upward. "I heard what your father said. I want to hear what *you* say." He bent over so his face was on a level to mine. "So, your brother has gone south, has he? *Why* has he gone—?"

"Begging *your* pardon, master," Papa interrupted as he moved between me and Iordan, closing his big, comfortable hand around mine. "I feel I gave you the answer you asked for. And you're frightening my girl."

"Oh, come now, Master Fallow," Iordan cooed. "Surely the truth isn't anything to be afraid of? Especially when it comes from the mouths of babes. Now, Miss Fallow, let us return to my question. Why has your brother gone south?"

I clenched my teeth, hoping to steel myself against what I knew my answer would bring. "Jonquin's gone down south to visit our auntie in . . . aaaah!" Before the rest of the fib could even make it past my lips, agony slammed into me like a runaway cart, knocking me to my knees. It was worse by far than the day in the lavender fields. My stomach heaved, and although there was nothing in it, I gagged, retched, and spit on the ground. The boy jumped back to avoid having his boots soiled.

Papa scooped me up and lifted me in his arms as if I'd weighed nothing at all. "Only! Only, what's the matter? Beulah!" His shout was loud enough for Non to hear him, even in the herbery. "Beulah, come quick, Only's having a fit!"

The last thing I saw before darkness swallowed me whole was the inquisitor's face, which told me he'd got exactly what he'd come for.

10

Anger is the vinegar that makes a bitter batter
And curdles kindness in its vat
The doves of peace it does scatter.
Rule thy temper, clear thy breast
And surely hold thy tongue
Bring to heel thy inner beast
Ere speaking, or become one.

—*A Child's First Book of Humors*

I woke to raised voices in the kitchen. I hadn't any memory of being put to bed, but I recognized the smell of my own sheets and the feel of my pillow beneath my head. A whimper escaped as I tried to sit up and failed, my head still beating out a lesson I'd yet to learn the first time.

"Hush. Don't try to speak. Drink this first."

Non was by my side. She lifted the vial to my lips, but I spluttered at the bitter taste on my tongue. "It's asper root," she explained. "Should quiet that thumping in your skull, but you might feel fuzzy after."

I choked down the rest of the liquid and was rewarded with a cup of ginger water to flush the terrible taste from my mouth. My face and hands began to tingle, but the ache in my head and the shouting in the kitchen dulled under the blanket of the medicine.

"There we are," Non said with satisfaction. "A bit better?"

"Mmmm."

Her eyes creased. "Feels a bit like someone's stole your tongue, don't it? Just means it's working." Another burst of voices down the hall drew her eyes to the door. "You don't need it now at any rate, but I expect your ears are working just fine."

"He's here 'cause of me, ain't he?"

Non bowed her head. "I do so like being right, but I wish I'd been wrong about that blasted bit of lore. Seems like that kingsman of yours had big ears and made his way back to the capital with a tale to tell."

So I was to be the gold coin in his ale after all. "How did he know about Jon?"

"There've got to be other kingsmen stashed away among the Ordish. News like a landwalker joining up with a clan is gonna travel pretty fast."

"I guess Mama and Papa know about . . . what I can do?"

"That old stickbug in a dress made sure they did. I won't say they weren't a bit sore with me for keeping it from them, but I hoped it wouldn't come to nowt." She put her hand to my cheek. "Ain't no sense wishing now. What's done is done."

"I want to see them," I insisted.

"Why don't you stay here a spell? Ain't no need for—"

"No!" I slurred, the medicine still tangling my tongue. "Please, Non."

She shook her head. "S'pose I know better than to argue with you once you make up your mind on something, but keep your peace, you hear?" She draped my dressing gown across my shoulders and took my arm to lead me out toward the kitchen.

Master Iordan stood in the middle of it, his eyelids low with boredom even with the clamor of Mama's and Papa's voices all around him. I hated him more than I had ever hated anyone. I hated him more than Toly. I hated him so much, I didn't even bother to offer up a silent devotion to Mother All to beg her pardon. Instead, I just stewed, watching the terrible, silver-haired eel standing in my house like he'd every right to be there. There was no sign of the boy. Perhaps he'd had all the entertainment he could stomach for one day.

Non and I appeared in the threshold in the middle of a hatefully calm sentence. "But I'm sure the crown is prepared to overlook your son's youthful indiscretion, so long as its other demand is met."

"Demand?" Papa bellowed. "And what demand is that?"

The inquisitor gave a light laugh. "Why, Master Fallow, surely you can see your child's gift would be best used in the service of the nation?"

Mama went pale as flour. "You want *Only*?"

"She'll be a valuable asset to His Majesty," Iordan explained, as if he'd just asked to borrow a hammer. "Times being what they are, it would be considered the act of a loyal citizen. What with new alliances being forged between Orstral and Thorvald and the continuing Ordish concern, your daughter could offer the crown a degree of protection a thousand soldiers cannot."

My legs began to shake. Was he talking about taking me away? I grabbed for Non's skirts, but she had already flown across the room and backed the surprised inquisitor up against the table with a long, pointed finger.

"Now listen here, you great, scrawny goosewallow, I don't give a flea's fart for the dictates of some old man with a lump of metal on his head. Only ain't going nowhere!"

"You're asking us to hand over our daughter and thank the king for the pleasure? It's absurd," Mama cried.

It could have been the braying of donkeys for all I understood. *He wants to take me away* was all I could think. *Away from the lavender, the trees, and the river. Away from the pressing barns, the kitchens, and the chickens. Away from Mama, Papa, Non, Ether, and . . .*

Non put her arms round me. "You just turn your bony backside round and go back where you came from, master. Don't think about darkening our hearth again."

"You can take that bloody warrant with you," Papa roared. "I'd rather lose a countinghouse full of coin than deliver my whelp into your tender care. We'll manage on our own."

The inquisitor was unmoved by all the bluster. "Then I'm sure, Master Fallow, that His Majesty could find another equally skillful and more dutiful subject to tend this estate."

There was a loud silence in the room. "Wh-what?" my father stammered.

"I'm quite certain I don't have to make my meaning any clearer, master?" He turned an insolent eye on my mother. "Mistress?"

"This. Is. Our. Land," Papa said in a voice that promised war. "My blood's in this soil back ten generations. Fallows tended these trees before the first regent was crowned in Bellskeep."

"Though you are the first to hold a royal warrant," Iordan droned. "Also, probably the first to be careless enough to lose a son to the savages of the river. And doubtlessly the first to have produced a child with such a rare gift. Her service to the king will—"

Mama lashed out, fierce as a bear. "My daughter is no man's servant!"

The bottom fell out of the world. That morning, I'd walked to halls, coat and scarf round my neck, watching the mist gather in the valley. And not six hours later, some sour, gray-faced scholar was threatening to take the very soil out from under us if I didn't go with him. The whole orchard—gone. Gone, for my parents' love of me. It wasn't something I was of a mind to allow.

"I'll come with you, Master Iordan. I'll serve the king. Just like Mayquin."

It was as if I'd stopped time for an instant. Four jaws slacked open in my direction before they all started flapping at once.

"You're going nowhere, Only!"

"Now, see here, Pip—"

"Master and Mistress Fallow—"

"He ain't takin the orchard!" I hollered.

"Only—" begged Mama, tears to match mine running down her face.

"No! There ain't no way we're losing the orchard 'cause of me and my stupid cunning!"

Papa knelt down and grasped my shoulders. "Sweetling, this ain't your fault. I'd rather walk the length of the country barefoot and begging for work before—"

"But *I* wouldn't rather that!" I rounded on the inquisitor. "Master, if I go with you, will you give your word that no ill'll come to my family? Not those here or my brother Jonquin with the Fairweather clan?"

The dour kingsman stared down his nose at me. "It is the king's word I give you, and it is unwavering."

I thrust my hand out toward Iordan. He looked at it as if I'd offered him a fish straight of the river.

"You ain't gotta do this, Pip," said Non.

"But I do." I looked at the sorrowful faces all round me. "'Cause if there's no orchard, and I know I'm the cause of it, there's no point to my breathing in and out."

There were plenty of words that passed between me and Non since the time I first learned to use 'em. Warning words, kind words, cross words, and all the words between that didn't always get said. But I didn't need words to say I wasn't budging, and she didn't need any to tell me she understood and that she was fiercely proud.

"I reckon Only's of an age to know her own mind," Non conceded. "And if her mind's bent on keeping that miserable old fool up north from thieving our rightful property, I ain't standing in her way. But I'll tell you one thing, you great cattle fly, no harm'll come to her or you'll wish you never heard the name of Fallow."

Iordan clucked like a ruffled rooster. "Are you threatening me, mistress?"

"You bet your backside. Weren't you listening?"

The inquisitor narrowed his eyes, ready to deal out some lip, but his book smarts were nothing against five feet three inches of Non. He might have been high and mighty at the castle, but in my house, he was nothing but a ransomer in fancy dress.

Finally, he shook my hand with as little of him touching me as he could manage. "We travel to Lochery in an hour. A carriage more suitable to the journey north will be waiting there. Make whatever preparations you see fit." He made for the front door, where he paused to give my parents a small bow. "His Majesty thanks you for the generous gift of your daughter."

He was forced to jump back as a plate shattered against the wall next to his head. A second sat clasped in Mama's white-knuckled grip. "Get out out of this house," she hissed.

The inquisitor didn't have to be told twice. He was nothing but a blur of gray robes and ill feelings as he whisked through the door, slamming it shut behind him.

NON ONCE SAID there's a part of your head you can use as a forgetting place—a little room where you can put troublesome things that won't give you peace if you let 'em loose. You can't keep 'em there forever, but it might give you time to do what needs to be done. That's where I put my fare-thee-wells to the orchard.

It's where I put Mama's tears and Papa's tight, sad face. It's where I put the rock my brother threw at the inquisitor before Mama could grab it from him. It's where I put the feel of Non's hand in mine when she kissed me and told me not to look back once the wheels started turning. It's where I put the smell of the cart that carried us over the hill until my home was just a speck in the distance. It's where I put the shift and shimmer of Master Iordan's fine robes in the early-evening light. It's where I put the pitying look of the liveried boy. And when my forgetting room was just about full to bursting, I shut the door and locked it up tight.

After that, there was only the rumble of the wheels, the dust of the road, and the greatest hurt my heart had ever known.

11

I must have drifted off between Presston and Lochery, the clatter and sway of the cart lulling me to sleep with my head on a bale of straw. I dreamed I climbed up into the branches of Grandfather, higher and higher until I ran out of tree. When my head popped out above the canopy of green, there were no lush fields and no river, but only Master Iordan, filling the whole sky, reaching his long, bony hands toward me. I gasped and lost my footing, tumbling back down through the branches, the ground rushing up to meet me.

The cart jolted and I woke with a start. It was nothing but a rut in the road, but from up front where the inquisitor was sitting next to the driver, I heard him grumble about "provincial byways" and hated him all over again. I hoped whatever happened once we reached the capital, I wouldn't have to see his thin, smug face ever again. I sat up, trying to concentrate on what was around me rather than thinking dark thoughts of shoving the inquisitor off his seat into the dirt.

Across from me, sat as straight as he could on a crate, was the young man in blue and silver. He'd given up pretending not to see me and was staring without apology. Who did he think he was, other than a fancy little serving boy to a glorified hallsmaster? I'd be horsewhipped if I was going to give him the pleasure of conversation, so I mustered my most ferocious glare. He looked away quickish, scooting as far back on the crate as he could without falling clean out of the cart.

We were just at the familiar stone bridge that spanned an offshoot of the river at the outskirts of Lochery. I often went with Mama or Papa into town if I could beg a seat on the wagon. Dressed neat as a pin, I'd be fair bursting with excitement at the promise of a honey stick from the goods shop after all the errands were finished, but that evening, the post marking the town limits filled me with nothing but dread. Wrapped in my best traveling coat and hanging tight to my nameday chest, I knew there was no honey stick waiting—only a long trip promising who knows what.

The cart trundled over the rough cobbled street into the town square. Shops were dark, but lanterns were burning in the windows of houses and in the Bird in'th Hand, where the merry chatter of the customers spilled out the open door. Men and women in from the fields hoisted tankards of ale and Scrump, grateful for the day's end, and my small heart was wicked with envy for them as we passed the pub heading toward the waystation.

I'd never been to the waystation at so late an hour before. The rattling of our wagon was deafening as we passed under the arch into the quiet courtyard, which would normally be bustling with hooves and coaches. Two stable hands, chivvied from some game or other, grumpily guided us in. A girl circled round to the back of the wagon and, with the help of Master Iordan's boy, began hoisting down what little luggage we'd brought. I clutched my nameday box tighter to my chest as the inquisitor extended a hand to help me down.

"Are we staying here tonight?" I asked. The waystation's inn was pleasant, with a huge hearth in the great room, but I was weary and mournful. Even a simple cot would feel like a luxury to my cart-sore bones.

Master Iordan shook his pompous head. "We're to keep to a schedule that will see you in Bellskeep within the week. We'll press on through the night and take on a fresh team at Oldmoor. If we make good time, we'll stay tomorrow eve in North Hallow."

Oldmoor? North Hallow? Bellskeep had seemed imaginary up to that minute—a place you found yourself after stepping into a faerie ring. Not a place you actually *went* to by way of two towns that I knew to be over sixty miles away. Bellskeep, as far as it was, couldn't bring me to tears, but Oldmoor and North Hallow sent salt spilling down my cheeks before I could stop it. I was glad the inquisitor's back was turned.

"Ain't traveling at night a bit on the dangerous side?" I asked sourly. "It's dark as old boots out there. Wouldn't take but a possum's sneeze to spook a horse. And what about the no-gooders waiting out there for folk with more haste than sense?"

"Do keep still, child. Do you really believe the king has made no provisions for your safe deliverance?"

As if to prove his point, a dozen cavalry riders made their entrance into the courtyard from the inn. At least six more stable hands followed with their mounts. They looked so grand, I forgot my fear a moment and drank in the sight. The silver braid on their leather surcoats shone as keenly as the edges of their swords. No one, not even the no-gooders in the woods, would be like to take a chance on this regiment of swordsmen and the enormous destriers being led out of the stables, nickering and tossing their heads.

Were they really all for me?

I glanced round, looking for some sign of the wagon that would carry us through the night, but could see none. I hoped they weren't planning on making me ride. I was at home in a saddle, but I was so tired, staying on a horse might well have proved impossible. I followed the inquisitor toward a small out-building in the yard I'd never noticed before when I visited with Papa. It wasn't till we got closer that I realized it wasn't a building at all—it was the most enormous coach I'd ever seen. Eight heavy carthorses were being hitched to the front, ready to pull the contraption nearly as large as Non's herbery. Clever lanterns, set into the frame of the coach, blazed from all corners, ready to bring the daylight to any dark path. Double doors on the side were open and Master Iordan stood by them, tapping his foot on the stone in impatience. "We should be gone by the eighth bell."

"Mother's breath!" I exclaimed. "What's that?"

"It's our transport and it's high time we were away," he replied irritably. "Now, if you please." He motioned to the coach. Inside was a narrow passage with sliding doors on either side. "You will have the rear compartment. I'll have one of the footmen stow that for you." He held out his hand for the box I had wrapped tightly in my arms.

"No!" I held it closer. "I mean, no, thank you, master. I'll keep it with me."

Iordan slid the door to my compartment open. "Suit yourself."

Inside the compartment were twin berths, one on top of the other, both with decadent quilting and a pair of lavish, overstuffed pillows at their heads. The same clever lanterns were set into the rich, blue-papered wall, making the small space cozy rather than close. In the corner was a tiny closet I took for a wardrobe, but when I opened it, it plainly wasn't for storing clothes.

"I ain't never seen a moving thunderbox before!"

The inquisitor's nose wrinkled distastefully, like it was trying to scoot off his face altogether. "Yes, quite. If you find yourself in need of . . . comfort . . . kindly utilize the box while we're in motion. Now, if you'll be settled, we'll be away momentarily." Quick as a gopher, he slid the door to his own compartment open and disappeared into it, closing it behind him, fast as he could.

Sliding my nameday chest onto the top bunk, I moved aside the thick velvet curtain covering the small window to my left so I could peer into the courtyard. The cavalry were all seated, their mounts champing restlessly at their bits, eager to be away. One rider stood out in the regiment—a bright silver breastplate gleamed atop the surcoat as the enormous mount carried the soldier around the coach, checking and double-checking the riders' formation. As the great beast came into my view, the lantern light revealed the rider to be a tall and stately woman, her sleek black hair pulled back and tucked into her collar. Her face was handsome and strong, her eyes dark and alert. I couldn't help but gape at her. I'd never seen a lady in armor before, but she looked fierce enough to eat most of the other horsemen for breakfast.

Her voice rang true over the courtyard. "Dahl, Rickard, you're to the front. Hutch, Emerick, you're bringing up the rear. Loosley, Farren, and Martin to the left. Ballard, Sweets, and Nafir to the right. Eyes and ears wide-open, understood?" The company barked their understanding and fell in around us in a racket of hooves. The rider took a last look at the formation and, satisfied, turned her own mount to the head of the carriage. Out of the corner of her eye, she must have noticed me staring, because she gave a sharp little nod in my direction before riding out of sight. From somewhere above, there was the crack of a whip and a shout of "Hi'yup!" and the enormous coach jerked forward, sending me staggering back onto the bottom bunk, where I sat down with a thump. The wheels were thunder on the cobbles as we rolled out of the courtyard and into the night. Most of Lochery twitched their curtains aside to watch the grand procession wind slowly out of town.

Before the stew of feelings bubbling in my soul's pot could overflow, a hatch in the roof flipped open and the top half the liveried boy appeared through the ceiling. It gave me such a fright, I banged my head on the bunk above.

"I'm sorry, miss, I didn't mean to startle you!"

"So, you've got a tongue after all," I spat, rubbing my forehead. "What are you doing creeping about the top of a moving coach?"

"I'm sorry we weren't introduced. Master Iordan . . . doesn't always remember I'm here. I'm Gareth. I'm one of His Majesty's stewards. If you need anything, just pull on the blue cord in the corner. Food, drink, water to wash with, anything."

"I don't need nothing." I know my tone wasn't pleasant and I could hear Non's voice in my head chiding me to mind my manners, but I wasn't of a mood to speak to anyone, especially Gareth.

His shaggy brown hair waved with the breeze coming in from the open hatch. "Oh. All right, then. Well . . . if you do . . ."

I thought he was about to disappear back through the roof, but instead, he just hung there. I folded my arms.

"What are you goggling at? Didn't get enough of a spectacle earlier when I got took away?"

The steward looked offended. "It's not like that! It's just that no one told me you'd be—"

"That I'd be what? In such a bad temper?" I felt the tears coming and there was no stopping them. "You'd be in a bad temper if some great, skinny beetle stole you from your own home."

The boy on the roof looked horrified. "No, they didn't say that you were so . . . young. I didn't realize that we'd have to . . ." He stopped short. "I thought you'd be a woman grown."

"Well, I ain't." I sniffed, wiping my nose on the cuff of my coat, not caring if he saw. "You and this whole party can go take a flying leap into the river for all I care."

He might have made a hurt face, but it was hard to tell as he was still upside down, jiggling with every bump of the road. Outside, one of the horses in the caravan whinnied loudly.

"Please pull the cord if there's anything you need. Good night, miss." Gareth's head vanished and the ceiling hatch clanged shut, leaving me alone with the rumbling of the wheels and my tearstained cheeks.

12

Non always said traveling was like stretching your legs in the world. But during the first day on the kingsroad, I did precious little leg stretching and saw almost nothing outside of the hateful wheeled box other than what I could spy through the small windows. Gareth must've come while I was sleeping, as I woke to the smell of good bread, butter, and sweet apricots. I'd had half a thought to make my displeasure known through refusing food, but my belly grumbled so loud, Master Iordan must've heard it in his cabin. At North Hallow, after a long night and day being bounced around like luggage in the back of the grand coach, we were bundled inside a large stone inn so quick, I didn't even have time to read the name from the sign.

I wasn't keen on being handled, especially by Master Iordan, who, thankfully, had kept to himself since we left Lochery. "Master, could I just have a breath of fresh air before we—"

"In case you'd not noticed, we're traveling in a large, formal caravan with a cavalry escort," the inquisitor interrupted, his mood after two days on the road plainly as sour as mine. "The less curious the locals are, so much the better. Now, up the stairs to your left, if you please."

I glanced longingly at the great room as we passed, with a fire roaring merrily in the hearth, glowing lanterns on the long tables and the smell of leek and potato soup and crusty bread wafting toward us. But the inquisitor chivvied me up the creaking staircase before the crowd assembled had time to give us a once-over. My belly rumbled loudly again. Gareth's travel rations on the coach had filled a hole, but I had a mighty need for something hot and nourishing.

Iordan seemed to read my thoughts. "I'll have the steward bring a meal up to your room. We'll not be making an appearance in the dining area."

My cold fingers itched to melt by the fire, but my belly, at least, would be satisfied. We reached the top of the stairs, and Iordan was forced to duck his head to enter the narrow hall with the rooms, where he pushed open the first door we came to. Inside was an enormous bed and a large, diamond-paned window overlooking a deep stream that ran behind the building. The inquisitor glided past me to draw the heavy drapes. I was a little cheered to see the room had its own fireplace with logs already ablaze to chase out the chill. The air had taken on a bite as we'd moved north. I wondered if Mama and Papa had lit our hearth yet, and my heart quivered a little.

Satisfied we were cloistered from the outside world, the inquisitor took his leave. "You're to keep yourself confined to this room. There is water for washing and a chamber pot beneath the bed. Dinner will be up directly." And for the second time in as many days, he shut the door in my face, leaving me with none but myself for company.

I sat down before the hearth. The hinges on my nameday box creaked as I opened it, filling the room with the scent of lavender that broke my heart open all over again. I pulled out the Allcloth to rub against my cheek, remembering the softness of it on my pillow when I was small and needed to feel it between my fingers before sleep would take me. Something sharp inside the cloth rasped against my face and I jerked up, only to find the Jack tangled up inside. I freed him, watching the dancing light of the acorn roll side to side as if it were just as restless as me, stuck in that blasted coach.

"I don't know if I can do this," I whispered to the little figure, fighting the hot, remorseful tears clinging to my lashes.

Lark and Rowan hadn't come this way in a fine carriage. They didn't have fine feather beds in an inn. They certainly didn't have a troop of cavalry to protect them from the no-gooders in the dark. They came this way with nothing.

The acorn flared and sparked its consolation.

Be brave, it seemed to say. *Be brave for us.*

I SUDDENLY FOUND myself sitting straight up, blinking into the dark of a room that wasn't mine.

I'd gorged on the soup, bread, and sweet milk that Gareth

had delivered, and now my bladder was complaining, but there was something else. Something I couldn't put my hand on. Prickles shot up and down my arms, tickling a memory of hiding in a cider barrel when I was small. It was dark and close and it wasn't long before I kicked the lid off, exploding into the world. I needed air. I needed it right then.

I jumped from under the quilt of the great bed and threw back the drape. Just the waning blue light out of doors eased the uncomfortableness of the room, but I still wasn't satisfied. I fumbled with the window latch and pushed open the pane, letting in the night air. It almost took my breath at first, but then I sucked it in, greedy for the fresh cold of it. Just below, a short trellis climbed up the wall—a ladder for flowering vines. At the bottom, a path led through the garden to the water closet, set far enough away from the inn as not to offend the patrons with its whiff. I glanced at the chamber pot beneath the bed and then back at the squat building out in the darkness. The inquisitor could go hang. I wasn't using that nasty old pot if I didn't have to.

Reaching out the window, I gave the trellis a tug and was happy to find that it was made of iron rather than wood. The leaves of the vine that snaked over it had already fallen off, so there'd be no rustling as I climbed. Once I hoisted my leg over the sill and found myself a sturdy notch for my foot, it took me no time at all to shimmy down the rest of the trellis. After years of hiding and seeking in the orchard, I was fearless and surefooted, but once my feet hit the dirt path leading to the water closet, all the grit went out of me. I wasn't in the orchard anymore. Every night sound was something fearsome just waiting for a disobedient little whelp like me to blunder into its path. I forgot my worry of being heard and all but ran to the water closet, yanked open the door, and locked myself into the fetid darkness to do my business.

Sitting there in the dark with the cold air against my nethers reminded me unpleasantly of the little wheeled prison I'd be forced back into the next day. It prickled my arms all over again. What would life be like once I got to Bellskeep? Would there be trees to climb or would I be locked in a little box like a toy for the king to take out and play with when he got the notion? The thought clung to me, hot and sticky as tar. *She spent her life in service to the crown.* I didn't even have the freedom to relieve myself in the dignity of a water closet. Would I ever be allowed to return to Presston, even for a visit?

Non said she did some of her best thinking in the privy. "Just don't sit there too long," she warned. "You never know when an idea might bite you in the rear end." Feeling well and truly bitten, I hoisted my bloomers and gathered the spirit I'd need for the trip across the garden. I cringed at the screech of the door as I slipped through, but just as I thought to make my way back through the dark, a hand closed fast around my wrist.

I pulled back, ready to lump my attacker, but even in the dark of the garden, I could make out the familiar, freckled face. I sagged with relief.

"Great All, it's a good thing I've already been to the privy!"

"What are you doing out here?" Gareth whispered.

"What're *you* doing out here?" I shot back angrily.

The steward scowled. "I went into your room to see if you needed anything and spotted you across the garden. You need to get inside before you're missed by Master Iordan!"

"Did you climb down the trellis?"

"Of course," Gareth snorted. "I can balance a meal tray on top of a carriage moving at full trot; a garden wall isn't much of a bother." He looked round nervously, peering into the night. "If you're caught out here, I guarantee the inquisitor will lock you in that wagon for the rest of the trip."

"What's it to you if he does?" I bristled. "All I wanted was a breath of air."

"Well, you've done that, so let's get—"

The sound of raucous laughter suddenly rang out in the dark. Both me and the steward flattened ourselves deep in the shadow of the water closet.

Before us, partly hidden by a row of stubby pine trees, were two soldiers of the cavalry regiment, stripped bare and bathing in the cold water of the creek. I squeezed my eyes shut. Living in a house with two brothers meant I was better acquainted with the sight of naked boy parts than I cared to be, but encountering soldiers bathing in a stream was quite another thing.

Gareth groaned. "Master Iordan's going to wonder where I am in a moment. I shouldn't've come out."

"Well, it ain't my fault, I didn't ask you to!"

The steward leaned his head against the wall. "Is everyone in your village a complete pain in the backside, or is it just you?"

"You sound like my brothers," I muttered.

"And you're more than a little like my sister. She's a pain in the backside, too."

"Reckon she'd know how to get across the garden without getting seen by a couple of naked soldiers?" I whispered.

Gareth sniffed. "My sister would have had better sense than to climb out a window of an inn being guarded by the royal cavalry."

The cavalry in question were taking their sweet time bathing. The man sitting nearest to us on the bank with a blanket wrapped around his waist was trying to shave his gingery stubble by feel. The long, straight knife he held in his hands glittered in the light of the lantern on the ground at his side. "Ach, Mother's breath!" he swore as he nicked a spot under his chin. He grabbed his undershirt from the pile of clothes next to him and pressed it to his skin to stanch the blood. His fellow, the only Acherian in the party, was still standing in the middle of the creek, naked as his nameday.

"You ought to leave that stain, Emerick. Your wife will think you saw some action on this little holiday."

"At least I've *got* a beard, Nafir. Perhaps your sweetheart would take you more seriously if you had one, too."

Nafir scoffed and ran a wet hand over his smooth cheek. "Your Mother All obviously thought my face was too handsome to cover with hair."

"A likely tale!" snorted his comrade, staring quite pointedly at a point farther downstream. An irritated woman's voice suddenly rang out.

"Emerick, could you at least *pretend* to turn the other way?"

I couldn't see who the voice belonged to, but I guessed it was the leader of the cavalry—the lady in armor. Only, without the armor.

Emerick laughed and scooted around to face the trees. Gareth tried to push us deeper into the shadows. There was no way to move without being seen.

"Apologies, Captain. Once a soldier, always a soldier."

"Well, unless a soldier wants his eyes poked out with a pine branch, he should move them somewhere else," retorted the captain.

"Aye, Captain, aye." Emerick chuckled as he took another long scrape up his throat with the dagger. "But you know, there are all sorts of old tales that start with a fellow who sees a beautiful woman bathing in a creek."

"Do those tales ever end well for the fellow who sees a beautiful woman bathing in a creek?"

"They usually end in a dungeon," the soldier replied. "Or being torn apart by wild dogs. I'll keep that in mind."

"See that you do. Or perhaps when we return, I'll decide that an officer of your quality is needed at the outpost in Sandborn."

Emerick groaned. "With greatest respect, Captain, I think I'd prefer the dungeon or the dogs."

She laughed. "Don't let Arfrid Sandkin hear you speak like that. He rather likes his little patch of wilderness."

"He's welcome to it," Emerick sniffed. "I've no desire to live in another man's paradise that's made up entirely of grass and cow dung. Besides, there's no decent pub for miles."

I was fast losing feeling in my fingers and toes in the chilly twilight, and the fear of being caught out of doors was mounting every moment that passed. Gareth's teeth were clacking together so hard, I was sure we'd be heard. I grabbed hold of his sleeve and we began to slither, inch by inch, out from the shadow of the water closet. The rough boards snagged our clothes, making tiny cracking sounds that were louder than a sanctuary choir to my ears. As we finally slid round the corner of the privy, out of sight of the bathing soldiers, I silently let out a breath and began to make a hasty retreat back to the trellis and the open window.

It was a good deal darker than when I'd first made my escape, and the path back to the inn was not as straightforward as I remembered. Squinting into the gloom, I tried to place each silent footstep on solid ground. I thought we were making good progress, but I heard Gareth's quiet warning just a moment too late.

"Watch out for the . . ."

My foot slipped under a tree root, sending me sprawling. A small, ornamental pond I'd not noticed on the way out was there to break my fall. I had only a second to pinch my nose before I hit the stinking, stagnant water with a splash. The pond wasn't deep, but the noise of my entry was loud. I gasped as my head broke the surface of the water only to find myself face-to-face with the point of three swords, one of which belonged to a very tall, very wet, and very naked woman with a wide-eyed Gareth behind her, his cheeks glowing scarlet in the light from the inn windows. Her two male officers, in varying states of undress, were trying hard to keep their eyes fixed on me. At least one of them wasn't succeeding.

"Emerick," she growled, her voice low and threatening, "think of the dogs."

The soldier's eyes flicked quickly back to where I sat, shivering in the pond. "Doing my best, ma'am."

The captain's mouth turned up at the corners. "I don't suppose we need three of the king's finest to guard one village rat. Make yourself useful and fetch my tunic. And don't think I won't know if you're looking as you go."

Emerick plodded off into the darkness and the woman's face grew serious. "What do you think you're doing, skulking around in the dark?" She whirled around to face Gareth. "I know you're coming to be of an age, master, but this is neither the time nor the place for dalliances with the locals."

The steward flushed even harder, each of his freckles standing out like a burning star. "Ma'am, I wasn't—"

But the captain's attention was already back to me. "You one of the kitchen girls?"

I didn't dare move, freezing, soaked to the skin and smelling of rotting pond plants as I was. I had to force my numb lips to work. "N-no, ma'am, I—"

"How long have you been hiding out here?"

"I just had to use the water closet," I sputtered, hoping maybe I'd just die of cold before I had to answer any more questions. "Please, I . . ."

Emerick trotted back out from behind the trees with a lantern and a tunic, which he handed his commanding officer while shielding his eyes with the other hand. The captain snatched the garment from him and quickly shrugged it over her head without giving up control of her sword. "Now, I think you ought to . . . Mother's breath!"

Her face dropped as she got a good gander at me in the light of Emerick's lantern. "How in name of All did *you* get out here?"

"I climbed out the window," I admitted miserably.

"I saw her out in the garden when I went in to check on her," explained Gareth quickly. "And I thought—"

Just then, there was a rattling of a lock from the back of the inn and the door flew open, spilling light into the small garden. I'd have recognized the gangly figure in the doorway anywhere. The flames on Gareth's cheeks were doused in milk as he stepped quickly behind the captain.

"What's going on out here?" roared the inquisitor.

Quicker'n I could blink, the woman yanked me out of the pond, thrust me behind her with Gareth, and shoved Emerick in. The clean soldier yelped in surprise as he hit the foul water, just as Iordan strode angrily toward us.

"It's nothing, master," lied the soldier, a dazzling halo of blue and white sparks igniting around her. "One of my men had a bit too much ale and stumbled on his way to the privy. No reason to be alarmed."

Iordan puffed up, all full of himself. "Your soldiers do realize we have a long day of travel ahead tomorrow. I trust I can expect everyone to execute their duty?"

Her face darkened. "I'll thank you not to talk to my men about duty, Master Inquisitor."

Iordan bit his tongue, thinking better of cheeking someone who could break him in half over her knee. Instead, he turned his disdain on the gawping soldier still sitting in the pond. "You're a disgrace, master. Be sure you greet the morning with a clearer head." Emerick made no answer other than an expression of disbelief from the depths of the smelly water. Satisfied, the inquisitor turned on his heel and marched back to the inn, slamming the heavy door behind him.

Emerick slapped the surface of the water angrily. "Beg pardon, Captain, but what in the seven hells was that about?"

"Think of it as penance for your wandering eye," the captain retorted, turning round to study me. "You think he wouldn't have been quick to tell the king we managed to miss the Mayquin sneaking around in the dark, unguarded?"

"The Mayquin?" exclaimed Nafir, stepping back, the point of his sword dropping to the ground. Emerick followed suit, climbing out of the pond quickly, as if something in the dark water had taken a bite of him. The woman let out a tired sigh.

"Are you two such old fishwives that you fright in the presence of a little girl?"

The soldiers didn't answer, but took another fearful step back. Their commander made a disgusted sound. "Get back to the camp, both of you." She wrinkled her nose. "Emerick, you should probably go back to the stream first. You're dismissed."

The men scampered away like two boys from their chores.

"And you," she said to Gareth, "went above and beyond your duties, master. I thank you. Now, quickly, back to your post before it's noticed you're gone."

The steward made a quick bow and made for the inn, throwing one last look at me over his shoulder that clearly said,

Pain in the backside.

13

Even in the dead of winter, I'd never been as cold as I was standing in front of the captain of the royal cavalry. Rotted water plants clung to my thin, wet shift. Mud trickled down my scalp. I smelled worse than cider mash. I, Only Fallow of the orchard, had just made a royal fool of myself.

"Bit colder up here than in Presston," said the woman, looking me over, head to muddy toe.

I worried if I opened my mouth, my chattering teeth might lop off the end of my tongue. "Y-yes, ma'am."

"I expect you'd like to be out of those muddy clothes, too," she continued, as if we were having a pleasant gossip over tea.

"If you p-please, ma'am," I said, shivering.

She rested her hands on the pommel of her great sword. "This isn't the place to be mucking around, you know. You must think you've drawn rather a short lot—and perhaps you have—but you must do as you're bid now, do you understand?"

"Y-yes, ma'am."

"I'm Captain Bethan Fisroy." Night might have been playing tricks with my eyes, but the world behind the captain wavered a little, distorting the view of the inn behind her. The long, sleek muscles in her arm flexed as she pointed the way to the creek with the sword. "Let's get you presentable."

I followed the captain to the creek, just a little upstream from the water closet. The water was shallow and fast flowing, but there was a hollow where it reached nearly past my knees. I let out a squeak as my feet sunk in. It was far colder than the pond.

"It's best done quickly," said the woman with a wry smile. "Give me your shift. I'll try to get the worst of it out."

I hugged my arms to my trembling body, glancing around into the trees.

Bethan laughed. "Emerick's gone back to camp, if that's what you're worried about. It's just you, me, and the moon. Come on, off with it."

Feeling more naked than I'd ever been in my life, I peeled off the muddy shift and my soaking drawers and handed them to the woman waiting on the shore. In spite of the cold, I hurried to hide myself in the little hollow. The icy water was a punch to the gut as it flowed up over my chest and arms. "Oh sweet All!" I yelped.

The captain scrubbed the fabric of my shift against a large, smooth rock by the bank. "It's fresh, I'll give you that. Get your head under and have done with it."

I dunked my head back and felt the current take the length of my hair like river grass. The cold water rushed into my ears as I scrubbed my scalp, trying to ferret out all of the pond dirt. When I was sure it was clean, I raised my head again, the heavy weight of my hair almost dragging my neck back down into the water. At home, after I washed, Mama would sit me before the fire while she used her sturdy boar's bristle brush to tease out the snarls. Sitting in the freezing stream, I wondered what would become of my unruly locks. Two days of travel had already tied it in more knots than Non's crocheting.

Bethan stood on the bank with a horse blanket she'd retrieved from the stable. "Out you come. Before you catch death."

My head tilted to the side as I picked my way gingerly out of the cold water and over the rocks to be wrapped up with the most beautiful, itchy piece of material I'd ever had the pleasure of warming myself in. The captain frowned as she took a length of my sodden hair in her hands.

"This won't dry by morning. And it's quite the rat's nest."

"My mama has the only good brush," I said in a very small voice.

Bethan's face gentled. "I'm sure you'll have a fine one when we get to the city. Until then, though, I think I have a duty to your mother to see to it that you don't come down with anything on the way, don't you agree? Don't want to venture farther north with damp hair." She unsheathed a large dagger from her belt. "Do you trust me?"

I nodded, keeping one eye on the blade.

Taking hold of my wet mane, she made a fat loop of it round

her hand. Before I could object, the dagger flashed and nearly two feet of wet curl and tangle was making its way down the creek. She looked at me approvingly.

"Long enough to be proper, short enough to be convenient. What do you think?"

My hands crept over my shoulders to explore the neat, severed ends. I'd never felt so light. "Feels like my head's about to float away."

She chuckled, running her hands through her own hair, which sat at almost the same length as mine. "You'll get used to it." She handed me a dry linen long-shirt and a pair of breeches. "One of the stable lads was about your size. It'll get you back to your room without freezing, at any rate."

I gratefully shrugged off the blanket, which, while warm, was beginning to feel like being wrapped in a nettle patch. I pulled the shirt over my head and the breeches over my legs.

"If anyone asks about your hair, tell them you didn't have a brush, so you decided to cut it and burn it in the fire."

I stopped in the middle of buttoning the breeches. "I can't, ma'am."

Bethan placed her hands on her hips. "Why not?"

"Because, ma'am, it ain't true."

One of the captain's eyebrows arched all quizzical. "Well, no, it isn't, but surely you understand the need to keep this from Master Iordan?"

"It ain't that, ma'am"—I tried to explain—"I actually *can't*."

"Can't what?"

"Can't tell a lie."

A look of genuine puzzlement settled on Bethan's face. "What happens if you do?"

"A bad headache. And you'd likely end up with a lot of leek and potato soup on your boots."

She grimaced. "Well, that's less than ideal."

"Yes, ma'am."

Bethan raised her eyes to the sky, where the waning gibbous moon was peeking above the tree line. "I don't like not knowing things, Mayquin."

"My name's Only Fallow, ma'am."

"Only." The captain shook her head in frustration. "I didn't know that either." She jerked her thumb back toward the stables. "I suggest, Only Fallow, that we adjourn indoors for a cup of tea and game of questions and answers."

IT WASN'T AN Ordish tent, but it had the same feel to it. The stables were blessed warm with the smell of horse and hay. It was the first time since the cart had carried me away from the orchard that I felt at home. If I closed my eyes, I could pretend I was in our own barn with the soft sound of old Waymer grinding oats between his teeth.

As we passed a glossy chestnut creature, Bethan dragged a hand over its flank and gave its soft nose a rub. "How's my boy?" she asked, bringing her forehead to the horse's forelock. He whinnied softly, shoving his head under her arm and nibbling at the pouch on her belt. She smiled, looking less like a warhorse herself. "I spoil him a bit," she said, reaching into the pouch and drawing out a handful of carrot, leek, and squash ends from the kitchen. The horse gobbled them up with a great flapping of lips and stuck his face back into the pouch, hungrily nosing for more. "That's it, greedy guts, that's all I've got," she said, laughing, taking his head in her hands and turning to me. "Do you know much of horses?"

"My mama does. She comes from a family of stablemen down near Farrier's Bay. The Pendricks."

The captain nodded knowingly. "Aye, it's a fine stable!" She rubbed the muzzle of her stallion. "Westdolph came from our own stables. He's a devil in a scrap, but a kitten in the fold. You can stroke him, if you like."

Putting a firm hand to Westdolph's shoulder, I ran it over the shining coat. I'd never seen a beast so fine. I wished that Mama were there—no doubt she'd have something to say about the length of his hock or the depth of his breast. The horse swished his tail, letting me know he was tolerating my touch for his mistress's sake. I removed my hand, polite as can be. A few well-placed kicks from Waymer had taught me never to test a horse's patience.

"This way," said the captain, pointing to the stable master's quarters just beside her mount's box. Inside was a small pot-bellied stove, a wooden chair, and a cot. More than comfortable for a stableman, but hardly fit for the commander of the king's cavalry.

Before I could stop myself, I blurted out a question. "Begging your pardon, ma'am, but why aren't you staying at the inn? I got a bed half the size of an Ordish barge. Surely there'd be one for a lady like you?"

Bethan laid her sword on the floor beside the cot. "A soldier doesn't need luxuries. The men are camped in the meadow on bedrolls, so this is quite comfortable enough."

A tall teapot steamed on the cool plate of the stove. Two tin cups appeared out of the captain's saddlebag, and she poured the dark liquid into them, handing one to me. The ice in my fingers began to melt against the hot metal of the cup. "Thank you, ma'am."

"It's been stewing for a while, so it might be a bit strong."

The warning came a second too late for my bitter sip. I must've made a face, because the captain gave an amused chuckle. "It's black tea from Achery. Nafir brought it back the last time he went to see his family. It's seasoned in crates with straw and pepper. Gives it a bit of a kick. It's a little better with milk."

I hardly wanted to say, but it tasted like licking the floor of a cow barn. I took one more neighborly sip before deciding that it was better as a hand-warmer than refreshment.

Bethan drained her cup and set it on the floor with a clink. "So."

"So," I repeated, hoping for some sign of what to say next, but the captain just stared at me as if I were a puzzle with missing pieces. "Questions?"

"What?"

"You wanted to ask me questions, ma'am."

"Well, yes, I do want to ask you some questions, but I thought maybe I could answer some as well."

I blinked at her. It hadn't really occurred to me I'd get to ask any questions. Everything had been so fast, so cruel. Master Iordan made it clear that I was nothing to him, so what regard should this soldier have for me?

"Um, I do have questions, ma'am, but . . ."

"You didn't suppose anyone would take any notice," she finished for me. "Well, I'm taking notice, although I am going to use the privilege of rank to take a few of my answers first. Is that acceptable to you?"

"Of course, ma'am."

"Good." Bethan leaned back against the wall, pulling her feet up onto her cot. "So, how does it work?"

"Ma'am?"

"Your ability. The augury. How does it work? What does it look like?"

"I can see an untruth, ma'am, but what it looks like depends on your aim in the telling. If you mean to cause harm by it, it's ugly, like a darkness. If it's to save your own backside or hide a shame, it's blues and purples. Pink is an exaggeration. Fear is green. Kindnesses look like twinkling flash fire. But it's not so direct as that, most of the time. Usually folk telling a lie have got more than one reason for it." I couldn't help wonder a second on what it was I'd seen when the captain introduced herself. It certainly wasn't like anything I'd seen before. Maybe it *had* just been a trick of the light. And as I'd used up all the goodwill I was owed with my nighttime tomfoolery, I thought it best to keep it to myself.

The captain gawped. "That's extraordinary! So, back at the

inn, when I told Master Iordan that Emerick had fallen in the pond, you could see it?"

"It was sort of a blue haze, with white sparks winking round the edges. I guess because you didn't want the inquisitor to know I'd got out, but you were also thinking about your men and what trouble they might catch." I looked down at the floorboards. "I'm sorry for sneaking out, ma'am. I just wanted a breath of air."

Bethan stared down at the folded hands in her lap. "I was rather like you when I was little. My mother died when I was very small and father cared more for his . . . duty than for anything else, so my care fell to a lot of tutors and housemistresses. I didn't half give them the runaround—I was out the nearest window the minute their backs were turned." She raised her eyes to me, her chin stuck out, resolute. "I'll try to see to it your journey from here on is more to your liking. There's little I can give you, but I can at least give you that."

The idea of a more exciting journey lifted my spirit a little. The captain pointed her cup at me. "Your turn."

"Ma'am?"

"Your turn to ask a question."

I had half a million buzzing around inside my head, but I could barely catch hold of a one to settle on. "What's Bellskeep like?"

"Have you ever been to a large city? One of the holds, maybe?"

I shook my head. "I been to Roundmarket a few times for the horse fair with Mama. We meet up with my auntie Rya when she brings the colts for sale. But I've never been farther than that."

"Bellskeep is rather larger than Roundmarket. If you put ten Roundmarkets together, they still wouldn't be as big as Bellskeep."

I'd a hard enough time imagining ten Roundmarkets. The horse fair was always a bustling place, full of buyers, sellers, and vendors. So many folk pressed in from all sides, I'd cling to Mama's skirts to keep from getting washed away in the tide of bodies around me.

"There's never been a city more beautiful," the captain continued. "But I'm guessing that's not what you mean."

I flushed. "I don't know if you can say, ma'am, but I was wondering what it'll be like for *me*."

"It's certainly an honor to serve at the king's pleasure. You'll have a fine chamber and clothes, private tutoring with Master Iordan . . ."

So much for my hope of leaving my grim-faced captor behind. "Master Iordan?" I groaned.

The captain stared in the direction of the inn. "He may seem a little inflexible, but he makes an excellent teacher. As for your duties, I understand you'll attend the king in council and at audiences and give a full and true account of what you see. Your impressions will be valuable. But in the time you're not attending to your duties or your studies, I imagine you'll have the freedom of the castle and its grounds. If you wish to go out into the city, you'll have your own guard."

Something warm began to uncurl in my stomach. "You mean I won't be locked in my room?"

The captain's mouth fell open. "Locked in your room? Of course not! What would make you think . . . ?" She slid off the cot and came to kneel at my feet, her hands grasping mine. "Child, listen to me, I don't know what sort of stories you've heard, but the king isn't a cruel man. Were I in your shoes, I would feel all of this is dreadfully unfair, and perhaps it is. I can't promise you the life you hoped for, but I can promise you that the life you'll have will be every bit as rich. Can you make peace with that?"

I thought of Lark and Rowan and the other indentured children of Bellskeep. Who else but a cruel man would do such a thing? Of course, I didn't give any of those thoughts a voice. What good would it do? I thought back to my jaw with Non in the sanctuary yard. *Sometimes we gotta be content to change what we got charge over.*

"I think I can, ma'am."

"Good girl, Only." The sound of my name from Bethan's lips put iron in my back. "Now, let's return you before you're missed, eh?"

The two of us beat stealthy steps from the stable across the inn's garden. I carefully avoided the inky smudge of the pond, and before I knew it, we found ourselves at the base of the trellis. "Do you need help?" Bethan whispered, looking up the latticework to my open window, where the curtains were drifting out into the night.

"Oh, no, ma'am. This ain't nothing compared with some of the trees in the orchard." Then I scrambled up, quick as a mouse, and sat boastful on the window ledge.

"Well, that certainly is something!" She crossed her arms, amused. "You as graceful on a horse?"

"I can ride, ma'am."

"Well, tomorrow morning, you can ride with me awhile. Does that suit you?"

I grinned so hard it hurt. "Thank you, ma'am!"

"Right, then, into bed with you. We start just after breakfast." She turned back to the stables, but stopped as if something tickled her memory. "Oh, by the way, what will you say if someone asks about your hair?"

I shrugged. "It needed cutting." Not a hint of pain from the inside of my head. I smiled.

Bethan gave me a small salute. "Good night, Only from the orchard."

"Good night, Captain Fisroy."

14

Master Iordan protested.

Thinking back, *protested* ain't the right word for what he did. He placed his scrawny, pompous self right between me and Captain Fisroy. Westdolph's tail twitched in annoyance as the captain was forced to leave off tightening the girth round the saddle to face the inquisitor.

"I won't allow it."

Bethan folded her arms with a lot more calm than I would have expected from a soldier who'd just been sassed by a jumped-up hallsmaster. "You won't allow it?"

The inquisitor tried to draw himself up higher. He and the captain were the same height, but she was wearing armor and looked much more formidable. "The king commanded me to make sure the Mayquin reached him unharmed."

"Funny," said Bethan, arching an eyebrow, "I'm sure he gave me the same command."

"Then you will know why allowing the child to ride in the escort is a ridiculous notion," Iordan answered.

"What I know," replied the captain, lowering her voice and entering her challenger's space, "is that the child has been ripped from her family and stuck into a rolling prison for two days. There are many different forms of harm, Master Inquisitor. To expect her to serve her kingdom for the rest of her life and not give her a glimpse of it seems cruel in the utmost." Satisfied she'd made her point, she went back to tightening her saddle's straps. "She'll ride with me. No harm will come to her."

Iordan's mouth opened and closed like a fish yanked from a creek. "You cannot guarantee that! The king has enemies."

"Most of the king's enemies reside solely in his head, garrisoned there by Lamia Folque," the captain said. The inquisitor's eyes widened, and both of them fell into the kind of silence that's louder than talk. I didn't have the first clue who Lamia Folque was, but I knew whatever Bethan said wasn't something meant to be spoken aloud. I also couldn't help notice Iordan didn't correct her. Instead, they seemed to have a whole conversation without saying a word, their eyes eventually darting back to me. The air round them was charged with the things left unsaid.

Finally, the inquisitor spoke, as if some of the hot air had gone out of him. "At the first sign of anything suspicious, you'll pass her off to the carriage master?"

Bethan nodded, looking a little deflated herself. "You have my word."

→×←

"WHO'S LAMIA FOLQUE?"

Gareth, who'd just walked in the door of my room, almost dropped a bundle of Master Iordan's books that he'd stashed under his arm.

My talk with Captain Fisroy the night before had put me in a slightly better humor, but it also made me hungrier for any information about where I was headed. I snuck a dried apricot from breakfast out of my pocket and popped it in my mouth. "Captain Fisroy said something to Master Iordan about Lamia Folque and the king. It didn't sound like she cared much for her."

The steward threw a nervous glance at the open door. "It's best not to speak too loudly of the Folques. I'm surprised the captain did."

I punched one of the fluffy pillows. "Yes, but who is she?"

The steward was taken aback. "Didn't you learn about the Four Families in halls?"

A rhyme from Mistress Averil's study hovered hazy on the edge of my tongue.

> Sandkins rule where cattle graze,
> And from the land springs wheat and maize.
> Molliers tend the fruitful vines
> That fill our cups with dark, sweet wines.
> Dorvans build their ships to last
> Against the strongest storm hold fast.
> Folques dig deep beneath the ground,
> Where treasures of the earth are found.

The Four do sit in wisdom round,
And by their council serve the crown.

"Oh!" I exclaimed. "She's a member of the king's council."

"She's the head of the council. The Folques have held the seat for almost two hundred years, but it's taken them a while to get back into favor after the last war with Thorvald."

My mouth fell open, apricot and all. "We had a war with Thorvald?"

Another book threatened to leap from under Gareth's arm. "Of course we . . . what do you learn in halls, anyway?"

There'd been a simple map tacked to one of the study's walls—one showing the outlines of enormous Thorvald to the north, tiny Achery to the south, and Orstral smack-dab in the middle. "What'd the Thorvald want with Orstral anyhow? They got three times as much space as us."

"Yeah, but it's mostly cold waste. There's a little fertile ground at the coasts, but they can only grow a few crops. A lot of their food and other resources come from us."

It was silly to feel sore over a war I didn't even know happened, but I didn't like the thought of the Thorvald stealing the orchard any more than I did the king.

"Guess they thought it was better to own the garden than pay the grocer."

"Exactly. It was a long time ago, mind. Our grandsire's parents probably weren't even born yet. But that doesn't stop people from remembering that the Folques actually helped the Thorvald when they invaded."

"Those snake-bellied eels!" I burst out.

Gareth shushed me quick. "Didn't you hear me say you shouldn't speak of them too loudly?"

"Sorry," I muttered, helping myself to another apricot. "If the Folques helped Thorvald, why're they still part of the council?"

The steward's mouth twisted the way Ether's did when he'd got a real good secret, but didn't know whether he wanted to share. His eyes flicked to the door again before he sat down on the bed beside me, putting Master Iordan's books in a neat pile on the quilt.

"The Thorvald only got as far as Oldmoor before the rest of the three families and the Acherian army managed to drive them back. The Folques claimed they were overwhelmed and had to choose between helping or losing their lands, but a lot of people think they were looking to bargain with them so they could take the crown and rule for the Thorvald by proxy. Lady Folque's great-grandfather splashed a lot of the family fortune around during his time on the council, helping to rebuild everything that got ruined, but it's never really stopped the talk. A lot of people still don't trust them."

We both jumped when the spindly form of Master Iordan suddenly appeared in the doorway, glowering like a spring thundercloud.

"The company is saddled and ready to ride. What foolishness is delaying us?"

The steward ducked his head. "Apologies, master."

Iordan's long arm swept toward the empty hall.

"The captain awaits her riding companion."

Riding a warhorse like Westdolph weren't nothing like riding a placid farmyard gelding like Waymer. The muscles of my thighs stretched in protest around the destrier's wide back and saddle as I leaned into Bethan behind me. I was thankful for the coarse, heavy breeches that not only kept out the worst of the cold, but kept the horse's rough coat from chafing the inside of my legs.

We rode in the middle of the left flank along the paved kingsroad with two of Bethan's company, Lovel Sweets and Raff Loosley. Sweets was a cheerful young man with a mop of honey-colored curls who took a great deal of delight in teasing the silver-headed Loosley for riding a few paces behind us.

"What's the matter, Loosley? You afeared of something?" he joked, winking at me.

"Shut your face, Sweets. You want to ride next to the augurer, be my guest," the other soldier growled.

But Sweets wasn't deterred. "Go on, Mayquin, do something scary. If you're truly an augurer, give Loosley the face of an ass." He gasped, looking back at his companion. "Great All! She *is* an augurer. Astonishing work, Mayquin!"

Loosley's face turned the color of a ripe apple. The captain's voice rose above Sweets's braying laughter. "That's enough, both of you. You know very well she can't do anything of the sort. I'll fall back, the two of you ride front. No bickering. Keep your eyes open."

Loosley spurred his mount, Bethan reined in Westdolph, and

the two soldiers fell into a trot ahead of us, the older man shooting murderous glances at the younger.

I tapped Bethan on the leg. "Beg your pardon, ma'am," I began shyly. "Why are they afraid of me?"

The captain snorted. "Don't pay them any mind. Some in the capital are more superstitious than others. The Great Cathedra recently got a new First Curate, and he's a little louder on the subject of augury than the last one."

"What's a curate?"

"Like a rector in a sanctuary. The First Curate is the rector of the Great Cathedra. He's got quite a lot of influence at court. And with the king," she added quietly, sounding none too happy about it.

"What does he say about augury?"

"Psht, the usual rubbish," said Bethan, waving her free hand. "That it's unnatural and that we should 'keep ourselves far from its path.' The last curate was more concerned about the welfare of the sick and the poor. This one is rather single-minded."

I pondered this as we swayed to and fro with Westdolph's gait. "He's probably not going to be very happy to see me, then."

"The king overruled his objections in bringing you to Bellskeep, so I don't suppose he will. Truth be told, I think the curate's a bit afraid of you, too."

"I just don't understand how anyone could be afraid of *me*," I mumbled.

"Can't you really, little one? You can see men's secrets. Take away their armor." She rapped her knuckles against her own breastplate. "Sometimes our only protection is in hiding the things we know. The things we feel. That's a frightening thing, even for me." She nodded in the direction of the soldiers in front of us. "But your augury isn't unnatural, no matter what those fool-born dunces might think. No matter what that buffoon of the Cathedra thinks. It's a gift, if it's anything."

The sounds of the road surrounded us—the low, rolling thunder of the coach, the strike of horses' hooves on the stone slabs, and the chatter of conversation between the horsemen.

"A gift," I whispered, trying to convince myself.

THE NEXT FEW days passed much the same, although after the first day's riding, my legs ached so badly, I barely wanted to take the saddle again. Bethan insisted, though.

"We're beginning to enter the timberlands at the edge of the Great Wood. It's incredibly beautiful." And so, though it felt like my thighs had been set fire, I dutifully mounted Westdolph in front of the captain, gritted my teeth, and rode on.

She was right about the beauty of the place. The little hills of Presston, which had always seemed mountains to me, had nothing on the great, rolling valleys and peaks of the north. Where the trees at home had almost lost their leaves, the woods of the timberlands were evergreen with pines and spruce. The cold, fresh smell of their needles made every breath I took a pleasure. The world seemed somehow bigger, making me feel like an ant among giant blades of grass.

After several days in the saddle, we passed through a fine

market town by a wide stretch of river. The whole place smelled of sawdust. Bethan pointed out the large lumber mills by the banks of the river, where huge flotillas of logs drifted downstream. "They're cut at the logging station and sent down the river to be milled. You can't throw a rock in this town without hitting a carpenter. Come on a market day and you'll see things for sale that you didn't ever think could be done with wood."

Just like I felt a glow in my heart when someone said something fine about the orchard, it was clear that the captain felt the same about the whole country. *But,* my traitor brain reminded me, *she serves the king who takes the Ordish's children. The king who took* you. *Have you forgotten where you came from so quickly?*

Truth was, I'd locked it all away in my forgetting room, where it couldn't trouble me. If my thoughts strayed too far toward home, I felt a physical tug on my insides that hurt worse than any gutsache I'd ever had. But the closer we got to Bellskeep, the harder it was to keep pretending this was all a jolly adventure instead of a long journey with a new life at the end, far away from my family and the orchard.

I swallowed down the lump in my throat. "How long before we get to Bellskeep?"

"Another two days," Bethan answered. "We'll stop tonight outside Timberwick. It's the town on the edge of the Great Wood."

The idea of the Great Wood made me shiver. Just about every fae tale I'd ever heard took place in a deep, dark forest. Though I was too old now to believe in brownies and snalighasters, the part of me that still checked under my bed at night took the idea more serious. I thought about the Jack under my Allcloth and resolved to carry him with me. Maybe the spirit of growing things in the pocket of my coat, along with thoughts of my Ordish friends, would give me some courage.

15

Mind you close the casement,
Mind you lock the door,
Tiny claws a-scraping
As they're creeping cross the floor.
Keep 'em from your bedside
With sage and ash and rue.
Mind the witching-hour beasties
Or they
Might . . .
Get . . .
YOU!

—Bedside rhyme

The morning dawned gray and dreary. The thin light barely made it through the thick curtains of the coach and I couldn't help but grumble as Gareth pleaded me awake for breakfast. As we walked down to the nearby stream so I could wash my face, everyone's mood seemed reflected in the sky. The soldiers, usually merry and joking, saddled their mounts in silence, talking to one another in low voices.

"Everyone's spooked as a cat in a thunderstorm today," I said, dipping my hands into the cold water. "If someone shouted 'boo,' they'd all jump half a mile." The stream's bite was even colder than the one at Oldmoor, and I gasped as it shot all the way through my bones. "Though maybe it's just the weather."

"I think it's the Wood," Gareth offered, turning to look at the road ahead.

"What do you mean?"

"I heard Ballard and Drake talking round the fire last night after dinner. Apparently, we're meeting up with a second regiment about halfway through the forest."

Worriment poked its head above the burn of the cold stream. What could be lurking in the woods that a dozen cavalrymen couldn't deal with? Probably more than brownies and snalighasters. "Why?"

The steward shook his head. "They kept their voices down after they noticed me listening."

"Only!" The captain's voice rang out across the encampment. "Ride with me."

I didn't move for a moment, thinking on what Gareth told me. When I didn't immediately go to her, she cocked her head. "Is there fog between your ears as well as in the sky?"

Gareth gave me a little shove, and I made my way through the bustle of boots and hooves to Bethan's side. "G'morning, ma'am."

"Thought you might like a little fresh air for a bit before you'll have to ride in the coach. The Wood can be a little . . . unpredictable."

I bit my lip as a light dusting of sparks fanned out from behind her, and understanding flickered across her face. "Ah"—she coughed—"of course. Would you like to know the whole of it?"

"Yes, please, ma'am. Non says it's best to have a lantern so when you meet the devil in the dark, you can see where best to kick him."

Bethan nodded in agreement. "I'm beginning to think that your grandmother comes from a line of exceptionally wise women."

"She likes to think so, ma'am."

"There've been some reports of unfamiliar camps discovered in the Wood, so we've been advised to take a little extra caution. Most likely just a few scoundrels logging without permits, but we'll take no chances." She stared over my shoulder to where the team of horses was being hitched to the coach. Master Iordan stood by Gareth, carefully watching the captain and me. "No doubt he doesn't approve of me telling you about the threat of danger any more than he likes you riding with me."

"I appreciate you telling me the truth, ma'am."

"It'd be rather pointless not to, don't you think?" Bethan put her foot into the stirrup to mount. "Now, it's time we were gone."

THE QUIET STARTED about half a mile before we passed under the boughs of the Great Wood.

It was as if we were sat in the middle of sanctuary. What little talk there was among the soldiers dropped off as the enormous green shadow of the forest loomed in front of us. There was no birdsong except for the occasional cry of a crow or scrubjay, so the footfalls of the horses and the rumble of the coach's wheels seemed extra loud in the stillness. I shifted uneasily in the saddle, glad for Bethan's sturdy frame behind me. Putting my hand in the pocket of my coat, I ran my fingers over the familiar shape of the Jack.

The trees were the biggest things I'd ever seen. They made even Grandfather look like no more than a green sapling. Long, ginger-colored trunks stretched into the sky, their scrubby branches not beginning for a hundred feet or more. Their bases grew so thick that a dozen folk might stand arm in arm round them before completing the circle.

"The great Orstralian pines," Bethan said in a reverent hush, her eyes cast up to where the tops of the trees brushed the low-hanging clouds. "I remember the first time my father brought me to see the Wood when I was a child. I thought they looked like giants who'd fallen asleep standing up."

"They're amazing," I whispered. Their dense trunks stretched out before us as far as the eye could see in either direction, making a living wall for us to cross. The kingsroad itself disappeared under one such tree that stood out from its fellows because of its size, but even more so because the road ran directly through it. Its great trunk had been carved out to allow for the passage of wagons and men, but the tree itself still climbed skyward, live and strong.

"One of the first Lamblin queens had the Mother's Gate hewn out so that the kingsroad could take a straighter path,"

Bethan explained as our caravan came to a halt before the living gateway. "Instead of going around the tree, her pride was determined to go straight through it." She turned to call to the soldiers. "Left to the front, right to the rear! Two by two!"

The soldiers at the left quickly filed to the front of the coach in order to pass through the narrow tunnel of the trunk. Sweets winked at me as he trotted by. Those on the right fell back until we formed a long, narrow procession. Bethan and I fell in between the coach and the rear guard. As we passed under the tree, there was just enough light from the other side to pick out carvings made inside the enormous trunk. IVE HEMERT PASSED THIS WAY. ALL SAVE THE KING. HERE WAS GIBIN AND FAIR KITT IN THE YEAR OF OUR MOTHER —. Names and initials of those living and long dead scored the inside of the passage. The tunnel was close enough that I reached out my hand and let my fingers run over the marks, wondering which way the folk who had left their names had been going. Into the Wood or out? Had their hearts been light or heavy when they came this way?

Bethan held up her hand, signaling for the procession behind us to stop. "Would you like to leave your mark? It might be something for future travelers to say they saw the name of the Mayquin in the Mother's Gate." She dipped her hand into the small pouch at her waist and handed a small whittling knife to me.

I stared at the blade in my hand. "What should I write?"

She maneuvered Westdolph closer to the wall. "Whatever you like. Best to keep it short, though. We need to be moving on."

It took a moment of searching to find a bare space on the wall, but I picked my canvas and quickly set to work gouging the bark, the horse under me standing patient. When I'd finished, my name, ONLY FALLOW, scarred the flesh of the tree, alongside a ham-fisted carving of an apple. Bethan nodded her approval. "A mark for the ages. All who travel this road will look and say, 'See? The Mayquin passed this way on the road to Bellskeep.'"

As we exited the tunnel on the other side, my breath left me in a whoosh. Seeing the trees from outside the Wood was nothing compared to seeing them on the inside. Non had always talked about the majesty of the Great Cathedra, but I could imagine nothing more holy or majestic than being surrounded by the towering pines. The weak, wintery sunlight fell in long beams to the forest floor and the kingsroad, which was peppered with needles. It felt like we'd walked through a door to another world, where the idea of brownies and snalighasters *weren't* so ridiculous after all.

It was a good number of miles before the spell of the Wood wore off and conversations began again. But I was happy to stay quiet, my eyes pointed upward.

"What do you think?"

Bethan's voice startled me out of my daydreaming.

"They make me feel very small," I admitted.

"It's good for a soul to travel through this Wood every so often," Bethan mused. "These trees have stood for hundreds of years. They'll stand for hundreds more, long after you and I are dust. It keeps one from getting bigheaded, don't you think?"

I'd opened my mouth to answer, when something whizzed past my ear.

"Are there bugs at this time of year?" I began to ask, but all the breath was knocked out of me as Bethan yanked me from my seat and laid me across her knees like a sack of flour. Shouts went up along the procession. Everything became a blur of color and sound as the captain dug her heels into Westdolph's sides, spurring him into a gallop. Both the horse and rider disappeared out from under me as Bethan heaved me upwards where a steady pair of arms was waiting to catch me. I could only make out the blue of Gareth's jerkin as he kicked open the steward's hatch in the top of the coach and dropped me through it like a stone into a well. My feet hit the floor of my compartment only a second before Gareth himself was beside me. He reached up to throw a bolt to the hatch and hurried to the door to throw another, hidden behind a bit of velvet drape, along with a short sword that he drew reluctantly. It was then I realized we were inside a fortress.

"Get on the floor, under the bottom bunk if you can," Gareth said, risking a quick glance out of one of the tiny windows before slamming the cover over it. "Now!"

I wriggled underneath the bunk quick as I could, still winded and confused. Gareth shot a look my way to make sure I'd done as he asked, but was suddenly on his knees next to the bunk, pushing my hair back from my face. "You're bleeding!"

I lifted my hand to my ear and it came away wet and red. "Something bit me."

"The caravan's come under attack," Gareth answered. To bring home his point, three solid thunks sounded against the side of the coach next to his shoulder. The steward flinched, pale and holding the sword as if it might bite him. "They've got bowmen."

I realized then why I was bleeding. I'd only been a gnat's wing away from an arrow through the head. The idea put the shakes in me, and suddenly, I was trembling all over, worse than after Toly had tried to spirit me away.

We could hear it properly now—the sounds of the battle outside. Bethan's voice stood out over the shouting and clash of swords, roaring orders to her surprised soldiers. It was impossible to tell anything about what was happening from where I lay, huddled under the bunk. It sounded to me as if our escort had been attacked by an entire army. Of course, I'd never seen a battle any fiercer than the occasional scraps the hired hands got into after a little too much Scrump, so the fighting outside sounded like a war that could end the world.

"Gareth!" I shouted above the din. "What's happening?"

"I'm not to open any of the doors or window ports," he answered, sounding queasy. "But you needn't worry. I'm sure they'll—" He was cut off by a loud thunk against the coach, followed by a bloodcurdling cry. "Make quick work of them," he finished, not sounding at all sure of himself.

"Do you know how to use that sword?" I asked as the crash of battle moved closer to the coach.

Gareth puffed himself up a bit. "Of course I do!"

A blue haze rippled round his head. "Gareth."

His shoulders slumped. "All right, I only know how to use it against a straw man in the training yard." Gareth threw up a hand. "I can lay a twenty-piece place setting, tell the difference between a fish and oyster fork, and starch a napkin so that you could almost cut your finger on it!"

"Well, unless you've got a whole lot of pointy napkins handy, I reckon the sword's our best chance!" I shot back. "Maybe they'll take care of them all before—"

And at that moment, the privy exploded.

Splinters of the door that modestly enclosed the moving water closet sprayed into the tiny space as a figure burst through it. The intruder was whip thin, like Master Iordan, but covered in lean muscle I could make out even under his loose gray tunic. His face was mostly covered by a dirty brown cloth, but such an entrance didn't leave much to the imagination regarding his intentions. Gareth stumbled to his feet and made a clumsy attempt to fell our attacker with the sword's pommel, but the man dealt him a blow to the cheek that put him right back on the floor. The corners of the villain's eyes creased in triumph as he spotted me huddled under the bunk.

"You come on out, then, whelp," he growled in a voice full of salt and dust.

The smell of the foul wood he'd just broken through mingled with the stink of a fellow living rough. I shrunk farther back under the bunk, but he was quickly on his knees, one arm thrust into my hiding spot, dirty fingers grasping.

I'd no other weapons available than the ones the Mother gave me, so I bit down hard on the soft flesh of his palm. The man howled, jerking his hand away, but his next try snagged the collar of my coat, dragging me from my hiding place. I fought with every ounce of vinegar I had. I slapped at him with my hands, tried to stomp on his toes, and nipped at his fingers, but still he dragged me back toward the ruin of the privy. It was only an extremely lucky kick—straight to a part of him where Mama told me I must never ever kick my brothers—that stopped him in his tracks. He fell to his knees, clutching himself and letting loose some especially filthy curses as I clambered up on top of my bunk.

It took him only a moment to recover and then he was on his feet again, enraged and ready to tear me in two. By that time, Gareth had managed to right himself and grabbed hold of the man's arm, but was quickly flung aside. There was the ring of metal on wood and the fallen sword was suddenly in the villain's fist, pointed straight at Gareth.

"It'll be a pleasure to put a little blood on the king's colors!" he snarled, his arm swinging back for a killing blow.

But it never came. From atop the bunk, I brought my name-day chest down on the back of his head as hard as I could. The good, sturdy oak box Papa built made a cracking sound as it connected with the villain's skull. The man staggered forward, stunned, then crumpled in a heap on the floor of the coach, the sword skittering into the ruin of the privy.

From outside, a shout of celebration echoed through the Wood. Gareth and I looked at each other with the same question on our minds.

Who had won?

16

We were answered presently by the pounding of a fist on the side of the coach. "Open in the name of the king!" bellowed Bethan. "In the name of the king, open these doors! Only! Gareth!" There was a note of fear in her voice.

Gareth was frozen, staring at the man lying crumpled at our feet, his mouth moving but no words coming out.

"Gareth?" I whispered.

Gareth didn't look up. I could only hear the weak thread of his voice repeating, "I'm sorry, I'm sorry, I'm sorry," over and over. He didn't even seem to notice the frantic pounding at the door.

"Gareth!" I shouted. My voice broke the spell, and the young man scrambled like a rabbit to undo the bolts. The door to the compartment flew open so fast, he was knocked backward against the bunks. Bethan, wild haired and covered in blood and dirt, burst in with Master Iordan a step behind. She took in the whole scene in an instant—the destroyed privy and the unconscious villain. "Sweet All! Are either of you hurt?"

"No, ma'am," Gareth answered shakily. "Though it was the Mayquin who brought down the fellow on the floor. I . . . I . . ."

"It seems you're a young woman of many talents," Bethan told me as two soldiers reached in to take away the senseless man. She laid a bloody hand on the steward's shoulder. "I commend you for your honesty, Master Gareth. You're an excellent steward—it would be foolish to expect a soldier's showing from you."

My heart swelled a bit when I saw the effect of the captain's words on my new friend. His head rose a little higher, and the flush of shame disappeared from his cheeks.

The captain took a deep, shuddering breath. "I also commend you for the strength and swiftness you showed getting Only to safety."

"A swiftness that would not have been necessary if she had been confined to the coach!" Master Iordan rebuked.

Bethan rounded on the inquisitor, who stepped back in alarm. "Master, three of my men died defending this caravan, including *your* miserable hide. I won't have my actions questioned at a time like this."

Three men died? Defending me? The thought was so horrible, I could hardly bear it—three souls gone because of my stupid cunning. I let my head fall to the pillow and gazed sightlessly at the ceiling. Even though the inside of the compartment smelled of blood, sweat, and privy wood, I didn't want to move. Didn't want to face whatever was waiting outside. I squeezed my eyes tight shut.

"Only?" Bethan looked into the upper bunk and spoke gently, as if I were a horse that might spook. "Only, are you all right?"

My fingers crept into my pocket. By some good luck, the Jack hadn't broken. The flame still danced, and I felt my hoofbeat heart begin to slow. Perhaps Lark's clever magic had been looking out for me after all. I cleared my throat to make sure I had a voice to come out of it. "No, ma'am," I answered, looking down at her. "But I'm not hurt much."

"Come on, come here." The captain stretched out her arms to me, and I allowed her to pull me from the bunk. I expected she'd set me on the floor, but instead she clutched me to her chest. "I'm sorry," she whispered in my ear. "I'm sorry for everything."

Before I could speak, she released me, brushing back the hair at the side of my face that was matted with blood. "There's a stream nearby. Let's get you cleaned up and presentable."

"Why, ma'am?"

Bethan's face was grave. "Because your duties as Mayquin begin now."

OUTSIDE THE COACH, darkness had fallen and our traveling party had grown tremendously. At least a dozen more cavalry riders and a small battalion of foot soldiers had joined us and now sat, jawing in low voices over fires. More'n a few were being tended by a patchwoman, groaning as bones were reset or stitches needled through their flesh. Others stood on the edge of the fires—burly men with wild hair and thick beards. Whispers told me they were lumbermen from Lake-in-the-Woods who'd followed the second king's company at the sounds of the battle.

I was glad of the dark as I followed Bethan back to camp from a clearing not far from the coach. I felt cleaner, but the icy stream water couldn't wash off the dread I carried. The night hid the blood on the ground and the broken arrows sticking out of the great trees. But far away in the woods were the sounds of shovels and pickaxes.

The clearing was alight and dancing with flames of a great fire. Soldiers were gathered in groups, their faces weary with battle. More warhorses were standing in the shadows, being fed and watered by grooms. But most noticeable was a small group of ragged men at the far end, bound at the hands and guarded closely by soldiers with pikes and axes. The men's fear was a presence in the Wood—it poured off them like a bad smell. An officer approached Bethan.

"Captain, it's nearly done."

"You've questioned them all individually?"

The man nodded. "Dahl's just finishing with the last one now."

Bethan introduced me. "Only, this is Captain Reynold. Joss, this is Only Fallow, the king's Mayquin. I thought she might be of some assistance to us."

Reynold gave me a sharp nod. "I'm sorry your journey was interrupted by these scoundrels, Mayquin." He looked round the clearing grimly. "This is no sight for a young lady."

I tugged at Bethan's sleeve. "Ma'am, may I please ask—who died? In your company?"

"Farren and Sweets in the first volley of arrows. Emerick took down two before he fell." The fire deepened the sad lines in her face. "If I'd known he wasn't long for the world, I'd have let him look his fill at the stream in North Hallow."

Mischievous Emerick and playful Sweets, gone in the blink of an eye. Though I didn't know either of them well, their loss was heavy on my heart. "Would you please tell their families that I'm awfully sorry?"

Bethan put a hand on my shoulder. "Of course. It's kind of you to remember them."

In my mind, remembering them was the very least I could do. How do you repay someone who died for something you spent your whole life trying to keep a secret? "What did you want me to do, ma'am?"

"Lieutenant Dahl is questioning one of the men who attacked us. I'd like you to observe. See if we can learn anything."

I squinted at the group of prisoners. There was something awful familiar about them. Though they were dirty, bedraggled, and beaten, the sun-kissed skin and green eyes were unmistakable.

"They're Ordish!" I gasped.

Captain Reynold sniffed. "Who else would be bold enough to attack a royal caravan?"

"Are these the same men who burned the grain store at North Hallow last week?" inquired Bethan.

"We haven't questioned them on that point yet," Reynold replied, "but I wouldn't be surprised."

"B-but . . . but," I stammered, "the Ordish don't attack folk! If anything, it's the king that—"

Bethan's head snapped round, her eyes flashing. "Be silent!"

The captain's command rang loud and harsh in the clearing, turning all heads in our direction. I couldn't help but shrink backward—any of Bethan's earlier good will toward me had vanished, leaving harsh correction in every tired, dirt-caked crease of her face. "Your duty is to serve His Majesty now, not question his judgment, is that understood?"

It was like I'd been bitten by a trusted guard dog. Chastened, I ducked my head so she wouldn't see my eyes welling up. "Yes'm."

Captain Reynold cleared his throat. "We'd be most grateful, Mayquin, if you'd assist us in the interrogations. These fellows call themselves the Woodland Scourge. They say they've been making a living thieving from logging camps and the odd traveler on the road while plotting attacks against royal properties."

I noticed one fellow at the edge of the bound pack listening close to our conversation with wide, fretful eyes that darted away nervously when I twigged him.

"Is that true?" I prodded. "What the captain said?"

"Yes," he replied roughly, turning away to reveal a bloody gash beside his ear. My heart twanged fiercely—the "scoundrel" was barely a man and looked so like Rowan—a fresh wave of longing for my friends and home crashed over me.

But man or no, he wasn't telling the whole story. Green fire lit his dark hair and eyes, dancing with flames of the campfire.

"Well?" Bethan's voice was still sharp and pointy.

I shook my head. "Whatever it is they're hiding, they're afraid."

Captain Reynold frowned. "Clearly our questioning techniques leave something to be desired. Perhaps we'll get more out of the last one. Mayquin, this way, if you please."

The two captains led the way down a dark path to a smaller clearing not far off, where there was only a meager fire, with three people beside it—one on his knees in the dirt, one looming above him, and Master Iordan watching sullenly from farther off.

"Dahl," Bethan called out as we approached.

The soldier turned. To my surprise, it was another woman, slightly shorter than the captain and thicker of limb. A scar ran down the side of her face from her eye to her chin, making her look every bit as fierce as the men in her unit. "Captain."

The thin young man on the ground was in a bad state, bound hand and foot and facedown in the dirt, groaning. Several livid bruises stood out on his neck and bare shoulders. I had a suspicion Lieutenant Dahl put them there.

"Anything new?" asked Reynold.

"I'm afraid his story's the same as the others, Captain," Iordan drawled, his sneer showing his distaste for the whole ordeal.

Bethan frowned down at the prisoner. "Attacking a royal caravan is a bit of a step up from petty theft, isn't it?"

The man spat on the ground, his face still in deep shadow. "We strike blows against the king when we can," he grunted. "Didn't reckon on the second company."

A dazzling display covered the prisoner—blues, greens, and reds shattered the darkness of the Wood, lighting up the clearing around him. I had to hold in a gasp of delight at the beauty of it. Men had died. Blood had been shed. I couldn't delight in villainy at a time like this. But as quickly as it had come, it vanished as the man mentioned the second company.

The three soldiers looked at me expectantly. Their attention

crawled over my skin like bugs. "It's true they weren't expecting another regiment, but the rest of it's a pack of whoppers."

Dahl turned on the man with a snarl, her arm raised to deliver another blow. "Do I need to rattle your brains a bit more, wetcollar?" She pointed at me and grabbed the man's chin to wrench his face upward. "It's pointless to lie. Do you know who this is?"

If the Mother herself had thrown back night's quilt and appeared in all her glory on the spot I was standing, I couldn't have been struck more speechless than when I found myself staring into the eyes of my brother.

Jonquin.

The long tongues of the campfire's flame licked up into the night, showing me what I couldn't believe was true. His hair, darkened with coal bark, had grown longer—long enough to cinch in a knot at his neck. His skin was a deep shade of gold from days on the river, but sure as eggs were eggs, it was Jon. I'd never been so happy or so terrified to see someone in all my life.

His mouth slacked at the sight of me. His lips even began to form my name, but Dahl's temper was quick, and her fingers bit into his jaw.

"I said, do you know who this is?" she barked.

I gave the slightest shake of my head I could manage. Relief ran cool through my veins to see his eyes harden, making him look more like the desperate men in the clearing than a boy from Presston.

"Some soldier's whelp? How should I know?" he spat, the falsehood exploding around him in shades of green.

Dahl's fist flew in the darkness, and Jon yelped, a fresh trail of blood blooming from his nose. "Don't!" I shouted, before I could keep it in. My hands flew to cover my mouth, but all the kingsmen in the clearing were staring at me. "I'm sorry," I said in a small voice. "I've . . . just seen enough hurting for one day." A knock echoed inside my head. I shut my eyes to drown it out.

Iordan drew himself up, trying to look as menacing as the soldiers. "How would a water-dwelling brigand such as yourself have any idea who this child is? Is she the reason you and your fellows attacked this caravan?"

Jon looked up, but pursed his lips, remaining silent.

The inquisitor turned to Bethan, his voice low and urgent. "The existence of the Mayquin was only known by members of the king's council." Iordan glanced down at Jon. "If *these* wretches knew about her, it probably goes without saying that we have a problem."

Even in the flickering firelight, I could see the blood drain from Bethan's face. I thought quick on the inquisitor's words. *Only members of the king's council knew I was coming.*

Bethan knelt down beside Jon. For a moment, I had a wild fear that she'd see it somehow—the same shape of our eyes or the way both our noses turned up just a hair at the end—but she was too full of battle rage to notice.

Her voice was soft, but with sharp knives in it. "Who told you about the Mayquin?"

"Captain," Iordan interrupted, "think carefully before you ask a question whose answer might be dangerous to hear."

But Bethan wasn't listening. "Attacks by your people on royal property have been stepped up recently, but this is madness, even for you. Your weapons?" She drew a sword from her belt, clearly taken from a prisoner. "The Ordish have never fought with blades like these. And the bows you used are finished finer than any Ordish hunting bow. These aren't your weapons, which means they were given to you by someone else."

The inquisitor took a wary step toward them. "Captain, please—"

"Hold your tongue, master!" barked Bethan, not taking her eyes off Jon. "Who gave you the weapons? And who told you about the Mayquin?"

The clearing held its breath. My brother, beaten though he was, didn't shrink beneath the captain's contempt. He wasn't the boy who'd been licked by the Bonniways in the orchard anymore. He was a man, staring down something bigger and scarier than him without flinching.

"We strike blows 'gainst the king when we can."

Bethan made a noise of disgust and turned her back on us to walk a little way into the darkness of the trees before uttering a cry of frustration. Those of us left by the fire looked at one another, not sure what we were meant to do, so we chose to wait and watch the captain of the king's guard set her hands on her hips and stare down at the dirt. After a moment, she rounded on her heel and marched back to us.

"Dahl, take him back with the others. Reynold, let everyone know we'll be away early tomorrow morning. Part of your company will escort the prisoners back to face whatever awaits them in the city. The rest of us will press on ahead with all haste and with any luck, we'll make the capital by nightfall."

Iordan cleared his throat. "Captain, the king is not expecting us until the day after tomorrow. There is the Mayquin's entrance to consider. The plans for the celebration—"

"The celebration and every one of its planners can go straight to the seven hells!" barked Bethan. "Three of my men are dead, and it's clear that *someone* is bent on the Mayquin not reaching Bellskeep. I won't parade her straight down the middle of the River when there are those that mean her harm. We leave at first light." And with that, she stalked out of the clearing.

Dahl grasped Jon's dirty collar and hauled him upright. I wanted to run to him, throw my arms round his waist, and tell the soldier not to touch him again. I wanted to ask him why he was here, why the Ordish were here. But I had to stand, as helpless as the day Iordan had ripped me from the orchard, and watch Dahl's rough hands on my brother, shoving him into the night toward the rest of the bound men in the clearing without a backward glance in my direction.

The inquisitor's thin hand fell on my shoulder. "It's about time you were abed, Mayquin."

"If you please, master," I began as we started back for the coach, "what'll become of those men?"

"I imagine they'll be questioned further back at the capital," he answered wearily. "I'm led to believe there are more . . . persuasive methods available there."

I didn't dare ask what those methods might be. And I wasn't

going to be able to get the answers I wanted from my brother, but some of the inquisitor's walls had come tumbling down and I thought maybe I could wiggle in through the cracks.

"Master, what didn't you want the captain to ask back in the clearing?"

The inquisitor spared a silent glance at the soldiers we passed. "These are troubled times, child."

"Are they?" I asked, surprised. "We didn't have much trouble in Presston."

Iordan pretended not to hear. "There are a great many things to consider. A royal marriage with a one-time enemy, the Ordish problem, and the king himself growing older and more . . . suggestible. The crown needs someone who can be relied upon to see through any deception. Despite your upbringing, child, you're neither slow nor dim-witted—can you not *see* how there would be those eager to prevent your arrival in the capital?"

"So, people who want to lie to the king—"

"Would very much like to keep lying to the king, yes," finished Iordan. "But it's best not to name names in the middle of a clearing, surrounded by the king's soldiers."

The flicker of the coach's lanterns greeted us as we approached. I was bone tired, but my heart was still singing *Jonquin, Jonquin, Jonquin* with every beat. The sooner I was shot of the inquisitor, the sooner I could see about finding him. Iordan opened the door and we both stepped into the narrow hallway.

"Master?"

The inquisitor had already begun sliding open the door to his compartment. "Could I persuade you to hold any further questioning until daybreak, child?" he said with a groan.

"No, sir, I just wanted to say . . . thank you. For telling me."

The prickly man paused in the doorway. "There's no one else who would tell you. I have no love for those who would use ignorance and fear to snuff out the light of reason. Though you're doing your duty, it's unfair to expect a young woman such as yourself to walk cheerfully into a den of vipers. Keep your wits about you, girl, and you may just keep the kingdom in one piece."

And with that, he slid the door into place, leaving me alone in the corridor.

17

It wasn't my brightest-ever idea.

The lumbermen had done some quick work on the ruined privy while we'd been gone. The boards, unstained and un-smoothed, looked as if they'd be murder on a bare behind. I wasn't keen to leave that way in the first place, but with the chance of splinters added into the smelly bargain of wiggling through the trap, it made what I reckoned on doing even more distasteful.

I made myself wait three-quarters of an hour to give the camp and Master Iordan time to bed down and be catching flies. In the meantime, my mind was racing. What in the world had brought Jon and these Ordish men to the Great Wood in order to waylay a royal caravan? And who'd told them about me?

The night outside the coach grew still. The voices of soldiers and woodsmen fell quiet in sleep or ponderation.

You're a Fallow of the orchard. Nowt you can't do. Just don't think too hard on how you're getting out.

As far as I could see, there was no other way to sneak out of the rolling crate without being twigged straight off. There'd be at least two soldiers standing watch outside, but likely they weren't expecting I'd try to leave the same way the villain came in.

Taking a deep breath, I quietly opened the new door and peered down the hole. It wasn't big—the man who'd bust in had been lean as a whippet, but bigger than me, surely. I didn't like to think of getting into a second spot of bother concerning a privy, especially if that bother included getting wedged inside one, but I knew if I stopped to think too long, I might lose my nerve. Shutting the door silently, I dangled my legs into the trap, keeping my eyes fixed on the dim light at the bottom. Arms quivering under the strain, I lowered myself down, the smell of waste getting stronger with every breath. I wished the villain had broken *that* part of the box as well, but he probably didn't want to touch it any more than I did. I gagged, my nose just inches from the damp wood, until I felt my toes hit the blessed ground below. It took everything in me not to drop out the bottom like a sack of flour just to get away from the stink, but I forced myself to take it slow until my head passed through the trap at the bottom and I lay under the coach, sucking in fresh air, quiet as I could.

Two pairs of legs stood straight and soldierly before the doors of the coach, and I hoped the soldiers attached to them weren't struck by a sudden fancy to have a peek underneath. Slow as I could, I rolled out from under the privy hole until I was faceup in the clearing, staring at the few stars I could see winking through the tops of the great trees.

As much as I hated to ask for help, I wasn't going to be able to get to Jon on my own.

Gareth made a sound like a drain unblocking when I gave him a poke. He was curled up on the steward's bench on the back of the wagon, his bedroll pulled up round his ears. He woke in a second, scrunched and ready to spring straight out from under the covers like an angry caterpillar.

What are you doing? he mouthed, sound not even passing his lips.

I crooked my finger, hoping he'd follow me without asking too many questions. Nights in the forest were inky dark—not even moonlight could penetrate the thick branches of the pines. The shadows were deep and good for secrets and mischief.

I crept into one far enough away from the carriage not to be seen, but not far enough to lose my way. It wasn't but a second before Gareth was by my side.

"Are you mad? How in the Mother's name did you—?" He broke off as he caught my whiff. "Oh, hells, you didn't."

"Never mind that. I gotta know right now, Gareth, can I trust you?"

"What?"

"Just yes or no, can I trust you?" I hissed.

The steward's silence stretched out almost as far as the dark. *I should've just left him snoring on his bench,* I thought, but he finally spoke up. "Yes."

I squinted at him real hard, but he and the forest stayed dark. I squeezed his arm.

"Thank you."

"I should have done better this morning," he murmured. "In the coach. I should have had that villain on the floor. You shouldn't have had to—"

"Didn't you hear the captain?" We didn't have time for nonsense. "You're not a soldier. Did that straw man in the practice yard ever try to hit back? I just got the drop on him, that's all."

He took a breath to argue, but I cut him off. "I need you to find out where they're keeping the men who attacked us."

"Why?"

I screwed up my courage. "'Cause one of 'em's my brother."

Gareth's jaw near unhinged.

"How . . . ? Your *brother*?"

"Story's too long for now," I said. "But I've got to know why he's here. You understand, don't you?"

"I do, but—"

"And you can't breathe a word to nobody. Not the captains, not Master Iordan, nobody." In spite of the steward's promise, I was still sore afraid of the words having been said out loud. "They'll take the orchard—my home—if they knew, and then my coming to Bellskeep will be all for nothing!"

Gareth was quiet, sorting over everything I'd dropped on him like a tangled bit of knitting. I couldn't afford to lose him.

"*Please*, Gareth. I'll be the quietest Mayquin there ever was."

In the dark, it was hard to tell what he was thinking, but

my heart leapt high when he stood up straight and squared his shoulders.

"What do you want me to do?" he answered finally.

It wasn't hard to find the clearing.

I'd a fragile hope of setting Jon free, but it was shattered when I saw the captives trussed together in small circles around thick stakes, pounded into the ground. Tricky ropes circled their hands, and each man's ankle was bound to his neighbor's with even more complicated knots. They were dozing best they could, slumped against one another's shoulders or leaning back on the poles. Four soldiers from the second cavalry unit milled round, still on edge from the day's fighting, eyes darting toward every shadow cast by the fire.

"The big one's Alfroy," whispered Gareth, pointing the men out by name. "Then Dafin, Calford, and Hale."

I was busy searching the captives for Jon. When I finally spotted him, I felt as though I'd been kissed by luck herself. He was tied on the outside of one of the circles, facing straight into the woods, only inches from a good, tall tree with a deep, dark shadow. His head was thrown back in sleep, his mouth slightly open, and Lieutenant Dahl's handiwork written all over his face. My heart hurt for the golden-haired boy who danced with his sweetheart by the river just a few months earlier.

Gareth squinted into the clearing, second thoughts written all over him.

"You ready?"

The steward bit his bottom lip. "No, but I guess that's beside the point."

"Just try to keep them looking the other way as long as you can. I'll see what I can get out of Jon."

"I'll do what I can. Good luck, Only."

"And to you," I answered, slipping farther back into the dark of the great trees. The steward took a deep breath and started into the light as if he'd every right to be there.

The four soldiers started at his approach, hands rushing to sword pommels, but relaxed as he drew near. "Evening, Gareth," hailed Alfroy, warming his hands to the fire.

"Good eve, masters. I've come to ask if there's anything I might get for you?" From between the trees, I watched the aurora of blue and green fan out from behind him.

"Not unless you can hasten the clock to the end of our watch," Dafin said, yawning and scratching at a row of stitching on his cheek.

"I can't move the clock, but maybe I could fill the time with . . . a song?"

I hadn't believed him at first when he said he could sing.

"When I was just a boy, I sang one of the songs I heard from the soldiers to my mother. It turned out the tune was more suited to an alehouse than her house. I got a switching, but I still enjoyed the singing of it."

"You still remember it?"

He blushed. "Every word, I'm afraid."

The soldiers chuckled. "G'wan, then, lad." Calford thrust a meaty thumb over his shoulder. "These scoundrels aren't going anywhere."

For a second, I thought maybe he was about to lose his nerve, but he smiled, took a deep lungful, and filled the clearing with his voice.

> 'Twas early one spring morning
> My sweet and I should wed.
> We'd say our vows and late carouse
> And then go off to bed.
> But the night before
> My mates they swore
> To give me one last fling,
> So to the tavern we did go
> And while we drink, we sing:
> Hoist the tankards high, boys!
> Hoist those glasses so high,
> In the morning you'll be married
> But tonight no cup will run dry!

Gareth sang so sweet and so clear, it took me a few notes before I remembered I wasn't there to listen. I felt round the earth till I found a long pine branch. Making double sure the soldiers were more interested in Gareth's song than the Ordish, I poked the branch out from behind the tree and gave the bottom of Jon's boot three sharp jabs.

He jerked his head up with a snort, peering into the shadows in front of him. "Mother's breath! Only!" His eyes, weary and bruised, lit up lantern bright.

"Shhhhh!" I bossed him, trying to cover up that I was so glad to see him, I was ready to burst into tears. "What are you *doing* here, Jonquin Fallow?"

"I could ask you the same!"

"They came to get me, Jon, all 'cause of some stupid cunning! They came to the orchard and told Papa if I didn't come, they'd take it all away from us." Before I could stop it, I was sobbing quietly. I wanted so bad to burst out from behind the great tree and bury my head in Jon's shoulder, but all I could do was watch him watch me, wishing the very same thing.

"Oh, Pip," he muttered. "Don't do that, you'll make me blub as well. What do you mean, 'cunning'? What's the king want you for?"

Across the clearing, the soldiers joined in Gareth's chorus with the gusto of men who'd lived to fight another day.

> *Hoist the tankards high, boys!*
> *Hoist those glasses so high,*
> *In the morning you'll be married*
> *But tonight no cup will run dry!*

This ain't time to be pitying yourself, I thought sternly. "I can see when folk lie. The king wants me to tell him the truth."

Jonquin tilted his head as if hearing a faraway voice, then gave a little gasp of astonishment. "That night by the river! You twigged Toly and he knew!"

I nodded miserably. Jon's face contorted with rage. "Still wish I'd a minute alone with him and that knife of his."

Across the clearing, the fella in Gareth's song was having problems of his own.

'Twas past the second morning bell
When I regained my head
Tied to the village hitching post
While wearing not a thread . . .

I didn't want to think any thoughts of Toly except what I'd do if I ran into him once we got to the city. "How in the name of All did you get here?"

Jonquin's face darkened. "After we got down to the Bay, Maura's brother Barrow disappeared. Toly must not have been the only kingsman with the clans. Then a fella turned up—he ferreted out some folk who'd lost whelps, including Maura's pa, Luc. He told us he was a servant to the king, moved by his conscience. Said the whelps were being moved to another of the king's holdings and we'd have a chance to take them back. Most didn't believe him. Most thought he was a kingsman himself. Most, like Master Fairweather, told him to pound salt, once he said what it was."

"Most men got better sense than to attack the king's cavalry!"

Jon looked at me helplessly. "Maura's family's been broken since Barrow was took. I said I'd go in Luc's place. His knees ain't what they used to be; he'd be no good in a skirmish."

The soldiers roared as the fella in the song hid his bare backside from the town bailiff. I could see why it earned Gareth a switching. How many verses did the steward have left in his pocket? Hopefully enough for the groom-in-waiting to find some threads and for me to learn more from Jonquin.

"What was the man like? The one who came to the Gathering?"

"Plain fella, mousy, all dressed in brown. Didn't look rich, didn't look poor. But he was right persuasive—said we'd out-number them two to one. Gave us all the weapons." He hung his head. "We were damn fools to trust him. But it was the first thing to give some of these men hope in a good many turns of the wheel. *Now* half of 'em . . ." He trailed off. Though the sound of the shovels had stopped, neither of us could pretend we hadn't heard 'em. "We were damn fools."

"The fella who . . . came into the wagon, he was definitely after *me*." I paused, not sure I wanted to hear the answer to my own question. "What was supposed to happen to me, Jon?"

"I didn't know about none of that, honest! All I knew was that there was something in the coach we needed, but only Wash Blackrudder knew what it was." Jon's face twisted in fear. "I think we're like to swing for this, Only."

"Don't even say it! When we get to Bellskeep, I'll find a way to get you out, Jon, I swear it!"

> 'Twas past the fifth bright morning bell
> When what should I a-spy
> But a line all full of washing,
> The clothes all nearly dry,

But hanging there
To my despair
Flapped gowns upon the breeze
Outside the tavern where
My mates had left me on my knees:

Surely the song was almost done. As the soldiers and Gareth roared the chorus once more, I boldly reached out from the shadow to squeeze my brother's toes through his boot. Jon's eyes filled up.

"I'm sorry, Pip. 'Bout everything. If . . . anything happens, you'll tell Mama and Papa and Maura that I love 'em, won't you?"

"Jonquin Fallow, you shut your mouth," I insisted. "You'll tell 'em yourself. The Mother Herself ain't gonna stop me, you hear?"

Jon nodded tearfully. "The king's gonna have his hands full with you."

"He's got no idea."

'Twas past the ninth loud morning bell
I arrived at sanctuary
To join my sweet before the altar.
I could not stop and tarry.
The rector frowned
Upon my gown
And then stood up to chide,
"How can I conduct a wedding
When I don't know who's the bride?"

I wanted to rain blessings down on Gareth as he led the soldiers into one last chorus, keeping a sly watch on our side of the clearing.

"I'll find you as soon as I can," I whispered, backing farther behind the pine. "Love you, Jon."

"Love you, too, Pip. Be safe!"

In the morning you'll be married
But tonight no cup will run dry!

18

I woke the next morning to an earthquake. But as I swam up through the sea of sleep, I recognized the sound of the wheels turning faster'n I'd heard them before. We were moving at a terrific pace. Whether it was toward Bellskeep or away from the Wood, I couldn't tell.

The bite in the air had grown fangs since we'd left the trees behind. I pulled the quilt up round my ears and burrowed down into the warmth. My heart gave a painful thump in my chest. Jon was out there with no quilt, being marched toward the capital to face All knows what. My promise burned in me, bright as summer. I *would* find a way to get him out.

The chill grew colder as the hatch in the roof popped open. Gareth's familiar legs, followed by the rest of him, dropped into the compartment, graceful as a cat, and bearing breakfast.

"Morning," he greeted me cheerfully. "Or, afternoon, I suppose."

"Afternoon? What hour is it?"

"Just gone two of the clock. We've put a lot of miles between us and the forest since dawn."

I sat bolt upright. "I been asleep ages! Why'd you let me laze round so long?"

"After yesterday I thought you could use a lie-in." The steward set the breakfast tray on my bed, stretched, and yawned. "Could have done with one myself."

"You were the buzz on the bees last night!" I exclaimed. "Maybe you should have been a balladeer instead of a steward!"

Gareth flushed down to his freckles. I grinned at him as I jammed a piece of the travel bread in my mouth. I hadn't realized how hungry I was—it tasted as good as a loaf straight from Mama's oven. The steward watched me wolf down breakfast as he leaned against the privy door.

"We're about an hour's travel from the Rivergate, but I think the captain means to bide our time for a while so we arrive after dark. Nafir was sent ahead to make preparations."

"Wath da Wivergae?" Too late, I put up my hands to avoid spraying crumbs everywhere.

"The Rivergate's the only entrance to the city," Gareth explained, ignoring my terrible manners.

I swallowed hard, the too-big lump of bread sliding down my throat. "There's only one way into Bellskeep?"

"There's a great wall that runs all around it. Nothing can get in or out except through the Rivergate."

"Well, rabbits always find their way into a garden," I pointed out. "They don't care so much about walls."

Gareth peered up at the hatch and lowered his voice. "My brother Gable once showed me the entrance to the smugglers' tunnels in the west of the city, but I was too white-feathered to go in."

Presently, the din of the wheels began to fall away and the great carriage slowed. Gareth made for the sliding door. "You'll be able to see Bellskeep in a few moments. Come out and look when you're dressed."

Eager to catch a glimpse of the capital, I shoved the rest of the bread in my mouth. "Ah'll be aught in a sehcont," I answered through another hail of crumbs.

Gareth smiled and made to go.

"Gareff?" I called, still chewing.

"Yes?"

"Fank 'oo. For wast nigh'."

He understood me just fine.

THE SUN HAD nearly disappeared over the faraway mountains when I got my first glimpse of Bellskeep.

The procession abandoned the road and continued to a middling-size farm on a hill just outside the city. Bethan came to fetch me from the coach and took me out behind the stables, where I got an eyeful of my new home. She'd not been wrong when she said it was bigger than ten Roundmarkets. It was almost bigger than *twenty* Roundmarkets and surrounded with the most enormous wall I'd ever seen in my life. It spread out over the valley—a colossal quilt of brick and stone.

"Great All," I whispered, clutching my chest. "I've never seen . . ."

Bethan bent down to point out landmarks that I could just about make out over the top of the city wall. "Those silver banners, fluttering there, can you see them? Those fly from atop the castle keep. And the little flame, far away? That's the Cathedra beacon."

I could just make out the banners, snapping this way and that, catching the last of the evening light. The Cathedra's beacon stood watch high above the city, atop the ivory towers of the greatest sanctuary in the kingdom. I didn't want to look like a gawping carp in front of the soldier, but the scale of the thing near took my breath.

"Quite a view, isn't it?" came an unfamiliar voice from behind us. It belonged to a kind-faced older man in the garb of a wealthy landowner. The pate of his mostly bald head was brown from years of work in the sun, but still had a few wisps of hair clinging to the sides for sweet All. "It's not quite the palace, I'll admit, but it's close enough."

"Emmory!" Bethan exclaimed, embracing the man. "It's good to see you, my friend. I apologize for bringing all this chaos to your doorstep."

The old man smiled warmly and kissed the captain on both cheeks. "Never any trouble for you, my dear, never any trouble at all." His smile broadened, noticing me. "Is this . . . ?"

"Only, this is Emmory Wickham. He used to be head gardener at the palace."

"Well," Emmory remarked, sliding his hands over his round belly, "I left the glamour of trimming the royal hedges for a quieter life out here some time ago, but I'm happy to be of assistance to you now. Shall we go see your transport?"

"Transport?" I asked as the old farmer led us to the handsome stone barn in front of the stables. "We're not taking the coach?"

"The coach is expected and will draw attention," answered the captain. "Whoever may have had something to do with the attacks yesterday knows their target. What they don't know is that you won't be in it."

Out from the doors of the barn came an ordinary wagon drawn by a tired-looking horse with one of Emmory's farmhands at the reins. As he steered the rickety cart toward us, Bethan began unbuckling her breastplate. "Did you find some cloaks for us?" she asked Emmory.

As the cart rumbled to a halt before us, Emmory reached into the back and tossed a large sack to the captain. "One big enough for you and two for the Mayquin and your steward. There's also a workaday dress of my wife's in there that should cover up your leathers." He patted his round stomach again and chuckled. "Both me and the missus are fond of our table. A trim lass like you might just get lost in it!"

Bethan smiled, shucking the large dress over her head. "I'm honored to wear it, Emmory. Thank Augusta kindly."

Gareth appeared from the side of the house, and the captain tossed a cloak into his waiting hands. The other one she gave to me, and I wrinkled up my nose at the scent.

"Smells a bit like sheep, ma'am," I said distastefully.

"Aye, but we're less likely to be bothered if we smell of sheep, wouldn't you agree?"

I couldn't argue. "I'd steer well clear of any folk smelling like this." The thought of the man who hoodwinked the Ordish at Farrier's Bay trotted unpleasantly through my head. I wondered whether he'd the news yet that his band of untrained soldiers had failed in their task.

Gareth had already climbed into the back of the wagon, piled high with timber. He stuck out a hand to help me clamber up next to him. The wood was stacked loosely, so we perched ourselves atop it best we could. Bethan vaulted into the driver's seat and took up the reins as she turned to our host. "I'll make sure all your goods make it back in one piece. Maybe soon, All willing, I'll be able to come for a more civilized visit."

"I'd like that very much, my dear, very much indeed," the farmer assured her. "Best be on your way. Curfew is in half of an hour."

Bethan spurred the horse on. "We'll be swift," she said over her shoulder as we began to move. "Thank you again, my friend."

And as quickly as we'd come to Master Wickham's farm, we left it. On the road, half a mile before us, the great coach thundered past, heading down the hill toward the city gates. The cavalry unfurled their banners, which waved proud in twilight. For a moment, I was almost sorry not to be part of the grand procession until the frightened face of Jonquin came back to me, chasing out any envy. Entering the city quiet like was definitely a better plan.

"What's a curfew?" I asked as we joined the main road that led to the city.

"The Rivergate doesn't admit anyone after ninth evening bell," Gareth answered. "Anyone outside the walls after has to wait till sixth morning bell, when they open again." He shivered in the night air. "We'll have to hurry if we don't want to get caught out."

"We'll make it," Bethan assured us, urging a bit more spirit from our sluggish horse, who was better used to the gentle speed of a plow. "Might be cutting it a little fine, but we'll make it."

The captain was right. By the time we reached the huge doors of the city, the guards were ringing the last warning bell. The clamor called out to any travelers on the road, warning them to spur their mounts or quicken their steps if they didn't want to spend the darkest hours of the night outside the safety of the walls. Those walls loomed large as the three of us, dressed in our ragged disguises, rolled toward the entrance.

19

Smile before your mother and your father and your kin,
Kneel before the rector so she'll take away your sin.
Clap before the players when they're finished with the show,
Dance before the fiddler as he plays so sweet and low.
Give silver to the taverner to fill your cup with ale,
Cross your heart before the captain as he puts your ship to sail.
Take your cap off to your sweetheart when you gift her with a ring,
You curtsy to a princess and you bow before a king.

—*A Book of Manners for the Young and Old*

Nothing could have prepared me to see the River.

On the other side of the Rivergate was a feat I thought must
have taken a thousand masons half a hundred years to finish.
The cart rolled slowly into a stone passageway so wide and grand
that two armies, both thirty men abreast, could pass one another
side by side with room to spare. The walls rose seventy feet into
the air, reducing the sky to a thin purple line of dusk. It was the
course of the long, dry branch of the Hush, cut off from the city
by Kester's Weir.

"It runs the whole length of the city—four miles in all, until it dead-ends at the Cathedra," Gareth explained. "It's really called the Kingsway or Queensway, depending on who's on the throne, but no one here calls it anything but the River."

A river made of stone, I thought. In the forest, the pines had made me feel small, but sort of comfortable like at the same time. Me and the trees were made of the same dust. But the bigness of the River threatened to swallow me whole. I wished we were back in the coach so I could retreat under my bunk, where I'd hid from the villain in the Wood, but I couldn't tear my eyes away from the towering walls that seemed to go on forever and ever.

Bethan turned over her shoulder, her face half hidden under her hood. "We're going to exit the River at Market Gate—we'll attract less attention that way. The coach has gone ahead to the Palace Gate."

"How do we get up there?" I asked, still looking at the city far above.

Gareth climbed into the front seat next to the captain. "We're coming up to South Gate in a moment. You'll be able to see the entrances to the underpassages."

Above the steep walls of the River, two towers came into view, one on each side. Stretched between them and supported by two giant stone columns sunk deep into the road below was the biggest bridge I'd ever seen. At least, I supposed it was a bridge, even though I couldn't actually see anything that might have been passing over it. My view was blocked by the walls of what looked like . . .

"Are those houses?" I marveled. "On the bridge?" In a few

of the grand, arched windows, figures moved to and fro in their nightly business.

"The city's grown a lot, even since I was a child," Bethan said. "There's precious little space left to build, so some of the wealthier citizens took to the bridges." She pointed ahead, in the shadow of the supports. "Those are the underpassages, up ahead."

Two dark, wide tunnels yawned out of the walls on either side of the River, the insides dancing with torchlight. Even in the gloom, I could make out the steep, upward slopes inside. Two guards in the king's colors stood beside each, jawing in low voices and stamping their feet against the cold.

"The River's the quickest way from one end of the city to the other," Gareth explained as the old carthorse's hooves echoed loudly off the walls. "The main streets are so crowded sometimes, it's easier just to pop down here to get where you're going. But anyone entering or leaving Bellskeep has to come through it."

"We'll be coming up on Market Gate in a few minutes," Bethan interrupted. "I think it's best you pretend to be asleep, Only. I'd rather not have the bother of one of the guards asking questions you can't answer."

I arranged myself best I could atop the uneven log pile. Even after the terrible, tiring day past, I couldn't imagine actually falling asleep on top of the lumpy, bumpy stack of wood, but I wriggled until I found a spot where I could be still for a bit. Gareth turned in his seat.

"When I came into service at the palace, I never imagined I'd be doing this," he whispered.

"When I got out of bed a week ago, I never imagined I'd be doing this either," I replied.

The wagon rattled over the flagstones. "I'm sorry you had to leave," Gareth said finally.

"Non says it's better to make friends with your lot rather than trying to fight it." I shifted uncomfortably. "Maybe it'll be easier once I ain't lying on a cold pile of logs."

The captain's voice, muffled by her hood, floated back. "Quietly now, we're coming to the gate."

I wrapped my cloak round me tight and tried to look as asleep as a very nervous and awake person possibly could.

The wagon rumbled to a stop beneath us, and Bethan greeted the guards. "Good eve to you, masters." The change in her voice, to the country tones I was used to from Presston, was followed by the telltale explosion of light around her in jaw-dropping shades of blue and green so bright that they lit up the inside of the passage. I had to squeeze my eyes shut so I wouldn't be tempted to watch.

"Evening, mistress," one of the sour men replied. "A bit late for deliveries, isn't it?"

"Oh, this ain't a delivery, sir. This load'll keep us warm for the next few months, I reckon."

The guards looked at one another suspiciously. "Where'd it come from? The market closed hours ago," the second asked.

"Ah, well, see, we was visiting my brother. He's a chopper out at the lake. Long day on the road." She pointed back to where I was pretending to sleep atop the logs. "I look after his whelps."

"Not a good time to be in the Wood," said one of the soldiers gruffly. Had news of the attack already made it to the city?

"Ooh, I'll say," Bethan answered. "Got passed by the royal coach on the way, moving along like it 'ad all the seven hells behind it. Must've been some excitement." Her fib nearly turned night into day.

A wary shadow passed over the older man's face. "They probably just wanted to make good time to the city and get out of the cold."

"It's got cold so fast this year," the captain agreed, trying to change the subject. "Cold's no good for no one. Me nephew here's got a terrible wheeze, haven't you, boy?"

"Oh! Oh yes!" croaked Gareth, launching into a coughing fit that would have got a troupe of players to their feet with cheering. Both men backed up, hoping not to catch whatever he was afflicted with.

"Yes, well, we'd better get you home sharpish, hadn't we?" Bethan had to raise her voice to be heard over Gareth's performance, which was getting louder by the moment. *"Hadn't we, boy?"*

"Oh, Mother's breath!" wailed Gareth, his gaspy, gurgling breaths putting more space between us and the soldiers.

The older man waved his hand at the underpassage. "Be on your way, mistress," he chivvied. "Good eve to you."

"Thank you kindly, masters," the captain said gratefully, bobbing her head and spurring the horses on. The glow around us faded as Bethan turned the cart into the tunnel and we began to ascend the steep slope up toward the city. After a few moments, she turned to Gareth, one eyebrow raised.

"Perhaps you missed your calling, master. You could have had a promising career on the stage." She spurred the horses onward up the ramp. "Let's see if we can bring the curtain down on this act of our journey."

NIGHT ALWAYS FELL on Presston heavy as a blanket, with quiet so thick you could cut a piece out with a pair of scissors. But even after dark in late autumn, Bellskeep was still wide-awake.

We came out of the underpassage into a bustling intersection. People of all sorts, both low and high, still crowded the streets, moving in all directions. Some wound their way to the west of the city over the bridge past its grand houses. Others clapped and roared at a bawdy dumbshow playing by lantern light at the wall of the market. My eyes couldn't take it all in fast enough. There were hardly this many people in the whole town of Presston, but this was just one crossroads in a city so big I could hardly fit it all in my head.

Gareth took in my wonderment. "It's not usually this busy so late. It's end of week, so taverns are allowed to stay open till the first morning bell. Grander folk use these evenings for calling or courting." As we rumbled through the intersection, he pointed down a side street. "My family lives just there, on Catchtail Alley."

"I'll make sure you can get away to see them soon, Gareth," Bethan said. "It's been a long few weeks on the road. You've more than earned it."

The young man's face lit up. "Thank you, ma'am!" He turned to me excitedly. "My mum makes the best bread pudding in all of Bellskeep. She's sure to have it on the table for supper." The thought of my own mama's bread pudding drove a sudden, sad spike through my heart. How long would it be before I would sit down to one of her suppers? How long before Jonquin broke bread with Maura and her family?

Just then, over the clamor of the street, a distant fanfare of trumpets sounded. The captain's shoulders tensed. "I'd hoped to be farther along before the coach reached the palace. We've only a few minutes before it's discovered that we're no longer with the company. They'll know we're somewhere in the city." Bethan growled in frustration as she was forced to slow the horse once more due to a tight knot of late-night revelers in the road ahead, wagering on the ability of one of their fellows to dance the four-step after drinking two pints of ale.

"We ain't far, are we?" I asked. "Surely no one can do anything about it before we get to the palace?"

"If someone sent a horde of assassins after us without managing to dirty their name, I wouldn't put anything past them," the captain replied darkly, adjusting the hood of her cloak. "But we're in sight, anyway."

As we cleared a tall, crooked pub, I got my first look at the castle. The walls were at least half as tall again as those of the River. Peeking out above, I could make out the high, square tower of the keep, but the huge walls kept all else hidden. The great barbican stood before it like a sentinel, ready to keep out the unwelcome. But as it turned out, we weren't headed that way.

Bethan turned the wagon down a side street lined with houses packed so tight together, you'd be able to hear a mouse squeak in your neighbor's kitchen.

"I don't intend to make any kind of grand entrance. The merchants' gate is round the north side of the castle. Hopefully, Nafir's managed to get two of my men down to watch for us. I'd rather not advertise the fact that we're outside the walls with no guard."

We crisscrossed a quiet warren of tiny streets, each more packed with close, cockeyed houses than the next. There were no gardens or green space to speak of but the weeds that burst out of the cobbles in the gutter. Even though it was dark, I could tell that what was running through it wasn't water.

"Sweet All, the stink!" I muttered into the hem of the fabric.

"You'll find the palace much more pleasing to the nose," Bethan remarked. "But I think if you grow up here, one of the first things to go is your sense of smell." She took a lungful of the night air. "I don't really notice anything."

Gareth's freckled nose poked out from under his hood. "Me neither."

Of all the things I could imagine getting used to in Bellskeep, the smell of night soil in the gutters wasn't one of them. I kept the cloak over my nose and mouth, preferring the smell of old sheep until we cleared the crowded avenues and finally came to the back entrance of the palace. Bethan steered the cart into a small courtyard, packed with empty barrels and wooden crates waiting to be picked up and filled once more. In the light of the gatehouse torches, we could see the outlines of two men playing at dice. They both stopped at our approach and came swaggering out to greet us.

Bethan stiffened. "Those *aren't* my men," she whispered nervously.

"Be off with you, skirt. It's well past the hour for deliveries," growled the taller man, stepping forward with his sharp pike in hand.

"Our arrival's expected, sirs," Bethan answered respectfully. "Sorry for the late hour. It's a long way from the Wood, and the streets are murder."

"Haven't heard about any arrivals," grunted the shorter man, rubbing his stubbly chin. I had to stifle a gasp as the air around him began to roil with darkness. I gave the back of Bethan's cloak a hard tug. Her head whipped round, irritated.

"Aye, whelp, just a sec . . . ," she began to chide me, but one look at my face told her all she needed to know. All the color drained out of her but two angry blushes high on her cheekbones. "Oh," she said quietly, her accent falling away. "That's how it is, is it?" She lowered the hood of her cloak, her proud face visible in the torchlight. "Gentlemen, I don't doubt you know who I am. In the name of the king, stand aside."

"I don't know you from the strumpet on the corner, love," sneered the first man, his darkness mixing with his partner's like oil and water. "See, we've only this week come to the king's service. We don't know anyone. Haven't even seen His Majesty yet." An ugly smile crept across his face. "Far as I can tell, you're just a mangy skirt from west of the River who hasn't got the right to use the king's name."

Fury clouded the captain's eyes as she threw back a fold of her cloak to reveal her sword. "Gentlemen, stand aside."

The short man laughed and slapped his fellow on the back. "Would you look at that, Tarique? A skirt with a sword!"

Then the captain did a strange thing. Despite being menaced by two armed soldiers, she looked back at me and said, "I'd wanted to discuss this at another time. I hope you'll forgive me."

"Ma'am?"

The captain stood up straight in the driver's box. Had I been either of the gatesmen, I would have been quaking in my boots.

"I am Crown Princess Saphritte Renart," she said through gritted teeth. "Stand. Aside."

The crown princess? Captain Fisroy is . . .

It hit me at once. The disturbance in the air behind her when we met! What a fool I'd been—twice now I'd not trusted my cunning and I cursed myself for where it'd got me. Why else would she know the palace's former gardener? Why would her father care more for his duty than anything else? How had I not seen it? I'd been double-crossed. Hoodwinked. We'd shared the same saddle for days and confidences at night by the fire. But she was the *daughter* of the man who'd ripped me from my home. And everyone in the unit must've known it. *Everyone.*

Including Gareth.

Wary of taking his eyes off the two menacing soldiers, he turned in his seat, his dark eyes rueful and sorry. But my hurt feelings would have to wait. The men at the gate had no intention of letting us through.

Tarique's mouth curled up at the edges. "A skirt with a sword and delusions, Marcel. I reckon impersonating royalty is worth a night in the cells, how about you?"

"She *is* the princess!" Gareth burst out. "Go find the king's guard that've just returned! Ask Captain Reynold! Ask Master Iordan!"

The steward's head jerked up sharply as the point of Tarique's pike stopped just a hair under his chin. "Make that a crazy skirt *and* a mouthy whelp," the guard snarled. "Sounds to me like you're keen to join your mad auntie in the cells." I sat and watched helplessly as the sickening colors around the two men rippled like living things, covering the torches behind. They *knew* who we were.

Marcel's hands tightened on the grip of his own weapon. "P'raps they could all do with a night behind bars. Might be a good lesson for the little one." He sought me out where I was cowering among the logs and showed me all his crooked teeth. "Didn't your mam teach you that you should . . . never tell lies?"

For a moment, no one moved as everyone realized that everyone else knew exactly what was going on. From the corner of my eye, I noticed that Beth . . . Saphritte's hand had slid to the hilt of her sword. Tarique noticed, too, but a little too late. Expecting the princess's sword to fly from its scabbard, he was caught completely unawares by her sturdy riding boot as it collided with his mouth. Blood sprayed from his face as he fell backward with an agonizing wail. Marcel's sword cleaved its way through the air, but Saphritte's was ready to counter it.

I was fixing to jump out of the cart when a rough hand grabbed me by the ankle. Tarique, with his destroyed face, yanked me straight out of the back of the wagon and slung me over his shoulder like a sack of potatoes. It was all so quick, I didn't even have time to shout as the soldier began to run from the merchants' entrance toward the steps that led up the side of the high wall separating the street from the River below. As I bounced along, Gareth's cries echoed off the high castle walls. "Highness! He's got Only!" But Saphritte was deep in a heated battle with Marcel, swords flashing and ringing in the torchlight, not able to break away from the attack.

Tarique reached the edge of the wall and mounted the steps, struggling under the extra weight of his wriggling cargo and snorting like an ox through a nose broken by the princess's boot. Up to that point, I'd been so surprised, it didn't occur to me he had a plan. But as I looked up at the parapet, it became crystal clear—whoever had sent Wash Blackrudder into the coach didn't care about taking me alive. Tarique had a mind to succeed where the Ordishman had failed. We reached the top of the wall and the sickening drop down to the River yawned beneath me. The soldier didn't hesitate—his meaty arms fastened round my waist to pry me from his back and launch me over the edge. Screaming and kicking, I reached down his back and grabbed hold of his belt so tight, the dull leather bit into my fingers.

"Let go, brat, and stop your squalling!" he growled. "It'll all be over in a minute." He pulled harder, trying to loose me, but I hung on for sweet All, wailing at the top of my lungs, hoping that someone, anyone, passing by, even at that late hour, might be tempted to help.

The soldier was in a rage now. Along with his shattered nose, he'd come by a fair few kicks to the head on the way up the stairs.

He twisted my body this way and that, trying to pry me from his belt. He shook me over the edge, where there was nothing but the darkness of the River and the faint flickers of torches far, far below. "Get off, you little witch!" he roared.

I felt my grip begin to give. I closed my eyes. *I am Only Fallow of the orchard. I'm as tough as a green apple in summer.*

Then there was a sound that I ain't likely to forget even if I live to be one hundred fifty. It was the sound of metal through flesh—a heavy, wet, ripping sound I felt all the way through my bones. Tarique grunted and lurched violently over the parapet, still gripping me round the waist; but a pair of hands grabbed me by the wrists, sliding me from the soldier's back as he tipped over the stone ledge, half the length of his own pike straight through him. His boots scraped the lip of the wall as he toppled and then there was nothing but silence.

Gareth stood frozen, staring at the space where the man had just been, my wrists still clutched tight in his hands. Far below, there was a soft *whump* and a splintering of wood, followed by shouts and footfalls that echoed up the walls. The sound jolted the steward out of whatever trance he'd fallen into, and he looked down at me. He was far paler than he'd been in the coach, but he sunk down to the ground and folded the ends of his cloak round my shuddering body.

"G-Gareth." I gulped. "Th-thank you."

"I'm . . . I'm a steward," he said, panting, his voice all flat. "I set the king's table. I fold napkins. I carry messages. I . . ." He stared down at his hands as if he couldn't believe what they'd just done.

I put my hands flat on the stone to convince myself I was really on solid ground. "A little different from a straw man."

Gareth gave a hollow laugh, resting his head against the battlement. "Just a little." I could feel him trembling where our shoulders touched beneath his cloak.

"Why didn't you tell me?" I whispered. "The future queen of Orstral? I *trusted* her." I turned my head away. "I trusted *you*."

His head bowed. "I half thought you'd be able to see it straightaway, even though it's not exactly a lie. It's part of her name, you see, and . . ." He bit his lip. "I wanted to tell you, honestly, especially after the Wood, but . . . it's what we all have to do when she's leading the cavalry. She's always 'Captain,' never 'Princess.' Just so we don't get any more trouble than we need on the road."

There were voices now—the shouts of soldiers calling across the streets, drifting up the stairs to the top of the wall.

He put his hand over mine, and his mouth close to my ear. "I swear on the Mother I've not told a soul about Jon, though. And I won't, either. You can see I'm not lying about that, can't you?"

Grudging, I peered out from behind my hair. There were no colorful shimmers, just his round, open face begging me to believe him. I looked away.

"Yeah, I see."

Heavy footfalls sounded on the stone steps.

A smear of blood made a sluggish trail down the wall before us. "I . . . can't believe I just did that," Gareth murmured. "Mother All says killing is . . ."

"I reckon Mother All's a mother," I told him. "I think she'd understand." The close-by voices of the guards let me know they were almost upon us. "Gareth, this city ain't safe for me. There's someone here who didn't count on me making it this far."

His eyes went wide. "They said they'd only just come to the king's service. But from where?"

I was in far more trouble than I'd ever imagined.

20

At the start of everything, there was just the Mother. That's what the testaments say.

They say there was nothing but the Mother and She was alone. She got fed up being the only thing there was, so She birthed the world and the sun and the stars. (Non said it must have been a fearsome labor what with the sun and stars and no midwife.) And when the first folk blinked into the first sunlight, She said, "Don't be afraid. All that is new, we will learn together."

At the beginning of my life in the palace, I realized being afraid might just keep me alive.

Saphritte was in a wild battle temper. Her skirmish with Marcel had ended right quick as members of the cavalry flooded into the courtyard and pried the two apart, whisking the soldier off for questioning. I imagined he was going to see a good bit of the cells he'd threatened to throw us in. Gareth looked queasy as the soldiers who found us on the parapets hoisted him on their shoulders and promised him tankards of ale back at the barracks. I gave him a sad little wave as he disappeared under a tide of arms, all trying to slap him on the back or ruffle his hair at once. Captain Reynold gathered me up in his arms so much like Papa, it made me wonder if he had whelps of his own. Together, we descended the stairs to where the princess was waiting. No words passed between us before she grabbed me by the arm and dragged me through a narrow, heavy door set deep into the castle wall.

She was moving so fast, I could barely keep up with all the twists and turns. We marched up staircases, through storerooms, out of doors, through a covered gallery, and back indoors again before I piped up. "Highness, could we stop a moment?"

Saphritte turned, suddenly mindful of my company again. Chest still heaving with pique, she cursed under her breath and pressed her palms and forehead into the stone. I jumped as she let out an unexpected roar and slapped the wall with her hands. "All take it!" she shouted. "What's happening in this kingdom? I was attacked at my own door—the door to my father's house! They tried to spill my blood on my step! On my . . ."

The princess whirled round, catching a glimpse of my face, still pale and frighted from being dangled above the dark chasm of the River. The red mist covering her eyes vanished—the royal tantrum well and truly doused. "I feel if I should sit on the throne till the sun goes out, I should not have enough time to beg your pardon." She let out a rueful laugh. "Look at you, creeping into this palace like a rat onto a ship when all you should be doing is sleeping in your bed in Presston."

The lock on my forgetting room rattled loudly, blocking out all my sense. "You lied to me. You ain't supposed to be able to lie to me!"

"Only, you've been through a great deal—"

"No!" I bellowed. "I'll not go one step farther, Highness, not one step!" It was as if I were floating above my body, watching some other whelp shout themselves red in the face at the future queen of Orstral.

The princess bent under the weight of my anger. "Saphritte Bethan Fisroy D'Abreu Renart, Heir to the Throne of Orstral, Duchess of East Reach and the Hatchings, Captain of the King's Guard. That's the whole of it." She squeezed her eyes shut and wiped them with bloodstained fingers. "When we're on the road, I feel very at home as Bethan Fisroy—more so than when I'm Saphritte Renart here. Perhaps your cunning takes into account how firmly a belief is held, even if it's not entirely true."

Though it satisfied my burning curiosity as to how the wool had been pulled over my eyes, I wasn't in the mood to aid the princess in her soul-searching while my rage was still boiling hot. "You don't care a fig about me! To you and the king, I'm just a tool to fix something that's broke. I'm just my cunning and nothing else! Lark and Rowan were right about your father, he—"

The sudden memory of the laughing faces of my Ordish friends finally put a cork in the bottle of my anger. Both my hands clapped over my mouth, too late to snatch back everything I'd said. Saphritte's own mouth was hanging open as if she'd swallowed it all and was trying to turn it over in her belly. I felt just as sick as I did when I told a lie. Quick as I could, I dropped down on my knees, my face so low, it almost touched the stone floor.

"Your Highness . . . ma'am, I'm . . . sorry. So sorry. I didn't mean . . ."

"Only, look at me."

Trembling, I stared up at Saphritte, who took a few deep breaths before she spoke. "You have every right to your anger. Every bit of it. But in these walls, you must school your temper. It's for your safety, do you understand?"

My head bobbed up and down like an apple in a barrel. I was grateful she hadn't decided to haul me off to a dungeon somewhere. "Yes, ma'am. I'll be quiet as a dormouse."

"My father doesn't need a dormouse, Only. He needs a champion."

"Master Iordan said that the king was . . ." I searched for the word the inquisitor had used, hoping it wouldn't slander the king under his own roof. "Suggestible."

Saphritte squeezed her lips in a prim line. "That's a diplomatic way to describe it. But then, Master Iordan *is* a diplomat." She stared deep into one of the torches that guttered and spit in the dark passage. "There's a good deal happening right now. And it's all delicate, but I think my father's being led by members of his own council to believe there are shadows round every corner. And it's resulting in decisions made from fear rather than reason. I know you meant all you said, and you're right, but consider this: The kingdom is like the pines of the Wood—bigger than you, bigger than me. And it will go on long after both of us are gone. I want it to grow tall and strong—to reach for the sun. I believe if it's sent down a path of despair and hatred, it will wither and die. And so, here you are." She took one of my hands between hers. "I need you. My father needs you. Orstral's about to walk across a chasm on a rope and we need you to be the sturdy pole to help us keep our balance, because it's a long way to the bottom. If not for me or for the king, do you think you could do it for Orstral?"

I thought about the feeling I'd had standing beneath the pines. About my dust and the dust of the kingdom.

"For Orstral," I said at last.

Saphritte laid a hand on my shoulder. "You're a brave girl, Only Fallow. Now, let's go and face the kingdom."

We emerged into the palace through a door hidden behind a thick piece of tapestry. The hallway was bright with lanterns and the stone floor smooth with wear. "This is the main route down to the kitchens and stores," Saphritte said. "I'm sure with a little exploration, you'll find the half a dozen other hidden ways in and out of the place. But I imagine you'd like a decent night's sleep first?"

My knees didn't feel so much like knees than jelly, but I didn't care for the idea of being too far from the princess's protection. "I'm all right, ma'am."

A wide staircase rose up before us, and Saphritte was nearly at the top before she realized I wasn't following behind her.

From the bottom, I realized I was looking up into the grand entryway of the palace. The pillars that melted into the vaulted ceiling were vast, and artfully carved to resemble the trunks of great pines. The branches formed graceful arches that criss-crossed the roof. High windows of green, yellow, blue, and tan glass glinted in the torchlight. In the day, the sunlight would cast the colors down upon the floor, making it look as if you'd found yourself in a forest grove. It was the Wood, turned to stone.

"Sweet All," I whispered, staring in amazement.

The princess came back down the steps to meet me. "Tomorrow, there'll be even more to see. But for now, let's—"

She broke off as the sound of footsteps echoed round the stone forest. At the top of the steps, there appeared a young woman wearing a long, elegant coat of blue and silver. Her blond hair was bound back tight in a tight plait and her hands were folded neatly before her.

"Highness," she said formally, bowing low before the princess. "It's good to see you safely returned."

"Thank you, Adria," Saphritte acknowledged. "I'm just taking the Mayquin to her chambers. It's been a very long—"

"You are summoned to council," Adria interrupted.

The princess's shoulders slumped. "Very well. Let me just—"

"You are *both* summoned to council. They expect you presently."

"Surely after the events of the last few hours—"

"The council has been informed of these events, and it's why they wish to see you." Adria gave me a sniffy look, and I suddenly came aware that I was still dressed in the same tattered cloak I'd put on hours before, which still smelled strongly of the barnyard.

"My father called the council?" the princess asked wearily.

Adria hesitated. "No, Highness."

From behind her, I watched all of the muscles in Saphritte's neck clench tight, from her shoulder to her jaw. The effect must have been even more striking from the front, because Adria took a careful step backward.

"Tell them," she said between tightly clenched teeth, "that we'll be with them presently."

The girl bowed and scurried away. The princess stared after her, robbed of the power of speech.

"Ma'am?" I said timidly. "Ma'am, you don't need to be sore. I . . . I don't mind meeting the council."

"It's not that the council is meeting," the princess intoned in a hollow voice, "but rather who has called it to order."

"Ma'am?"

"The only person with the authority to call a council other than my father is Lady Folque."

THE PALACE WAS a confusing jumble of corridors. Half of them seemed to have just sprouted right out of the stone and started growing in any which way they fancied. Any spirit I'd had left wilted with every change of direction, and I tried not to imagine losing myself in some dark corner where a dark deed might befall me. But despite my confusion, I was fair certain that we were heading into the heart of the building.

"If we walked this far at home, we'd near be in the center of town by now," I wheezed.

"It's just here," Saphritte assured me, pointing to a doorway ahead flanked by two guards. They snapped to attention as we approached, each pulling open the heavy oak door beside them.

The council chamber was one of the fanciest rooms I'd ever set foot in. Thick, rich drapes—embroidered in the king's colors—hung on the walls. A great iron chandelier hung from the ceiling, guttering with candles. A polished wooden rack held dozens of bottles with dark red wine in them. Silver goblets gleamed round the enormous table, whose legs were carved with climbing vines and morning glory. The three figures gathered round the table stood up and bowed respectfully to Saphritte. "Highness!" bellowed the man in the far corner, coming forward to meet us. He grasped the princess's shoulders. "Good met and well returned!"

The fellow was nearly as large as his greeting—arms and legs like oak logs and a fermenting barrel for a chest. He wore a salt-beaten, floor-length leather jerkin and golden hoops in his ears. Fastened round his large belly was a black leather belt with a huge golden buckle, intricately carved with swirling waves and mermaids. His long, graying hair was pulled back behind his head in a loose braid. Even more wondrous was the dog that padded faithfully by his side. It matched its master in size, standing past the man's hip, its bristly gray coat making it look just as windswept and salty.

Saphritte chuckled, slapped the man's meaty shoulders in return. "Good met, Dorvan. How's work on *The Bountiful* going?"

"Oh, well, well," said the man, hooking his thumbs into his belt. I couldn't help notice the faded letters that adorned his hairy knuckles. They read *Hold Fast*. "She'll be ready to sail on the winds of the new year."

The princess knelt to bury her fingers in the dog's scruff. "Good met to you, too, Mizzen. How's my favorite sea cur?" The hound's tail began to whip back and forth, its eyes closed in pleasure at the attention.

Waiting, with his arms folded, was a smaller man dressed in a fine woven tunic and breeches in shades of green. He had a short, neatly trimmed beard, and his hair was cut mixing-bowl style. Soft leather boots, trussed with sheep gut, rose up his legs to his knees, and the expression on his face reminded me of Master Iordan when he disapproved of something.

"Sandkin, good met," Saphritte said, extracting herself from Dorvan and taking hold of the shorter man's hand. "I know you like to retire early. I'm sorry this matter couldn't have waited till morning."

"I'm used to the palace keeping odd hours," he grumbled. "I hope this won't be long."

An older woman rose from her seat at the other end of the great table and motioned to me. "Come here, child, let me look at you." Her white hair was piled high on her head in elaborately braided ropes, and her wine-colored gown had a high, straight collar that made her neck look long as a deer's. "I've heard you've had a terribly hard journey."

"That is a generous description of our progress, Constance," Saphritte agreed, shepherding me over to the lady. "Our poor Only has been much abused along the way."

"I'm Constance Mollier, child, and you're very welcome here," the grand dame said as I came to stand before her. If Non had been high-born, she might have looked like the lady in front of me. Maybe that's why I liked her straightaway.

"So, where's the honorable head of this council, then?" barked Dorvan. "She rouses us from our chambers at this hour and isn't here to greet us?"

"You know as well as I do, Everard, that her ladyship does things in her own time," Sandkin answered sourly.

"Well, I wish she'd've called this council on her own bloody time!" Dorvan countered.

"It's as well she did call it." Saphritte's voice cut through the arguing men. "I would have a word or two with her."

"My dear," said Lady Mollier, stepping forward, "you must be careful what you say. Even here. Even now."

I'd begun worrying the inside of my cheek with my teeth when the door to the chamber opened.

Since the moment I heard her name at North Hallow, I'd been conjuring up pictures of Lamia Folque. She'd become just as fierce and terrible as anything in my imagination, with eyes like a cat, terrible claws, and snakes for hair. The woman who strode into the council chamber had none of those things, but she didn't need them for anyone who laid eyes on her to know she was dangerous. Her crimson, gold-trimmed gown set off her deep golden skin and chocolate-brown hair. From her ears dangled a pair of gold droplets that glinted in the light of the lanterns that filled the room. A mesmerizing green-and-blue jewel lay at her throat. I'd never seen anyone take up so much space in a room before.

"My apologies, masters, mistress, Your Highness," she cooed smoothly. "Matters of my estate detained me."

"This could not have been put off till morning, Lamia?" complained Sandkin.

"I felt, Arfrid, that in light of the events of the last days, not to mention the last few hours, we ought to come together to discuss—"

Saphritte started forward, dangerously. "I'll tell you what we must discuss, Lady Folque. We must discuss—"

"The measures that we must take to keep our Mayquin safe now that she's within our walls, I'm sure, Your Highness?" interrupted Lady Mollier, who lit up like a torch with the force of her untruth. It exploded, crackling white and green around her as she begged Saphritte's silence with her eyes.

Lady Folque's head slowly turned to where I stood in the corner. Maybe it was just the leftover fear from my almost-trip over the wall into the River or that I was so weary, I could hardly keep my eyelids from drooping, but everything seemed muffled, like I had my head underwater.

"Yes, of course, Your Highness," she purred. "She must be kept quite safe."

I expected the darkness of a sinister lie to blot out the whole of the chamber, but instead, as she came closer, the light of the blazing lanterns dimmed. All the other human noise in the room stilled. There was the sharp smell of iron, copper, and fire. The world became narrow until it was only as big as me and her bottomless eyes. Torchlight licked out from behind her bejeweled head like a crown of flame, just waiting to burn those who came too close. Waiting to burn me.

"Mayquin," said Lamia Folque, in a voice that sounded like a blade on a whetstone. "Welcome to Bellskeep."

21

It was hard to remember the whole of the night we arrived in Bellskeep, apart from Tarique trying to pitch me into the River. That part stood out quite clearly in my memory. If it hadn't been for Gareth, my story would have ended in the long-dry riverbed that ran the length of the city. All that came after the kind Captain Reynold delivered me back to Saphritte was a blur of dark corridors and angry words—all until the moment I met *her*.

As Lamia Folque turned to lay eyes on me, everyone else seemed to disappear. It was just her looking into me and me looking into her. Her regard was fire, and her voice, iron being wrought on a blacksmith's anvil.

And then I was back in the room, the chatter around me almost too loud to bear, but I wasn't listening. I'd just recognized Lady Folque for what she was.

Cunning.

I couldn't tell how I knew, but there was no question in my mind. Me and Lamia Folque were two of a kind, and her cunning had called to mine in a way I couldn't explain. She'd felt it, too—her eyes went wide and some of the pride she'd carried in with her fizzled away like water on a skillet. No one else in the council chamber could tell what happened, but *I* knew. To cover her discomfort, she turned smoothly to Saphritte. "Your Highness," she said, concern in her tone, "I owe you a thousand apologies. The men who met you at the gate were new recruits from the Motte—rogues to a man and obviously ill suited for service. Rest assured, the one who remains alive will suffer the consequences of his actions."

Tarique and Marcel were Folquesmen?

It took a moment for me to realize Saphritte wasn't looking at Lady Folque while she was speaking. She was staring at me. *She wants to know if Lamia Folque's lying, you newt.* I shrugged at the princess, helpless.

Lady Folque's face fell, wounded. "Surely Your Highness doesn't believe that *I* had anything to do with this dreadful occurrence?" The beautiful woman fell on her knee in front of the princess. "Your Highness," she murmured, "I know that we have had our differences in council. I know you do not share my fear of the threats our kingdom faces, but you must believe that I would never . . ." She seemed to choke on the words, overcome with genuine emotion. "That I would *never* seek to do any harm to your royal person." Her eyes, brimming with tears, turned to me. "Or to *any* person, let alone a child. I'm a mother myself.

Please do not let our past disagreements lead you to believe this of me."

There was nothing. No telltale hues of purple or malicious black. Not even a *hint* of a falsehood in her tearful plea. As far as I could tell, Lamia Folque *wasn't lying*.

Saphritte glanced, astonished, between me and Lady Folque. Her thoughts were as clear as if they'd been written across her forehead: *Did I do all of this for nothing?* I couldn't help but wonder the same thing—*did* she do all of it for nothing? Was I dragged, scared and sorrowful, all the way to the north just to settle a quarrel between the princess and the councilwoman?

Constance Mollier stepped to the princess's side and laid a hand on her arm. "I'm sure, Lamia, that Her Highness doesn't believe anything of the sort. We all have the best interests of the kingdom at heart, don't we?" Her fingers tightened on Saphritte's arm, willing her to end the matter.

Saphritte looked like someone whose house had just fallen down around her feet. Though the angry whooshing of blood through my ears was loud, a tiny voice inside my head lifted itself to be heard. *But Folque's cunning. Who knows what she can do? Maybe she could be false to my face and I wouldn't know.*

"If you'll excuse us, my lords, my ladies," murmured the princess, the whole burden of the days just past falling on her all at once. "This might be best discussed when we've had a chance to rest. The road has been . . . difficult." Her jaw tightened—maybe her thoughts had turned to the faces of her men lost in the Wood. She paled and clutched her left arm, as if all that had been holding her up to begin with had been her rage. Now that it was gone, she was spent. Anticipating her fall, Dorvan appeared at Saphritte's side just as her knees buckled.

"Your Highness? Shall I send for a healer?" asked the big man worriedly. "Are you hurt?"

"An injury taken yesterday," she admitted, swaying on her feet. "It should probably be seen."

"I'd say so, Highness," declared Dorvan. "Do you need me to carry you, ma'am?"

"Do I look like I need carrying?" the princess said, her voice no louder than a light breeze.

"Begging your pardon, Highness, but you most certainly do."

Her pale face twisted in embarrassment. "If you ever mention this to anyone else in court, I'll have your guts, Dorvan."

"Wouldn't dream of it, ma'am," he answered, the hint of a smile on his face. White lights twinkled round his head, and I cleared my throat. He looked guiltily in my direction, but his smile grew as he scooped Saphritte into his arms and whisked her out into the corridor, the hound trotting along behind.

"Adria," Lady Mollier called out the open door, before turning back into the chamber. "This council is adjourned. All business is carried forth until the morrow." Lamia looked as if she had something to say, but Constance cut her off sternly. "*All* business. The Mayquin has had a trying journey." The young woman who met us in the entrance hall entered, still looking fresh and calm, despite the late hour. "Adria," Lady Mollier instructed, "please show Miss Fallow to her chamber with all haste. She's dreadfully weary."

She took my hand between hers. "I'm sorry for the way

you arrived, my dear. Rest yourself now. And when you're prepared, we will show you that Bellskeep has much more to offer
than woe."

As we were bustled through the heavy door by the page, I
caught the eye of Lamia Folque. The expression I saw there made
me think that there was probably more woe ahead than Lady
Mollier could possibly imagine.

My chamber could have been a horsebox in the royal stables
for all I cared. My body was heavy with sleep, but my brain wasn't
quite ready to let go of my meeting with Lady Folque. What if her
cunning could hinder mine? What if she wasn't behind the fellow
who sent the Ordish and Tarique? What if I can't get Saphritte to
believe me when I tell her . . .

But I was simply too tired for any more what-ifs. I hardly
noticed as unfamiliar hands peeled the layers of my journey from
Presston from my body, reeking of sweat, fear, and the long road.
They guided me into the washroom, where a huge cauldron of
steaming water had been prepared. I sank into it like a pebble,
letting it warm all the places in me that I didn't even know were
frozen. Sleep would have taken me then and there, but rough
fingers began to scrub me all over, just like when I was a babe
and washed in the water pail. The rich soap smelt strongly of rose
and gardenia, and soon the cauldron was awash with perfumed
bubbles that popped round my ears. It drifted my fears away,
along with all the what-ifs. I would have drifted away, too, like a

fish, but the hands lifted me back up into the air, where I remembered that I had to breathe again.

A thick white bath sheet was wrapped round me, and a night shift was pulled over my body. Then there was the delicious warmth of a mattress with a coal pan at its foot, and I knew my fight was done. I sank right away into a deep, fragrant, and dreamless sleep.

22

I was certain the coach had stopped. It was still dark and I couldn't feel the rumble of the wheels. Had we come under attack again? Were there more villains waiting outside in the night? I reached for the comforting shape of the Jack in the darkness, but found only the soft form of another pillow. I stretched my hand farther, exploring with my fingers. Gone was the familiar, rough wall of the coach at my back—in its place, an acre of mattress. And then it all came back to me.

The room was pitch-black. The fire in the grate had long since burned itself out—not even a glowing ember remained to light my way. I lay back on the pillow and stared up into the dark. All the what-ifs I hoped had been tossed into the gutter with my bathwater came creeping back, sneaky like. I tried to put them in a neat line, but they all crowed loudly for equal attention.

Jon's a prisoner. I'd been so weary the night before, I'd barely remembered my own name, but my heart gave an urgent thump at the memory of my brother bound in the clearing. If the Ordish from the Wood were carted from where we were attacked, they might arrive come noon that day. I hadn't the first idea how I'd free him, but I needed to do it before he faced whatever kind of justice the king had in mind to visit on him. There was also the problem of the mysterious fella who'd set them on the path toward the caravan in the first place. Was he here in Bellskeep? Did he hire them for himself or was he working for someone else?

Lamia Folque is cunning. That fact worried and confused me most. For all my fear, I still didn't have a good idea of what cunning really added up to. *You know, medicines. Birthing. Seeing. Things like that,* Rowan had said. Lady Folque didn't strike me as the kind to dirty her hands with the mess of birthing or grinding compounds with a mortar in an herbery. I supposed I was a "seer"—my cunning made it impossible for anyone to tell me an untruth. What might Lamia Folque's be?

Saphritte believes I can help the kingdom. That idea troubled me more'n any other. What could I do against an Ordish plot? Against sneaky meddling from Thorvald? Against some other force that meant me ill, hiding somewhere out of sight? Now *that* was an uncomfortable thought.

"Mistress?"

A voice in the darkness near made me soil the nicest bed I'd ever slept in. "Y-yes?" I stammered, white knuckles gripping the edge of the quilt.

"Oh, good, you're awake." There were sounds of a pail scraped near the hearth along with the thud of logs and kindling being placed in the grate. Then, a sharp strike of flint and the beginnings of flames outlined a figure, kneeling to gentle them higher with her breath. "Master Iordan wanted you straightaway, but Her Highness insisted you be allowed to take your ease."

The heavy drapes were thrown open, near blinding me with the early-morning light. I groaned and pulled the quilt over my head.

Footsteps pattered across the floor to the bed. "I'm afraid hiding won't do you no good, mistress," she said, tugging the cover from me. "I'm meant to . . . *Great Deep!*"

Blinking furiously into the light, I shot up from my pillow. "*Lark?*"

Even though she was wearing a plain white shift and dull blue pinafore, with her lovely dark hair stripped of its beads and pulled back into a sleek pile atop her head, I would have recognized her anywhere. She gave a laugh that was nearly a sob and flew to me, our arms circling each other, tight as sailor's knots.

"Only Fallow!" She wept into my shoulder. "I shouldn't be joyful to see you, but, tides, am I ever."

I almost couldn't speak. "There ain't been a day I haven't thought of you since you were took."

She held me to arm's length and looked me up and down like she was committing me to memory. "You, the Mayquin! How . . . ?"

"I tried to tell you that night, honest I did! I could see Toly was up to no good, but he twigged me. Oh, Lark, you tried to save my skin and we both ended up here anyway," I cried miserably. "Are you well? How about Rowan?"

Her shoulders slumped, and she sank into the mattress. "Aye, well enough. Ro's drawn a rougher lot down in the kitchens. He gets . . . hotheaded and ends up getting beatings from the porters."

I bristled to think of some great lunk raising his hand to my friend. "And you?"

"Seamstress's assistant. I'm good with a needle and thread." She slid off the bed and went to open the wardrobe. "It's why they sent me to you this morning—to help fit your new clothes."

"Will you be coming every day?" I asked excitedly.

She shook her head. "You'll get your own waiting girl, I imagine, to help you dress. These clothes ain't exactly something you can just throw on before you walk out of doors."

I'd not given much thought to what I'd be expected to wear, but I hardly had room in my brain for fripperies. "Come back and sit a spell. I've got loads to tell you."

But Lark had already begun pulling pieces from the closet. "We can jaw while I fit you."

"But we only just—"

"I ain't my own mistress anymore," she said peevishly. "The seamstress might not raise her hand to me, but I'll be buried in a pile of dirty washing a mile high if I don't do what I'm told. We might both have got took but . . ." She pulled a fawn-colored gown out from the sea of shifting material. "It ain't quite the same, is it?"

Shame rolled through me, deep as a river. I picked at a loose thread on the quilt. "No, it ain't."

Lark came back and laid her hand on my knee. "Come on, we've got three-quarters of an hour. Let's use it well—tell me everything."

"Sweet All, how many layers does one dress need?"

"This would go a lot quicker if you'd stop wiggling!" Lark chided through the pins between her teeth.

"It's these stockings!" I complained, shifting back and forth. "They're itchy as sin."

"You'll be glad of 'em about the castle—it ain't half drafty. Just hold still a second, I only got a couple more pins to place." There was a tug to the waist of the gown. "All right, that should do it. Now, what did Jon tell you about the fellow at the Southmeet?"

I'd tried to impart as much as I could to her over the last half hour in between slips and gowns and surcoats being tugged over my head. "Just that he was silver-tongued enough to persuade a handful of men to attack a royal caravan in the hopes of getting their whelps back."

"Arms up," she said, slipping the blue gown off, carefully avoiding pricking me with the hidden pins. "Only, Papa wasn't one of them . . . was he?"

"No," I answered quickly. "Jon said he didn't give the fella the time of day." The sound of pickaxes and shovels deep in the woods resounded in my ears, making me powerfully glad Bula had the sense to still be safely wintering in Farrier's Bay.

Her shoulders relaxed a little as she pulled out the last

remaining pieces left in the wardrobe. "These should fit well enough for today."

On went an indigo woolen shift that warmed me from beneath, along with a pair of cotton stockings and soft leather boots with fur inside to keep out the cold. A brilliant salmon-colored coat stretched to the floor, with velvet cuffs and trim the same shade as the shift. A leather belt with intricate stitching went round my waist and, at my collar, a large gold coat pin. As I ran my fingers over its finely wrought edges, I realized that it was shaped like an eye. *The Mayquin, looking into places I got no business looking into.*

"Come sit at the vanity, I'll try to do something with your hair before Master Iordan arrives."

Obediently, I let her lead me to a low stool before a huge looking glass. The princess had made good on her promise—a fine silver boar's-hair brush sat waiting.

Lark's reflection in the glass was somber as she brushed. "What are you going to do about Jon?"

"I don't know," I replied helplessly. "I can't just *ask* anyone about it neither. Not without giving him and me away."

Her clever fingers twisted and plaited, fastening strands of my unruly hair with gold pins from a dish on the vanity.

"Do you think it's daft to wish Papa *had* joined them?" she asked quietly.

"Of course it ain't daft!"

"It ain't good, though, is it? Hoping one of 'em might be . . ."

"It ain't daft to hope someone came for you!" I declared.

"There's not a second gone by since I left the orchard that I didn't hope Mama and Papa would show up and take me home. They took you and forced you to serve 'em months gone now! Wishing someone might come for you just means they ain't managed to kill your faith in folk you love."

I grabbed her hand and looked straight into her eyes in the glass. "You're right. We both got took, and it ain't the same. I don't know if I got any kind of charge over anything, but if I do, I'll change it if I can. I promise."

Both of us were startled by a sharp knock on the door. Lark straightened with a jerk. "That'll be the inquisitor. Sounds like he was a hard traveling companion," she whispered in my ear. "I think I would have throttled him in his sleep."

"Mistress Mayquin," came the dry voice from the other side of the door. "May I enter?"

"Of course, master, just a moment," I called. Lark, with a mischief smile on her face, went to open the door.

In place of his traveling clothes, the inquisitor now wore the robes of the lyceum—purple and deep burgundy, trimmed in gold. Around his neck, he wore his heavy inquisitor's chain, leaving no soul in any doubt of his importance. He seemed bigger than he had the night we spoke in the Wood.

Lark stood by the open door, casting sneaky glances at the inquisitor as he circled me, inspecting my new appearance. "Yes, this is much better."

I brushed my hands down the coat. "It's a little fancy."

Iordan raised one of his enormous eyebrows. "You didn't

think you'd be allowed to run around the castle in stableman's breeches, did you?"

"No," I admitted, fidgeting, "but I didn't think I'd have to be dressed like I was going to sanctuary every day, neither."

"*Either*," he corrected me, "not *neither*. We'll have to work on that rural vocabulary of yours."

Out of the corner of my eye, I could see Lark trying not to smile. Iordan stared down his nose at me. "Are you ready?"

"Ready for what?" I asked.

"To learn about the kingdom," he said, sweeping his long arm toward the door. "Let's begin."

23

Mother of all things,
This day we live is Yours.
Guide my hands to good work,
Guide my heart to good deeds,
Guide my mouth to good words,
And guide my mind to good thoughts.
So as You ask,
So shall it be.

—#260, Litanies for the Mother

In halls back in Presston, Mistress Averil would begin our morning lessons with a beseechment, but Master Iordan wasn't going to waste time on that kind of ceremony.

The study was large and airy and filled to the brim with wonderful things to look at—none of which the inquisitor seemed disposed to show me. My eyes flitted over curious glass flasks filled with mysterious liquids, the golden spines of books, and even a small, moving model of the heavens made lovingly of brass, but Iordan was insistent on beginning with maps.

From one of the small cubbies nearby, he pulled a tightly

rolled scroll and, with a flourish, unspooled it across a worktable, trapping its curled edges under heavy glass weights. I gawped in wonder—it was a far cry from the crude outline in Mistress Averil's study. Shades of green and brown melted into an ocean of white under an outline of finely drawn pine forests and tiny mountains, all set against the royal blue of the sea, where strange serpents breathed fire from toothy jaws. In the corner, a cluster of spidery writing declared it to be . . .

"Is this *Thorvald*?"

"Have you never seen a map, child?" Iordan asked, in the same tone of voice he used for the word *provincial.* But I was so amazed, I couldn't summon an ounce of ire.

"I have, but nothing like this," I admitted.

"As you observed, it is indeed a map of our neighbors to the north. In the weeks to come, it will be important for you to learn as much about the nation as you're able."

"Oh!" The cross words between Papa and Master Anslo in the sanctuary yard seemed like another lifetime ago. "The wedding! The princess is going to marry a walrus called Eydisson."

A large vein popped out on the inquisitor's neck. "The princess is most certainly *not* marrying a walrus!" he bristled.

"That's not a fancy Thorvald word for 'prince'?" I asked.

"No, it isn't! A walrus is a large, blubbery sea creature with flippers, whiskers, and tusks. The Thorvald hunt them for meat and ivory." He sniffed. "I suggest that your source of information on Thorvald matters may be . . . unreliable."

Stupid old Anslo, I thought. *Should have asked Gareth about walruses.* "But we did have a war with them, right?"

Iordan's nose came down out of the air, just a bit. "Yes, though it was quite some years ago." He folded his arms and looked at me suspiciously. "I'm surprised your hallsmistress would have felt that topic of value for your study."

The last thing I wanted was to get Gareth in hot water for running my mouth when I oughtn't. "I must have heard it . . . somewhere else."

Lucky for me, the inquisitor was more than happy for a chance to give an unscheduled lecture. "The Quartern War only lasted five months, but it's taken nearly one hundred years for Orstral and Thorvald to restore cordial diplomatic relations. The marriage between the princess and Hauk Eydisson will be one more step in erasing old grievances."

"How about the Folques?" I asked. "Will it erase grievances against them, too, for helping the Thorvald?"

Iordan blanched, turning to look round the room, though he knew it was empty. "Were you not listening that night we spoke in the Wood?" he squeaked in a breathless whisper. "The den of vipers I mentioned? You are in it now. Such questions are not wise."

As quick as his calm had frayed, it knitted itself back up once again. "Now," he said, laying a long finger on the map. "We'll begin with the cities of the western coast."

MISTRESS AVERIL OFTEN said a pair of attentive ears and a curious mind were all a body needed to learn, but after an hour with

Master Iordan, I could see I'd also need the patience of a midwife and the wakefulness of an owl.

Thorvald town names were devilish hard on the tongue, and mine certainly wasn't going to win any praise from the inquisitor.

"It's pronounced Kaupstefeyr," Iordan informed me for the second time.

I pointed to the town on the map. "That's what I said. Cup-stay-fear."

"No, no, Kaup-ste-feyr. Say it slowly."

One night of sleep hadn't erased the weariness of a week on the road and I was flagging. "Kaup-stay-fear."

Iordan buried his face in his hands. "Perhaps it's time we moved on to something else."

What with my worries over Jon and Lamia Folque now fighting for space with cities of western Thorvald, if I had to remember anything else, it was all going to come spilling out my ears. "Master, could we . . ."

But the rest of the sentence never made it out of my mouth as the inquisitor unrolled a second map before me.

A week before, Orstral had been the deep valley of the orchard, the rough road to Lochery, and the bustle of Roundmarket. Then, on the road it became the mountains, the timberlands, and the great pines of the Wood. But on the piece of paper was the *whole* of it, sat in the middle of a jewel-blue ocean with its name in gold script above. The whole of Orstral, a shape I could carry in my two hands. It was *beautiful*.

"Is this . . . ?" I choked out. "Is this what it looks like?"

"Orstral? Just so," confirmed Iordan.

I moved beside him, greedily following the tracks of rivers and roads and drinking in the names of towns I never heard of. "Where's Presston?"

The inquisitor pulled a pair of spectacles out of his robes and balanced them on the end of his beaky nose. Leaning over, he traced the kingsroad down the length of the country until he tapped the middle of dark green smudge near a bright blue squiggle. "Here, I believe, just to the right of Lochery."

I put my finger over the smudge as if somehow touching it could open up a window and let me look down on it from above just like the Mother. I could skim the treetops in the orchard like a tern, dipping low over the river for a swallow of water. I could swoop over the roof and watch the smoke curling from the chimney. I could glide over the pressing barns and watch the men stamp against the cold while brewing the winter cider.

"There's great value in knowing where you are in relation to the rest of the world," said the inquisitor, tracing the coastline with a long finger. "But it's hard to judge how far you've come unless you know where you started."

I dared a sideways glance at Iordan and found the look in his eyes not unkind. I gave a little nod, not wanting to speak further.

There was a knock at the chamber door. The hinges creaked, and a familiar freckled face appeared.

"Gareth!" I cried.

"Decorum, if you please, Mayquin," Iordan said with a sigh. "We do not greet stewards and other domestics in such a familiar fashion." He swung round. "What is it?"

Gareth, now in palace livery rather than traveling clothes, stood straighter, his hair freshly washed and tamed. He looked every inch the king's man. I wasn't sure how I felt about that.

"Master, the Mayquin's presence has been expressly requested by His Majesty."

The inquisitor slid the glass weights off the map, and Orstral disappeared into a neat curl once more. "His Majesty's wish is my command." He waved me off. "Tomorrow I expect you to have retained a good deal of the knowledge imparted to you today— from the capital at Eyrfell to the southern coast at Skipver."

As if I've not got more important things to worry over! "Yes, master," I parroted. I wasn't exactly chomping at the bit to be presented to the king, but I was eager to speak to Gareth.

"Very well. You're dismissed."

It's FUNNY WHEN you meet someone you know and suddenly feel like you don't know them at all.

We walked together in silence with only our own footsteps for company. Did two new sets of clothes really mean we weren't still Gareth and Only? I plucked at his sleeve.

"You clean up all right."

A little of his stiffness fell away. "And I hardly recognized you, as you weren't climbing out of a privy."

I poked him hard in the arm. "Cheeky."

He grinned sideways at me. "Pain in the backside."

My heart lightened a little, but I noticed the dark circles cut under his eyes. "You look a little beneath the weather."

He blinked at me as though even just being upright was a chore. "I'm not used to fighting like a soldier, but I'm even less used to drinking like one."

I thought back to the first time Jonquin and his mates nicked some Scrump from the cellar and how the next day, seeing his red eyes and pounding head, Mama declared that his crime had been his punishment. "No good comes from overindulging. That's what my folks say."

"I didn't *want* to," protested Gareth, "but they kind of insisted. Luckily, I managed to move over by the window so when my tankard was refilled, I could just dump it out. I don't think anyone noticed." He pinched the bridge of his freckled nose. "Didn't really seem to be something to be celebrating anyway."

I didn't envy him the memory of his deed. "No, but you know I ain't half grateful, right?"

"Mind you, I'd do it again," he said quickly. "The saving-you part, though. Not the drinking."

We came to a halt in front of a set of enormous doors where two decorated guards stood, eyes straight ahead, gloved hands on pikes.

"The Mayquin, to see His Majesty," Gareth announced, with a ring of command in his voice.

The guards snapped to attention and moved to part the great entryway. Fear made a sudden, unwelcome nest in my belly. Behind those doors was the man who'd had the power to take me from my home. To rip countless Ordish children from *their* homes. The man who might soon lay down a judgment on the head of my brother. I'd known from the beginning of my journey that it would end here. But I still wasn't ready.

"The first day I came to work at the palace," Gareth whispered in my ear, "I'd never been so scared in my life. My mother said something that helped a little, though."

"What was that?"

"'What you do, Gareth,' she said to me, 'is when you're before the king, remember that he puts his underthings on one leg at a time, just like everyone else.'"

My mouth fell open. "Are you saying . . . I should try to imagine the *king* in his underthings?" The idea alone sounded like something that might get me thrown in a dungeon.

"No. Well, if it helps, I suppose you *could*, but just remember, he's not the Mother. He's just a man. Just like any other man."

The doors reached the end of their swing, the way before us clear.

"What d'you reckon a king wears beneath his clothes?" I whispered back, grasping at anything that might give me some comfort.

"I'm not sure," he replied. "But just remember, whatever it is, he puts it on one leg at a time."

24

Come not before Her like a child before a throne.
Run to Her arms with joy and gladness,
And be lifted in your Mother's strong embrace.

—Second Lesson of Lucia, the Prophet

When Hatter Leyward's sister, Hettie, married the son
of a merchant from near Sandborn, her hand-fasting band had
boasted a Renart sapphire about the size of a pinhead. It cost her
intended half a shipment of goods from Achery to get hold of and
was the talk of Presston for weeks.

As I stood in the high, narrow antechamber, waiting for
Gareth to announce my coming to the king, I ran my fingers over
the pin at my throat. In the middle of the great golden eye sat
a sapphire larger than my thumbnail and no doubt worth more
than the whole of the orchard.

If only Hettie could see this, I thought, bitter as bark. *I'd hand it
over to her in a second if it meant I don't have to go through those doors.*

The thunderous boom of those very doors cracking open
made me leap right out of my boots. After the darkness of the
antechamber, I had to squint against the white light that poured

in from the room beyond. A dark figure approached from the heart of it, resolving into a face that gave me a helping of comfort.

"How are you, Only?" asked Saphritte.

Weariness dogged her eyes, but the princess stood upright and proud, her hand upon the pommel of her sword. Washed clean from the dirt of the road, her black hair and blue-and-silver surcoat gleamed in the sunlight. Surely none of the Mother's hosts ever looked so fine or noble as the princess did to me that moment.

"Good met, Highness," I said, trying not to let my voice wobble like a babe's. "I'm well, thank you. I'm glad to see you looking more healthful."

She gave me a light smile and cocked her head to the side. "It'll be some little time before I'm able to take on another army of brigands, but the healers did good work." Her steady hand lit upon my shoulder, and she lowered her voice. "I know you're afraid now. Just answer the questions the king puts to you and all will be well."

Thoughts of Lamia Folque galloped to the front of my mind. "Highness, I hoped to talk to you. Last night—"

The princess cut me off. "After this is done, you and I will speak privately, but my father is impatient to meet you."

"But, Highness—"

"Stop trifling, daughter! I would see what you've brought me."

The voice was as loud and thunderous as the doors, and it shook my bones to hear it. Saphritte turned into the dazzling light. "As you wish, Majesty," she answered, taking my hand and giving it a squeeze. "Come, Only."

The throne room was truly wondrous—narrow and high, like the antechamber. The same pillars I saw in the entryway, cut to resemble the Orstralian pines, rose to the ceiling, their branches forming the vaults overhead. Dozens of intricate silver lanterns, decked with shimmering blue gems, hung on long chains, white candles guttering within them. But the most coldly beautiful thing of all was the dais where the king himself sat. The throne was in the middle of a great apse with long, pointed windows that showered light down upon the thousands of silvery tiles running up the walls. It looked like the work of some notable magician— as if winter itself had been brought indoors in all its frozen finery.

The king's fingers danced, restless upon the horns of the two silver-winged bulls that made up the sides of the seat of Orstral. I clutched Saphritte's hand more tightly. The king himself looked like he'd been touched by snow—from his long white hair and close-clipped beard to the glittering silver plate on his chest beneath his furs. The council was gathered on the petitioner's stand and their eyes followed us up the long cornflower carpet— Constance Mollier, Everard Dorvan, and Arfrid Sandkin took us in with relaxed ease—but the stare of Lamia Folque went right to my marrow.

As we mounted the steps into the glittering apse, I noticed Gareth, standing dutifully a ways behind the throne. I was glad I knew the boy beneath the mask, who'd not twelve hours since dispatched a villain to save my life, because the serious statue by the king's side gave me a cartful of disquiet.

At the king's left hand stood a solid fellow, an enormous gray fur slung across his shoulders, looking like a wolf he'd yanked straight out of its den. The pelt's head, now flat, empty and staring with blank, jeweled eyes, gripped the tail between its jaws to fasten it. The man was handsome enough, though his full beard put me in mind of a garden hedge. A braid ran down its center, fastened with bronze beads—a fashion I'd never seen before. With a jolt, I realized this must be the Thorvald walrus, Hauk Eydisson.

Though the prince cut a fierce figure, none looked so fierce as the portly rector standing just behind the king's right shoulder. He looked nothing like mild, old Rector Wither—this fellow was dressed in rich gold-and-white vestments with jewels glittering upon his thick fingers. He had downturned jowls like a hunting hound and bushy gray brows that near covered his eyes. But no amount of extra eyebrow could cover the barely concealed hate that glittered there. There was no other man it could be other than Theodorus Heyman, the First Curate.

As we came to the gathered council, Saphritte let go of my hand, making a light bow to them and a deeper one to the king. "Your Majesty, my lords and ladies, it pleases me to present the Mayquin, Only Fallow."

My curtsy was less manners and more my knees turning to water. "Your Majesty," I managed to squeak.

The princess made her way up the steps to stand at the right of the throne. "Only's journey's been difficult. I don't think more than a gentle test will be needed, Father."

"We'll come to that in a moment," the king replied gruffly,

waving a hand at her. "First, I should like to know about the attack upon my daughter's person last night by members of our palace guard recently come from the Motte, Lady Folque."

The woman bowed her dark head. "Majesty, as these two men came from my family's house, I myself will take responsibility for their actions. They were taken on by my captain and arms master at the Motte and only recently brought into the city to bolster your own forces." Regret was heavy in her voice. "Obviously, the threat to your rule runs deeper than we'd feared."

Saphritte's eyes rolled round in her head. "Lady Folque, I don't believe—"

The king held up his hand. "Pray be still, daughter. I would hear what the head of my council has to say."

The princess's face became a picture of bottled temper. If eyes could murder, Lady Folque would have been stone dead.

A sly smile touched Lamia's lips. "As I was about to say, Majesty, the remaining man was questioned extensively by the sergeant-at-arms, and what was discovered was alarming, to say the least."

Lady Mollier frowned. "You didn't mention this last night, Lamia."

Lady Folque blinked at her from under heavy-lidded eyes. "The news only came to me this morning, Constance. Apparently, the man required some gentle persuasion in order to make his confession." I thought of Lieutenant Dahl and her "persuasion" of Jon in the Wood. What kind of "persuading" had Marcel needed?

"And that confession was?" demanded the king.

"Majesty, much as it pains me to report, the men known to my captains as Marcel Vaine and Tarique Hoorwood are in fact Rhys and Flint Breakwater, members of a prominent Ordish clan on the Blue. Yet more evidence of a growing Ordish resistance against the crown."

There was a hiss as the council all drew in sharp breaths. Disbelieving, Saphritte sought me out, silently willing me to say it wasn't so. I could do nothing but shrug and wish I'd had just a few breaths to tell her what I'd ferreted out about Lamia Folque's cunning before I'd been trapped not three paces from the woman. There were no signs the councilwoman was speaking anything other than the truth.

The princess's disbelief didn't go unnoticed. Lady Folque narrowed her eyes. "Her Royal Highness mistrusts this information?"

Standing next to her father with the council and His Majesty waiting on her answer, Saphritte cleared her throat, looking suddenly no more than a whelp like me. "It simply seems unlikely that the Ordish would be planning open rebellion against the crown. They would be outmanned and outarmed."

"I find it hard to believe you would be so quick to dismiss evidence, Highness," Lamia shot back. "Especially since you yourself came under attack during your journey from an entire band of river savages!"

Without thinking, I opened my mouth to protest, but a sharp look from Saphritte closed it again.

The king cut the disagreement in two. "We shall come back to this matter shortly, but first, the Mayquin."

"I had thought to let her rest this afternoon," interrupted

Saphritte. "Perhaps, Majesty, we could dispense with the formality of a trial?"

"Of course we can't!" snapped the king. "Would you have me climb on the back of a horse that hasn't been tested? Taste a dish made by a stranger? Why would you ask me to put my faith in a child whose talents are unknown to me?"

"I wouldn't, my lord father, if I hadn't seen them for myself," the princess replied stiffly. "After the attack upon us in the Wood, she assisted us in the questioning of the prisoners."

The king grunted. "I would still see it with my own eyes. Call in the heads of house."

The chamber doors opened to reveal three figures. One was a short, plump woman in a sober navy dress with an apron like one Mama wore when she baked. Another, a nervous man wearing carefully polished stable boots, holding his fur-trimmed hat like it might try to escape back to the forest where it came from. The third was a tall, upright woman in battle leathers, her graying hair close-cropped to her head. As the three approached the base of the steps, they all stopped and bowed. "Majesty," they said as one.

Saphritte descended from the throne to stand by my side. "Mistress Abbot is the head of kitchen and stores, Master Piers is the steward of stable, and Mistress Coppervale is the keeper of the armory. Master and mistresses, your reports, please."

Mistress Abbot stood forward. "Majesty, Highnesses, Mayquin, my lords and ladies," she began, acknowledging all of us in turn, "it's been a busy week below the stairs, I don't mind saying. The bricksmith's begun to build the new, larger ovens and the mess it's created has been dreadful. We've had a shipment of Acherian orange, though, so the whole of the stores smells divine. I've got some of them drying for the Yule grog—the ones from down in Blessing aren't as flavorful. The two new indentures need a bit more training, and if it pleases Your Majesty, I'd like to do a pheasant stew for your luncheon with the master of coin on Monday next."

Saphritte looked up at her father, who nodded. "Thank you. Mistress Coppervale?"

I tugged on the princess's sleeve as the armorer stepped forward. "Highness, I don't understand. What am I meant to be doing?" I whispered.

"Just listen and watch," she assured me.

"My good nobles." Mistress Coppervale planted her strong, leather-clad legs upon the carpet. "The forge is nearly halfway through the new blades for the reinforcements arriving from Folquemotte and Thorvald for the wedding, though the steel they've brought with them is certainly good enough for the moment. The kingsguard's leathers have come to be oiled this week, so I expect to find myself knee-deep in goose fat. And lastly, the squires have begun with quarterstaff this week. They've taken to it well, and I've only had to send one to the healers so far."

And there it was. A blue wreath flared to life round the mistress of the armory. I must have flinched, because Saphritte's hand closed on my wrist, willing me to be still. "Thank you. Master Piers?"

The stableman nodded timidly. "Well met, my betters. We've had two foals this week—one from Druskine, one from Lillithe.

Rayolian took a hit to his flank during the battle, so he'll be box-bound till it can heal. Otherwise, it's just the winter shoeing and exercising till Yule."

Saphritte nodded, dismissing the man, who scuttled back to his place between the armorer and the kitchen mistress. "Thank you, master." She squeezed my hand and returned to stand by the throne.

"Mayquin, upon my order, one of my servants is lying to me," he rumbled. "Which one is it?"

I didn't hesitate. "Mistress Coppervale, Majesty. When she said she'd only sent one squire to the healers this week."

One of the king's frosted brows raised as he turned to Mistress Coppervale, who nodded in approval. "As much discipline as you give, boys will be boys when you hand them a big stick. So far," she confirmed, "we've had four broken fingers, three broken ribs, and more bloody noses than I can count."

"I thank you all for your diligence," Saphritte proclaimed. As the heads of house filed out to return to their duties, the princess turned to her father. "Does that test satisfy you, Majesty?"

"It does not satisfy *me*."

All eyes turned to the glowering curate, who had, until then, been silent. The princess's hands unconsciously tightened to fists.

"I beg your pardon, Lord Curate, but I feel that it's the king's place to—"

"It is my place to look to the spiritual well-being of this kingdom," Heyman interrupted. "This . . . *thing* . . . you've brought"—he shuffled forward to look down at me with undisguised loathing—"its unholy abilities may have some use, but surely such a creature cannot be trusted."

"Her own trustworthiness is not an issue," the princess said through clenched teeth. "She's unable to lie—it's painful for her."

The king leaned forward on his throne. "Have you witnessed this personally, daughter?"

"No, sire, but Master Iordan assures me—"

"Master Iordan is not here," barked the king.

"We would see for ourselves, Highness," added the curate.

My heart skipped a beat, remembering the pain that exploded inside my head when I tried to lie to the inquisitor by my garden gate. What did the old men mean to do? Still glaring hellfire at me, the curate leaned down to whisper in the king's ear, the rest of the council exchanging worried looks around us.

Finally the king spoke. "How many siblings have you, child?"

"Two brothers, Majesty," I answered warily.

"I think you're mistaken," the curate interjected. "I believe you have four."

I looked at Saphritte and found nothing but sorrow in her eyes. "I'm sorry, Majesty, but I only have two—Jonquin and Ether."

Struggling to stay calm, the princess answered. "What my father is saying, Only, is that he would like you to tell him that you have four brothers."

"But, Highness . . ."

"I know and I'm sorry," she said, regret in her tone. "Please do as you're bid."

I'd promised myself I'd not cry in front of any of them. Not ever again. But in an instant, it all came down on me—I was an untested horse. A plate of food cooked by a stranger. No matter how fancy my clothes, no matter how big the jewels I wore, I wouldn't ever be more than a thing he owned to do with as he pleased. And right then, it was his and the curate's pleasure to see me hurt. Tears pooled in my eyes.

"Majesty," I said, "I have four brothers."

I yelped as a wave of misery swept through my head, making my ears pound and squeezing unshed salt water from my eyes.

The king didn't wait to pile the next question upon me. "What is your father's name, child?"

I stared up at the throne, squinting through the pain. "Ellis, Majesty."

"Surely his name is Otto," the curate prompted.

Saphritte leaned closer to the throne. "Father—"

"Be silent, daughter! Child, what is your father's name?"

"Otto, Majesty," I said, gritting it out, as another fit of agony erupted inside me. I fell to my knees with a wail, clasping my hands to my ears and trying to ignore the roiling of my stomach. Through the noise in my skull, I heard the king's voice once again.

"Tell me one last thing, child. Are you happy to be here in Bellskeep?"

Above the high whistle splitting me in two, I heard voices—Saphritte's pleading with the king to stop, the concerned whispering of the council, and even the silken tones of Lady Folque asking me if I was well. I could faintly make out Gareth's horrified face across the chamber.

I heard the curate above it all, bound and determined for an answer, his voice cruel and haughty: "Did you hear the question? Is it not an honor to serve at the pleasure of your king?"

"Yes, Your Majesty," I gasped out before the glittering light in the chamber faded into blackness.

25

For one blessed second, I believed I was at home. But like any dream, it faded before I could wrap my fingers round it.

Sharp, green smells pricked at my nose as I cracked my eyes open. The taste of asper root was on my tongue and the heavy wool of it in my head. A cool cloth that smelled of mint rested on my forehead. The bed beneath me was no more than a linen canvas, but it was more comfortable to me at that moment than any feather bed in the kingdom. Truth was, I didn't want to be awake with the memory of the winter king sitting in his terrible silver chair. I whimpered, pressing my head into the pillow.

A soft hand fell on mine. "Are you back with us, child?" The hand moved to my brow as one of my eyes, then the next, was pried open, unwilling, to face the light. "That's a bit better. Your pupils aren't pinpricks anymore."

"Where am I?" I croaked.

"You're in the herbery, my dear. Can you sit up? I've prepared a goldleaf tea."

The hands slid under my shoulder blades, supporting me as I slowly sat up. Unsteady, I crossed my legs beneath me and accepted the warm clay cup that was tucked between my fingers.

The herbery was snug and familiar, even though it was much bigger than Non's. Cream plaster and deeply stained beams reflected the dancing flames under the cauldron in the fire. The ceiling boasted carved, curling wooden vines that snaked around every iron candle sconce and down behind the enormous herb dressers. But the smell was savory and sweet, brackish and clean, strong and mild—the smell of things from the earth. Women in heavy leather aprons chattered at the counters as they mixed, ground, and poured.

I took a sip and sighed. The Acherian woman sitting beside the cot smiled. "I'm Vasha Devi, head of the herbery."

"Good met, mistress," I said, taking another deep draft from the cup. "I'm sorry I can't curtsy just yet."

Vasha laughed, her dark face creasing in mirth. "Oh, you haven't got to curtsy to me, I'm not that fine. But I can tell daggeroot from spidergrass."

"How did I get here?"

"I brought you." Saphritte appeared in the herbery's arched doorway, grim and drawn. "Mistress Devi, I know your patient is still delicate, but I would have some private words with her."

I didn't trust myself to look the princess in the eye. The

herbist inclined her head politely. "Of course, Highness. If she shows signs of tiring, I'd ask that she be allowed to rest."

"Of course, mistress," Saphritte answered.

Vasha disappeared around the corner, and the cot creaked as Saphritte sat down beside me. Her mouth opened and closed a few times, as if each time she'd expected something to come out, but nothing did. Finally, she spoke.

"In North Hallow, I told you my father wasn't a cruel man," she said quietly. "He's made a liar of me."

I didn't know how to answer. I was an empty thing, all my words used up.

"Even the council was shocked. I don't think they realized how far he'd go, especially with Heyman egging him on." Her shoulders slumped. "It's become worse just in the time I was away. You must believe me, Only, it won't happen again."

I shook my head. "It don't matter, Highness."

"It *does*," the princess insisted, but I cut her off.

"It's just like I said when we arrived—I'm a tool to fix something that's broke, and before he used me, he wanted to see what I was made of."

I knew my tone wasn't fit for speaking to the next queen of Orstral, but I reckoned I was through with begging the pardons of folk who'd stolen and abused me, royal or not. Papa always said there was more worth in striving to be *good* than *Great*. The king might've been *Great*, but he certainly wasn't *good*.

But Saphritte took my choler without flinching. Weary, she leaned against the wall behind the cot and absently ran her fingers over the thick sleeve that hid the bandages covering her wound. "Before, in the antechamber, you wanted to tell me something. You have my full attention."

I'd near forgotten about Lamia Folque after the drama in the throne room. "Last night, ma'am, when we arrived before the council and met Lady Folque? The minute I saw her, I could tell she was cunning."

"Cunning?"

"Like me, ma'am."

Alarmed, Saphritte sat upright. "What do you mean, like you?"

"I mean, she's got some kind of cunning." The princess stared at me blankly and I tried to explain. "Like a talent, a gift. I can't tell what it is, but it's a strong one, like mine."

"Are you telling me," the princess hissed, "that Lamia Folque is an augurer as well?"

"I never met another one," I confessed, "but I'm as sure as I can be."

"And yet, you say she wasn't lying last night about the attack. Or today?"

My head had finally begun to clear and all my late-night what-ifs came pouring back. "Not that I could tell, ma'am. But ain't that a worry? What if her cunning can block mine? She could be lying and I'd never know it."

"Have you seen nothing from her?" Saphritte asked.

"Not a thing."

The both of us looked at each other, caught up in our own

thoughts. "Highness," I asked, almost fearful of her answer, "you don't think the Ordish are really behind all this, do you? You don't think they actually mean the king any harm?"

"It's not that they don't have reasons to be angry," said Saphritte.

"Ma'am, they've been round the orchard most of my life and . . . they're good folk. Why does everyone here hate them so?"

"Because people are easily frightened of things they don't understand. And it's even easier to rule when they feel you can protect them from something frightening, whether it's true or not. All this city has is the memory of a great tragedy caused by the people of the river. It was so long ago, we can't even be sure it's true. But doesn't matter—people believe it. There haven't been any Ordish barges north of Timberwick in nearly three hundred years. All that people know about them is what they hear from loud, ignorant fools like the First Curate, shouting about augury and sin."

"*You* know better, though," I complained. "Why don't they listen to you?"

"People take cues from their leaders, and right now my father leads." Saphritte stared hard at the winged-bull sconce above the door. "When I take the throne, I'll do my best for *all* the citizens of Orstral."

My heart swelled like a bellows. "I want to go home, ma'am, but if I *have* to serve as Mayquin, I'd just as soon serve someone like you."

The princess gently tousled my hair. "While I appreciate your offer of service, what I came here to tell you is that I wish to make you a bargain."

"A bargain, ma'am?"

The princess nodded. "My father is one kind of ruler, but I know in my heart that I am quite another. Therefore, here's my offer: Serve my father well until the end of his life, and I swear by my crown, I'll release you from your service when I come to the throne."

The long, dark tunnel of my future suddenly sprung a light at the end of it. The king was an old man, but he'd still a good many years ahead of him. I might be a woman grown by the time he met the Mother, but it was a better thought than being a pampered captive in Bellskeep until the end of my own days. I searched her for any glimmer of untruth, but there was none. "You mean that," I said in surprise.

"Kings and queens have ruled for many generations without the benefit of a Mayquin, and the kingdom hasn't fallen apart yet." She offered her right hand to me formally. "Do we have a bargain?"

I'd hardly dared hope such a thing'd come to pass, but I knew the princess was being true. "We do, Highness," I answered, taking her hand. "So, you spoke it over with Prince Hauk?"

"Prince Hauk?"

"Well, when you take the throne, you'll be queen and king, won't you?"

"Royal marriages are a little different," Saphritte interrupted. "While I'm sure we'll grow . . . fond of each other over time, decisions of state belong to me."

So, Saphritte was determined to change what she had charge over. I wondered if I could risk trying to do the same. "Can I ask you something, Highness? For . . . a favor?"

She spread her hands. "If it's in my power to give to you, it's yours."

"I was fitted for my clothes this morning by an Ordish girl," I began, picking my words carefully in order to avoid any more pain. "She made me feel . . . at home. I was wondering, if I'm to have a . . . waiting girl, could it be her?"

"The indentures aren't usually placed in serving positions to the court . . ." The princess frowned. "Especially with the current unrest. And after what happened in the Wood, we still don't know if this is part of a larger plot to—"

"I understand," I said quickly, not wanting to lose any of the pity that might be tugging at Saphritte's conscience, "but I know I could tell if she meant me any harm. She's ever so kind. Please, Highness?"

For a second, I thought she'd dismiss the idea altogether, but she finally nodded.

"I'll see to it. But you must see to it you guard your tongue in her presence, just in case."

I wanted to say more, but Saphritte held up a hand. "I need to return. Remember my promise, but in the meantime, be watchful and wary. Serve my father with care and keep Lamia Folque at a distance. I'll try to investigate if there's any truth in her claims of an Ordish plot." She cocked her head to the side. "Mistress Devi," she called, "you can join us now."

Vasha's head popped guiltily round the corner. "You knew I was here, Highness?"

"I could feel you hovering," answered the princess, amused.

"Maybe you've got some cunning, too, ma'am."

"Mother forbid!" Saphritte exclaimed. "If you're right, this castle has all the cunning it can handle right now. Are you feeling well enough to return to your chambers?"

My head still felt stuffed with feathers, but my arms and legs weren't so heavy as they'd been. "I think so, ma'am."

"Mistress, I'm going to send for the Mayquin's new girl to escort her back to her rooms."

Lark! If there were anyone who might be able to shed some light on things, it'd be her.

Vasha inclined her head graciously. "Of course, Highness. I'll send some more goldleaf tea in a bit."

Saphritte bent down, putting a hand on my shoulder. "Remember what I said, Only. Watchful and wary." And with that, she nodded to Mistress Devi and strode from the room.

"I AIN'T NEVER heard such a load of sheep spit in my life," Lark announced as we made our way down the drafty halls of the castle. "Ordish plot. I ain't heard so much as a whisper of such a thing, not ever, even at the Southmeet."

"My family was pretty sore when I got took," I pointed out. "Maybe your folk have got sore enough over all their stolen whelps to do something about it."

"There's gettin' sore, and then there's wishin' to meet the White Lady before your time. You seen this place—swords outnumber folk. How'd you reckon anyone could get close enough to Bellskeep to do any harm without being cut to ribbons?"

"It doesn't make much sense, does it? Why pick a fight you can't win?"

Lark stopped dead as we reached my chamber door and snagged me by the elbow. "I swear to you, it's not a fight that's being picked!"

I frowned. "Non would say something about this smells worse than leftover cabbage."

Two girls, far out of their depth, stood silent in the castle corridor.

"It's probably best to jaw on this behind a solid door," Lark whispered.

The moment the latch clicked up, I could tell we weren't alone. The early-winter sun was setting and the rooms were dark but for the freshly lit fire and lanterns, so it took me a moment to notice the figure in the seat by the window. All thoughts of scheming with Lark scattered like leaves in the wind as Lamia Folque rose to greet us.

26

If **Alphonse Renart** was king of winter on his shining silver throne, Lady Folque looked the queen of summer as she stood by my window. Her cloth-of-gold gown trapped the oranges and pinks of the dying sunlight, turning her into a woman burning—more dazzling than midday in a hot wheat field. All the air seemed to go out of the room as the door shut behind us. Lark tensed at my shoulder.

"Lady Folque," I squeaked. "G-good met."

"And to you, Mayquin," she answered silkily. "After this afternoon's excitement, I wanted to assure myself that you were well."

"Well enough, my lady."

She advanced as I retreated. "I wondered if we might have a little chat, just you and I?" Her dark eyes flicked over me as I shuffled my feet back slow, not wishing to give any offense. "You're not *afraid* of me, are you?"

I pulled my heart out of my boots. "Yes, ma'am, I am a bit."

Lamia laughed like the tinkling of a hundred golden bells. "You are delightfully forthright, Mayquin—a quality so lacking in palace life. I rather respect the idea of telling truth to power." She placed her hand over the great jewel at her breast. "On the honor of my family, you will be as safe with me as you would in a room by your own good self."

There was nothing I could see to make me think the woman wasn't honest, but everything in my gut was telling me to hide under the bed till she got bored and left.

"I reckon I'm dressed for running if I have to," I replied.

Lady Folque burst out in another peal of laughter. "I must say it's rather rich to be thought so frightening! I'll tell you what—I shall sit over here." She glided back to her seat by the window. "And you may sit upon your bed. If I should make any alarming moves in your direction—which I shan't, of course—I shouldn't fancy my chances of catching you before you were able to make your escape through the door. Is that acceptable?"

I'd outrun a nest of hornets I disturbed in the orchard the summer before, so I knew for sure I could outrun Lamia Folque. I nodded.

"There now," the councilwoman said, gracefully settling herself back into the chair. "We are both comfortable." She turned to Lark, who was still half frozen at the door. "You may return in fifteen minutes to assist the Mayquin with whatever she requires."

Lark looked ready to grab me and flee. "Only?"

"It's okay," I told her, half to calm her and half to calm myself. "I'll be okay."

She nodded and, with a last suspicious look at Lady Folque, pulled the heavy chamber door shut. Not turning my back on the councilwoman, I hopped up on the edge of the great bed and sat uneasily.

Lamia blinked slow and easy like a cat before a hearth. "You don't like me, Mayquin," she observed, as if it didn't trouble her one way or the other. "And please, don't deny it. I wouldn't want any more harm to come to you."

I bit the inside of my lip. "I don't know you, lady. I just know what I heard on the road."

"Ah, from Her Highness, no doubt. And you also know that two men who came from my service—though they turned out to be Ordish rebels—tried to kill you," she said, matter-of-fact.

"That didn't boost my notion of your ladyship," I admitted. There was no way I was risking another fib. My head might just split clean open.

"I should think not. If I were in your place, *I'd* certainly be of the opinion that I was trying to kill you."

Uneasy, I scooted back to the middle of the bed. Lamia laughed again. "Oh, don't be foolish, child. I'm here for exactly the reasons I said I was. I wanted to make sure you were well after the king's questioning. I am sorry that you were made to endure it."

"Like I said, your ladyship, I'm well enough." Feeling a bit bolder, I leaned forward. "Don't suppose anything like that happens to you?"

Lamia cocked her head, curious. "Anything like what, my dear?"

"You know, if you use your cunning wrong."

"My cunning?"

"You know, whatever it is you can do. I saw it when we met yestereve, though I couldn't tell what it was."

"A cunning," Lady Folque mused. "Funny, I never knew it had a name."

So I'd been right! "That's what the Ordish call it. If I ain't being too bold, ma'am, could I ask what it is? Your cunning?"

Lamia sized me up. "How old are you, child?"

"I been round the sun eleven times just before harvest, ma'am."

The lady nodded. "I was nearly of your years when I realized what it was." She tapped a long, painted nail against the jewel at her breast. "I suppose, down south, such things are not quite so uncommon?"

Curiosity was near busting out of me to learn the truth, but I bade myself be still. "What, cunning? I'm afraid I wouldn't know, lady. I never met anyone else with one like mine. The Ordish have got little magics—glamours and the like. But you ain't got one of those, have you? You got one like mine."

Lady Folque rose from her seat with a quiet *swish* and went to the hearth, resting her elbow on the mantel, where the flames danced with the gold in her gown. "Do you know, I have never thought to speak these words aloud to anyone? Then again, I never thought to meet anyone so well suited to understanding."

Somehow, I'd stopped worrying about her trying to do me a mischief. "How do you mean, ma'am?"

"My father used to like to say that I could sell timber to a woodsman. Even when I was a child, my brothers and sisters complained that I could have almost anything I asked. I used to think it was simply because I had some skill in argument that they lacked or some particular favor of my parents, but it took a grave misfortune for me to discover the truth."

"A misfortune, ma'am?"

The councilwoman heaved a sigh. "My family and I were picnicking by the river one spring when it was very warm. All the snowmelt had swollen the banks, and the water was running very fast. My elder brother and I were playing by the bank when my little dog, Tot, wandered to the edge and was swept away. I cried and begged my brother to save him, but he didn't want to risk the river's fury. I was so frantic, I kept trying to persuade him, and finally, under the thrall of my words and against all sense, he waded into the cold river." Lamia grimaced at the memory. "Neither my brother nor my dog returned."

I sat in shocked silence, thinking how awful it would be if my cunning was dangerous to other folk. But then my heart beat heavy, remembering Sweets, Farren, and Emerick, who were all cold in the ground. For the first time, I felt something approaching gentle toward Lady Folque, who sank down on the corner of my bed.

"I didn't realize until then that I had something more than a silver tongue. I'd put too much of my 'skill' into my plea to my brother, all at once. I didn't tell anyone, of course. How was I to tell my grieving parents that I might be responsible for their suffering? It was especially knotty as my brother's death made me the heir of the family estate, so I let them follow their own beliefs that he perished in a misguided act of heroism." She stared down at the rings on her fingers. "I loved my brother," she continued softly, "and would not have harmed him for every last coin in our family's countinghouses. And yet, here I sit, the mistress of all of those treasures, and he is dead and gone."

A terrible thought struck me and I shrunk back. "So, Saph . . . the princess was right! You *do* hold power over the king!"

Lamia put her hands up in a frantic denial. "No, no, you must believe me, since that day, I have never exerted control over anyone. While I still fancy myself a persuasive speaker, I vowed I should never use it to its full extent again."

"I don't understand," I protested. "If you're not the one trying to keep me from arriving in Bellskeep, who is?"

Lady Folque pursed her lips as if she were weighing up an answer. "You'll no doubt be brought to council tomorrow, so there is little harm in telling you that we have had reports from our confidants within the meeting of the South Council this year. The Ordish are indeed planning some sort of action against the crown. Whether it is an action against the city or the king himself, we can't be sure."

"The fellows in the Wood knew we were coming," I said carefully, not wanting to give away anything having to do with Jon. "Does that mean someone here told them?"

The councilwoman smiled, but it had no light in it. "There

may be someone working for Ordish purposes inside the palace. It would certainly explain the attempts upon your life. I don't suppose I have to tell you it's imperative this is all brought to light, especially with a royal marriage forthcoming."

Saphritte had begged me to keep my distance from the woman. Non, who I trusted with all I was, had told me always to trust my guts. Lark knew her people better than anyone. So, why was I so ready to believe in Lamia Folque? I still didn't know if her cunning could influence mine—for all I knew, at any moment, she could tell *me* to go take a walk into the River. But what I couldn't explain to Lark or Non or the princess was if I looked hard enough into her eyes, there were still echoes of that sad, scared whelp, missing her brother.

"What can we do?" I asked.

"I'm afraid there's little room for compromise while the king sits upon the throne. His policies of dealing with the river people are at the root of the unrest. His daughter, however, is much more reasonable."

My fire sputtered out as quickly as it had come. "By the time the princess takes over, it'll be too late."

The councilwoman rose from the edge of the bed and crossed back to the window, where night had already lit the clear, dark sky with stars.

"Ma'am?" I asked. "Did I say something wrong?"

"No, my dear, not at all. But you've hit upon the problem," she said cautiously. "A problem it may be within my power to correct."

Her meaning didn't take root right away, but when it did,

the dread it carried was colder than the icy stream in the Wood. "Ma'am, ain't that . . . treason?" I whispered.

"Sometimes, child, we must do the things that we know to be right, no matter what the cost. I serve Orstral. And if I can make certain that there is no more bloodshed, I will do whatever needs to be done."

"So, you'll just . . . *ask* him to give up the throne for the princess?"

She nodded her regal head. "If I can do it subtly. It must appear to everyone, including Her Highness, the decision be of his own will, so I must be cautious—make sure all in the council know what's at stake before I attempt such a thing. After it's done, I shall retire to my estate, leaving my council seat to my daughter, Adalise. It simply wouldn't be right for me to remain. Not after that."

Just over a week ago, I'd been in Mama's kitchen, peeling apples. Now, suddenly, I was sitting at the heart of the kingdom, whispering treachery in dark corners. Everything in me wanted to run and hide, to disbelieve Lamia Folque. But my cunning— the same cunning that saved me from Toly—told me she was true. A seed of hope cracked open inside me. Saphritte's promise was stamped on my heart, deep and unfading as if it had been done by a smith with an iron brand. With the princess on the throne, I could go back to being Only of the orchard in time measured in months rather than years. The whole terrible journey could come to be nothing but a bad memory. I imagined the rumbling of the cart's wheels as I rolled up to my house in the valley, Mama and Papa waiting for me at the gate, their arms open wide. I imagined myself watching for the Ordish barges at harvest, eager to see Lark, Rowan, and Jon. Not only that, but with a new queen on the throne, they'd be safe from the kingsmen ever after. The thoughts were so real, I could near taste 'em.

"What say you, Mayquin?" Lamia's voice broke in on my happy thoughts. "You are unsettlingly quiet."

I wrung my hands. "Ma'am, now that you've told me this, if anyone asked me, I'd have to tell the truth."

Lady Folque raised her chin. "It is a chance I am willing to take. I needed you to know my aims, Only. I hope to never have need of a falsehood, but if I do . . ."

"You don't want me to say anything," I finished.

The councilwoman had the grace to look repentant, but searched me for my answer all the same. "You would be doing a great service for all the people of Orstral."

And I'd be back in the orchard again.

"Ma'am, not that I don't believe you're meaning well, but . . . could I think it over?"

"I'd be more concerned if you didn't," Lamia answered. "It's a simple mind that follows blindly without concern for consequences. And should this come to light, there could be some grave consequences indeed."

I shivered. The orchard. Jon. Not to mention the lady herself, risking her own neck and her family's safety.

Lady Folque could see the struggle writ plain on my face. "I'll give you leave to wrestle your conscience a while. When you're ready, send me a message."

She swept toward my chamber door, but turned back with

a last thought. "You're a brave girl, my dear. I know it'll be difficult, but I hope we can rely on your courage when you assist in questioning the prisoners tomorrow."

My heart jumped straight into my throat. "The men from the Wood, they're here? Now?"

"You mustn't fear, my dear, they're locked away quite safely."

She thinks I'm afraid. "If I might ask, ma'am, where are they being kept?"

Lamia patted my arm. "In the cells next to the barracks. I assure you, child, it's quite impossible for them to do you any more harm. They'll be questioned and then . . . justice will be done."

"When you say justice, ma'am . . ."

Lady Folque looked down at the floor. "Ordinarily, the king is quite merciful, but what with the recent attacks on grain stores and talk of rebellion, I fear he'll wish to send a message to the Ordish that dissent will not be tolerated."

"What kind of message?" I squeaked.

The councilwoman looked at me with pity. "It's not I that will sit in judgment on them, my dear, but I expect they'll hang."

LARK BORE MY tale with patience, even when it got messy. Even as I carefully skirted around Lady Folque's plan. I trusted Lark more than anyone else here, but I didn't want to burden her with treason on top of her forced servitude.

"She said they were gonna hang," I moaned, sinking to the

bed with my face in my hands. "How foolish was I to think I'd be able to do anything?"

"You weren't foolish!" Lark insisted. "You're trying to do right by your kin, and mine!"

"They can't send me down there tomorrow! Someone'll ask a question I can't answer without giving Jon away and then it'll be over for my family, the orchard, all of it."

Lark frowned as she opened the wardrobe to retrieve yet another new bit of frippery I was expected to be turned out in. "I wish we knew who the fellow was who spoke to them in Farrier's Bay. My folk are wary of landwalkers who turn up at the Southmeet. He must have seemed on the level for two dozen men to up and do something so foolhardy."

"It doesn't really matter who he is now. Most of 'em are buried in the Wood and the other seven are gonna join 'em in short order if I don't do something."

"It docs matter!" she insisted. "You think anyone's gonna care *why* they attacked the caravan? No one's gonna hear that story. They're just going to know it happened." The girl ground her teeth together. "They'll just know that some *wetcollars* raised swords against the king. It'll give that old eel leave to do whatever he likes to us."

The fury in her eyes gave me pause. "What if . . . what if that's why the fellow at Southmeet wanted them to attack the caravan?"

"What d'you mean?"

"I mean," I began slowly, my thoughts unspooling like thread, "he knew those whelps weren't traveling with us. And if all they wanted was me, there must be other no-gooders, ones who were better fighters, that would have been easier to persuade to do something foolish."

Lark threw up her hands. "So why send my folk? To get them slaughtered?"

"You just said it yourself! People are going to think the Ordish raised swords against the king. It'll give him leave to do whatever he chooses."

"So . . . you think it was done to turn folk against us? More against us, that is?"

"I don't know, but it seems more likely than a stranger with a conscience wanting to help a group of desperate men get their whelps back."

We silently chewed on that bit of gristle until my stomach interrupted with a deep growl. Lark ran her hands over the gown she'd taken from the wardrobe. "We've got to get you proper for dinner. The king's expecting you."

If there were a thing I didn't fancy, it was sitting round a table, supping with the king. What if he wanted me to demonstrate my "gift" again? "I don't suppose I could just take a bit of bread and cold meat here, could I?"

"Not likely! The whole court'll be dining tonight with the aim of gawking at the new jewel in the king's crown," she said, unpinning the brooch from my coat.

"The council's already met me!"

Lark slipped the coat from my shoulders. "You don't think the council's all there is of the court, do you? You can't throw a rock round here without it bouncing off the head of some lord or another. Not to mention the First Curate."

I shuddered to think of his hateful voice, urging me to lie to the king. The dinner sounded less agreeable than a tooth pulling.

"There's no time for this," I declared as she slid the new gown over my head careful like to avoid mussing my hair. "I only got till tomorrow morning to make sure I don't have to face Jon in that cell and to keep them getting hung!"

My belly kicked up a loud fuss once more. "Perhaps something'll come to you once you're fed," Lark suggested, clipping a gold chain to the sides of the hateful pin and clasping it round my neck. "In the meantime, I'll think on it, too."

She pulled a stray lock of my hair back into place and fastened it with one of the many gold hairpins from the dish on the vanity. Tucking more into place, she touched them all in turn, leaving behind soft points of honey-colored light behind. My hair shone, alive with orange and umber. I gasped with delight at my own reflection.

"Can't let you go to dinner this way. Any little magics are taken serious round here, but . . . it looks well on you, don't it?"

The beaming faces of Jon and Maura, glowing in the light of crowns of nightmoths, filled my head while the dancing flames of the Jack's acorn filled my heart.

"Something *will* come to me. I know it."

27

After all the fancy rooms I got trotted through that day, I didn't think I had it in me to be dazzled by another, but I'd not reckoned on the banqueting hall.

The shapely stone tree trunks and branches that vaulted the walls elsewhere in the castle closed in overhead, all cozy like, to make diners feel they'd happened upon some fae entertainment in an enchanted clearing. In the center of the long, narrow room, a huge dome made of blue glass and set with silver stars bowed up above the table. From the middle, as if it'd grown straight out of the roof, descended an enormous, upside-down silver tree, with what must've been a thousand crystal leaves that caught the light of hundreds of candles, cleverly lit from behind. The table itself was set with glittering silver, glass, and fresh greenery that released the scent of warm pine. Tall white candles guttered in the boughs of miniature silver trees along the whole length of the board.

I wasn't the first to arrive, so I was treated to the sudden stares and whispers of the crowd of chattering nobles when Adria thrust me through the doors into the hall. My stomach did an uncomfortable flip under the attention, but thankfully, Lady Mollier swept from the middle of the throng, regal as an empress in a purple gown, and took my hand in greeting.

"My dear child, you do my heart good! It was awful to see you so terribly affected this afternoon—I wasn't sure if we'd have the pleasure of your company this evening!"

A tall woman with salt-and-pepper streaking her once-red hair emerged from the crowd. A gold circlet with an amethyst shone warmly on her forehead, complementing a handsome rust-colored gown. She slipped her arm through Constance's and gave her hand a chiding tap.

"My sparrow, you always abandon me with the most frightful characters when I come to court. That Thorvald fellow could talk the hind legs off a donkey, provided the donkey could understand a word he was saying! You seem to have found more pleasant company."

"That 'Thorvald fellow' is one of their premier vintners, my dove, but you're right, as always, I have found better company. This is the Mayquin, Only Fallow. Only, this is my wife, Mariel Hawliss."

Mariel kissed me on both cheeks. "I heard of your welcome, my sweet. How dreadful! If you ever need anything, you'll let Constance know, won't you? Can't have you wanting for anything while you've got fellow cantonswomen around!"

Mollier's Hold was about two days' ride from Presston—both towns sitting snugly in the canton of Mothervale.

"That's kind of you, Lady Hawliss." I felt a warm glow of

thankfulness to be in the company of the two women who worked the same earth as the orchard. "If there's any way of getting word to my mama and papa that I arrived safe, I'd be much obliged to you."

"I'll have pen and paper sent to your chambers at once, my dear, so you can tell them yourself after the banquet," Constance declared. "Mariel will deliver it personally when she journeys back south again, won't you, dove?"

"I'd be more than glad to make a detour to your orchard, my dear," Lady Hawliss assured. "Wrennet and Ellonie will be pleased as pie if I bring back some apples to dry for Yule."

"My nieces and heirs," Constance explained. "We are a hold made up entirely of women, making us the most sensible holding in all of Orstral!"

A loud *clang* reported sharply through the hall, silencing conversations and gossip alike. Lady Mollier put a hand on my shoulder. "The king arrives, child. Come this way."

The crowd parted, its members arranging themselves in neat lines against the walls as the doors of the room swung wide to admit the royal procession. The king came first, dressed in formal robes of state, glittering with silver trim. Behind him came Saphritte, trying hard to seem as relaxed in a gown and on the arm of Prince Hauk as she did in the saddle. Her father might not have tormented her in the same way he did me, but him making her marry some walrus she didn't care for made me hate the old man all the more.

As the noble threesome took their places at table, Saphritte to the king's right and Hauk to his left, the rest of the throng glided quickly to their seats.

"You're over there, dear, beside the princess," Lady Mollier whispered as she and Mariel moved toward their own chairs.

At least I'd have the sturdy wall of Saphritte in between my body and the king's.

IT'S EASY TO forget you're sitting next to a king when there's a fancy dinner to be had. Especially after you've had nothing but road grub in your belly for over a week. It seemed only fitting that my first proper meal at the palace should serve as inspiration fuel for mischief. It tasted even nicer as it was served by Gareth, who winked me a big wink as he laid the first dish.

I had to keep reminding myself of table manners as plate after plate of the most delicious food I'd ever had appeared in front of me. Creamy soup served in bowls made of sour, crusted bread. Dainty dishes of fruit ice. Rare and dripping roasted rabbit. It wasn't till I tried to sip from a saucer with flower petals floating in that the princess gave me a crafty poke in the arm.

"That's a finger bowl. For cleaning your hands."

I brought it from my lips to see the rest of the table dipping their bejeweled fingers in theirs, then dabbing at their napkins. Shamed, I put it down on the table, hoping no one had seen.

Saphritte laughed. "You were enjoying yourself so much, I didn't want to interrupt you, but rose water doesn't taste all that good."

The princess stole a glance at her father before leaning closer to my ear. "How are you feeling?"

"As well as I can be, ma'am," I murmured, not wanting to be struck again by my cunning. It would've been a shame to empty my belly of all the lovely things I'd just put in.

"I'm glad to hear it."

The table stewards were streaming in again, whisking away the finger bowls and replacing them with platters of cheese and grapes. I speared a bit of cheese with a long, thin fork and popped it in my mouth, stealing a glance down each end of the long table at the nobles picking at their own platters. I'd been so knuckled into my food, I'd not noticed the silent row of well-dressed men and women standing outside the golden glow of the feast.

"Beg your pardon, Highness, but who're the folk behind the chairs?" I asked, reaching for another slice, dotted with red currants.

"Proctors. They manage estates when their masters are at court," Saphritte explained through a mouthful of blue cheese. "They also take care of personal business between families at gatherings like this."

My eyes drifted across the table to the man standing dutifully behind Lady Folque, waiting to be bid. He was wiry, with a neatly trimmed beard and lively, darting eyes, all dressed in the crimson of Folquemotte. Lady Folque herself was having an earnest talk with the young woman to her right, who so resembled her, they could have been cut from the same cloth. To her left sat a serious young man of the same complexion, who didn't seem to have much appetite. He raked his fork through the cheeses on the platter without fixing on one.

"So, that fellow behind Lady Folque is her proctor?" I asked, popping a grape in my mouth.

"Yes," the princess answered, her ill feelings writ clear on her face. "Maddock Beir. He's almost as well respected as Lady Folque herself."

"And the two she's speaking with—are they her children?"

Saphritte shifted uncomfortably in her seat. "Adalise and Borin."

I shall retire to my estate, leaving my council seat to my daughter, Adalise. They already looked so alike, scarcely anyone would be able to tell the difference. My jaw with Lady Folque bit at my conscience like a flea. By all rights, I should have turned to the princess and spilled the whole tale. A plot to unseat the king was too big a burden for someone like me to bear. *But then again,* a small voice whispered in my head, *Lady Folque wasn't the one who took you from the orchard, was she?* It shouldn't have been a hard choice to make, but somehow, it was.

My belly now full, other worries besides treason began to creep back. As I passed the time in the beautiful banqueting hall, my brother was passing his in a miserable dungeon, not at all far away. And tomorrow morning, if I didn't think of something, I'd be forced to betray Jon and my family. I didn't have a lot of hope that being the brother of the Mayquin would keep him from the gibbet neither. I was so caught up in my own thinking, I didn't notice the king rise from his chair until he called for quiet in the hall.

"My lords, my ladies, tonight we celebrate a great boon for the kingdom of Orstral. My daughter, though danger waylaid her not once, but twice, has delivered to us a most valuable gift."

A polite round of applause swept through the room.

"Though none of her like have been seen for many generations, we rejoice in the return of a Mayquin—a heartseeker—to the service of the throne of Orstral. She has been tested to our satisfaction, and as we enter into this new era of cooperation with our Thorvald neighbors, I trust in her to keep both our person and our kingdom prosperous and safe from all who seek to do us harm."

The stewards moved through with jugs to fill empty goblets. A familiar smell rose over the table, sweet and sour, plucking at my memories like a fiddle. I ducked my head so all those looking my way wouldn't notice. The king intended to salute my health with Scrump.

One of the heralds, clad in a blue surcoat and standing stiffly behind the royal seat, called out loudly over the hall, "My lords and ladies, I pray you to be upstanding for the king's salute!"

The moan of chair legs scraping the floor and the swish of velvet and satin filled the room. The bases of cups rang as they were lifted from the table. I wasn't sure if I was meant to stand as well, so my backside stayed glued to the chair while the members of the court towered above me.

All but one, that is.

Across from the king, Theodorus Heyman sat glowering, his arms crossed over his chest.

"My lord curate"—Saphritte's voice was velvet with an iron

rod through it—"perhaps you didn't notice, but His Majesty is about to salute the Mayquin. Has your glass been charged?"

The curate harrumphed and narrowed his eyes in a challenge. "I will not drink, Highness, I pray you pardon me."

The king cleared his throat. "Theodorus, the demonstration this morning has closed the book on this matter."

"As I said this morning, one cannot close the book upon a threat like this at the heart of our nation!" roared the rector, pounding the table with his fist. Glass and silverware rang like chimes, startling the standing nobles. How was the puffed-up partridge allowed to speak to the king in such a way? And in front of the whole court?

Saphritte obviously felt the same way. "This is neither the time nor the place, Lord Curate!" she insisted, using the same tone she did with the cavalry. It would have sent most folk scurrying, but the rector was not moved.

"I have been silenced in every other time and place. I've expressed my fears to the council and have been shouted down. I have been bid to hold my tongue behind the lectern. But, by the Mother, I will be silent no more!" He heaved himself out of his chair, his face near as red as Master Anslo's, and pointed a thick finger at me. "*That* has no place in Bellskeep!"

I'd been called all manner of things by Jon and Ether, some not repeatable in polite company, but never *that*. I shrank back in my chair.

"She is a child, my lord!" Lady Mollier's voice rang out across the table. "It's a small man indeed who sees disaster in the face of innocence."

There was some tittering round the room. The curate's face grew redder still. "There is no innocence in this, lady! Augury has been embraced to the bosom of the kingdom! I have seen it with my own eyes!"

"My lord curate—" the king began, less patient than before, but the rector had well and true gone over the garden fence.

"In these times, when the savages of the rivers lead attacks upon us, we bring one with the same deviances to our city to be our savior? No, Majesty, I will not drink to the health of such a creature! I would sooner see its wickedness drowned at the bottom of a well!"

Or at the bottom of the River? I thought, a cold hand gripping my heart.

A protest rose up around the table. "How dare you call yourself a servant of the Mother," bellowed Saphritte. "Though I'm not a rector, I'm fairly certain of my understanding of the testaments when they say, 'Do no harm to each other, for harm to one is harm to all.'"

"As you say, Highness, you are not a rector. If you were, you would see that bringing this vessel of augury into the palace *does* harm us all!" The curate pushed back his chair. "I beg the pardon of Your Majesty, but I will tarry here no longer. I fear it is the company and not the food that shall give me gutsache!" In a great swirl of vestments, Theodorus Heyman marched defiantly from his place at the table. The acolyte who'd been standing in place of a proctor was forced to scramble on his robe hems to keep up.

A swell of chatter rose up in the wake of the curate's exit. Saphritte still stood, trembling with anger.

The king's voice soared above the din. "My friends, please, let us not dwell on unpleasant divisions! I pray you, raise your glasses." He lofted his great goblet, glittering with sapphires. "To Orstral. To the Mayquin!"

"To Orstral. To the Mayquin," echoed the hall. I couldn't help but notice some of the cups never touched the lips of them that raised them.

"Now, if you please, my lords, my ladies, seat yourselves. Eat, drink, and enjoy. I leave you in the capable hands of my daughter and near son-in-law. My good councilors, I would have your ears awhile."

The court sank to bows and curtsies as the king scooted his own gilded chair back. Saphritte tried to stay him, keen to have a word, but he shook her off. The four council members mumbled apologies to their guests and hastily followed. Across the table from me, Adalise Folque watched her mother go, as her brother stared pointedly at Saphritte and at Hauk, who'd come to take her arm. I might've been imagining it, but I thought I noticed the princess meet Borin's gaze for just a moment before turning a strained but charming smile on a small, elderly lord.

In the autumn, when spiders began spinning in the trees of the orchard, I loved to watch them work—from the messy anchors they put in place, to the neat spirals in the middle. I was entirely surprised to find that my brain was weaving a web of its own out of bits of the evening. Out of Gareth and Lark. Out of dinner, and most important, out of the curate's "gutsache."

I felt I owed the old loudmouth the teensiest bit of thanks.

He'd given me an idea.

———

291

28

The herbery was dark after the glittering light of the banqueting hall. A few night lanterns burned on the walls, casting twisty shadows on the carved ceiling vines, but the room itself was empty. The cheerful space of the afternoon had become a forbidding cave of gloom and strange smells.

"You sure on this?" Lark whispered, her toes just barely poking over the threshold of the door.

"Sure as I can be," I answered, trying to remember the lay of the place in the light. "Can you think of any other way to get a whole watch of soldiers out of the way long enough?"

She shook her head. "Just wish we had a little more time, that's all."

The feast had gone on ages longer than I'd hoped after the curate threw his toys out of the crib. In the confusion, I'd pulled out a messy strand of hair and snagged a busy Gareth to send for Lark to fix it. In the few moments she and I had together,

I'd painted a quick picture of my notion and then left to rejoin the gathering and make my apologies. But no sooner was I in the door than I got waylaid by Saphritte, who wanted me to do my curtsies to some two dozen or so lords, ladies, and Thorvald nobility. As she steered me round, I got the notion she was looking for an excuse to give Prince Hauk—her husband-to-be—the slip. The party from Thorvald had taken over a corner of the hall and were singing loud drinking songs. By the time I managed to leave, it was already first bell. I just had time to hike up my gown and hightail it back to my chambers. Lark had managed to lay her hands on the stable breeches I'd traveled in and the frayed cloak from Master Wickham's farm, but I felt colder in them than I ever had on the road. It wasn't the weather I was trying to keep out this time; it was the fear that any moment, the whole desperate plan I'd stitched together would come unraveled. It came down to one stitch in particular.

"I know it was your brother and such, but . . . they attacked us!" Gareth complained when I cornered him just outside the banqueting hall.

"I told you back on the road—it's only 'cause some slippery fish told 'em they'd be able to get their whelps back if they did. They're going to hang, Gareth!"

The steward bit his lip. "This isn't something I can hide with a song, Only. This is—"

"Do you know the way or don't you?" I pressed.

"I do, but—"

"You've already done so much for me, but I can't let Jon . . ." My throat closed up tight. "Please."

I hadn't any right to expect him to be part of this desperate, half-brained plot, but I held my breath, waiting on his answer. His face twisted this way and that as he chewed it over. Nervousness started to creep on me. I was asking the same of him that Lady Folque had asked of me, and there we were in the corridor, for all to see—not even protected by a closed chamber door. Just when I thought I might have to turn tail and haul my britches back to the dinner, he finally spoke up.

"When and where?"

"Third bell, the gate outside the barracks," I put in hurriedly, before he could change his mind. "They won't give you no trouble. Jon'll make sure of that."

Gareth closed his eyes. "I can't believe I'm even considering this."

"It's 'cause you know the real villain's still out there! The one who wants me dead. The one who found a bunch of sad and angry folk to do his dirty work." I seized him by the shoulders, his wine pitcher sloshing alarmingly. "I'll never ask anything of you again. I'll owe you, in fact. If you ever need someone stabbed in the guts or have to break someone out of prison, you only gotta ask."

The steward gave a little huff. "You'll be the first person I'll come to if I ever need either of those things."

"Does that mean you'll do it?"

He nodded gravely. "But I'm out at the first sign of trouble. My wages keep my family in food and shelter, and I won't risk them. You understand, don't you?"

"There're half a million ways this could go pear-shaped, but I'm much obliged to you for even giving me an ear, let alone going along."

"Third bell?"

"Third bell."

He swept away, looking unruffled and sure of himself as if he were dangling from atop the carriage roof again. I envied the easy way he put a face on, as if there were nothing going on in his heart—like swans that look graceful above the water, but underneath, they're kicking their scaly little legs for all they're worth. It wasn't a talent I'd ever have, not with my cunning waiting to give me away at every turn.

But, in the dark of the herbery, I didn't need worry about my cunning giving me away—only the sound of Lark's and my feet as we crept round tables, boxes, and copper pots and pans.

The great herb cupboard stretched the length of the room, and even in the dark, it was an impressive sight, glass jars shining in the candlelight. It was three times the size of Non's cupboard, easy. I thought Non must've had every remedy that grew above or below ground, but the palace cupboard was another thing entirely. I brought the candle closer to the jars nearest me on the bottom shelf.

"Devil's salt, chewsop, usceolla . . . I haven't heard of any of these."

"Maybe Mistress Devi'll give you a tour in the morning if you're interested," hissed Lark. "But we're looking for just one thing, right? Where do you suppose we start?"

I looked from one end of the cupboard to the other. "If they're ordered like Non orders them, they start with remedies for complaints of the head and end with complaints of the feet."

"Why don't they just go by name? That's how Auntie Maven keeps them."

"When you got as many herbs as this, it's easier to have all the bits you need for one problem in one place," I explained, holding the candle closer to the lines of neat jars in the dark. "Non'd give her big toe to have a gander at this. Oh!" In the guttering flame, I spotted my prize, two shelves up, way beyond my fingertips. "Drat."

Lark tapped me, pointing to a rolling ladder fixed to the side of the enormous case.

"That'll squeak to high All. We've gotta do this quiet like." I glanced round, spotting a few low stools, but nothing quite tall enough to stand on to reach.

"You're smaller'n me," Lark suggested. "You can sit on my shoulders. Think you can grab it?"

I squinted up at the shelf. "Pass me the candle."

She handed it to me. "You ready?"

I braced myself as Lark bent down, gripping my knees as they bumped up against her shoulders. She began counting softly. "One . . . two . . . three!"

Lark stiffened her back as she heaved me up, settling my weight against her neck. I swayed wildly, trying to balance, leading her on a stumbling dance before the full herb cupboard.

"Stars and muck!" she swore as drops of hot tallow from the

candle splashed against her cheek. "Stop wiggling! And try not to set anything on fire!"

I reached out a free hand, gripping the edge of one of the shelves. It managed to stop our clumsy thrashing, but shook the cupboard just enough to jiggle the hundreds of jars against their neighbors.

Neither Lark nor I dared breathe. "So much for quiet like," I whispered finally.

Her legs were already starting to shake. "Quick, now, in case someone heard."

I licked my fingers, snuffed out the candlewick, and carefully handed it down to her. Reaching out, I slid the jar off the shelf and silently removed the lid. I began stuffing my pockets with the earthy herb. "This should be enough to clear out a whole stable of stopped-up horses."

Lark grunted. "I can't hold you much longer!"

"I'm near finished!" Shoving one last handful into my borrowed britches, I slowly slid the jar back into its place on the shelf, but as I went to return the lid, Lark's poor knees decided enough was enough. She crumpled like a cornstalk, bringing me crashing down with her. The lid of the jar flew from my grip and smashed to the stone floor in shards—a noise louder than the end times.

I rubbed my bruised backside as we both twigged the patter of house-shoed footsteps from round the corner.

One of the corner mixing tables was covered with floor-length oilcloth—the kind Non used to chop things she didn't want seeping into the wood. Scrambling for Lark, I dragged us across the floor and under the cloth. I was glad for the dark—my hands brushed over some things best left to my imagination as we frantically gathered in Lark's skirts and stray leaves that'd escaped my pockets. We clapped hands over our gasping mouths and fought to keep still as the footsteps entered the herbery. There wasn't much we could see from below the cloth but a pair of slippered feet with colorful Acherian embroidery. While an apprentice might not take too close of a look at what was missing, Mistress Vasha Devi would surely notice which canister's lid lay scattered on the floor.

"Hello?" Mistress Devi's voice echoed around the empty room. "Who's there?"

I reached for Lark. The Ordish girl was shaking something fierce. If I got caught, it'd be terrible. I'd be forced to confess the lot, but it wasn't likely the king'd want to waste a perfectly good Mayquin. But the thought of Lark caught made me cold all over. What was her life to the throne of Bellskeep? No more'n my brother's in the dungeon below. I cursed myself blue inside for bringing her to do such a fool thing.

Mistress Devi's slippers scraped over a piece of broken glass and she made an annoyed chuffing noise. Holding her candle down to avoid stepping on the shining slivers, she picked her way carefully toward the cupboard.

Any second, she's going to see. Any second . . .

Suddenly, there was a screech and a shout from Mistress Devi along with the ring of glass on glass. Several canisters smashed to the floor, some of their pieces spinning under the oilcloth bench. A sharp mix of smells stung at our noses.

Vasha Devi swore roundly in Acherian. Lark gripped me all the tighter. *What just happened?*

"Oh, you furry devils, look what you've done to my cupboard!" shouted the herbery mistress. "Do your mousing somewhere else! Shoo, shoo!"

Two striped tails streaked close by the hem of the oilcloth, trying to escape Mistress Devi's wrath. Me and Lark shrunk farther under the table as the bristles of a broom swished close behind, disturbing our hiding place. The herbist made a disgusted sound. "Ay, what a mess!" She was grumbling still as her slippers retreated back toward the hallway.

"She's gone for soap and water!" hissed Lark. "Quick!"

We clambered out from under the table and sprinted for the door. Pieces of glass poked through the leather of my boots, the pungent smell of clashing herbs stung at my eyes, but we didn't stop till we'd skidded round several corners and thrown ourselves down a winding staircase that led to All knows where.

"Sweet Mother!" I exploded. "We ain't half lucky! Were those cats?"

"Balon and Bonnet—they mouse the pantries. I could kiss those little hairy little malkins!" said Lark, panting. She opened her pockets of her apron so I could dump the dark brown leaves inside. "I'll get this to Rowan in the kitchens."

"And then?"

She pouted. "I still think I should go with you. You ain't never been there and—"

"We already been over this. We almost got twigged, and I ain't putting you in any more danger!"

I wanted to tell her everything, tell her she might not have to wait too much longer to get back to the river if only I could rouse my own nerve, but some helping of canny kept the words stuck tight in my chest. "Where're you going after the kitchens?" I pressed.

Her shoulders drooped. "To your chambers."

"You pull those covers up tight round your ears, just in case anyone's of a mind to check on me."

"I can give my hair a little glamour, make it look a bit more like yours."

"You're sure you'll not be missed?"

She shook her head. "It ain't unusual for some of us to get called up at night. An empty bed ain't nothing to get in a flap about."

"That's good. You'll tell Rowan thank you for me, won't you? I know he's putting his neck out, too."

She stood up again, smoothing her skirts. "I will."

Sitting on the steps, I knew I could still back out of this dangerous business, but the sinking feeling at the thought of meeting Jon face-to-face with a group of interrogators was more fretsome. But it wasn't only the business to come that evening weighing heavy on my mind. "Lark, if someone asked you to do something, something big you knew was wrong, but could lead to a lot of right, would you still do it?"

She shrugged. "I guess that would all depend on who'd suffer for the wrong and who'd profit from the right." She raised an eyebrow at me. "After all that, you ain't having second thoughts, are you?"

"No, no," I said quickly. "I just . . . wanted to know what you thought." I looked up the stairs, into the uncertain future. "I ought to get going."

Lark kissed me on the cheek. "Wind to your back, Only."

The bewitching harmony of the Ordish parting song rang sweet between my ears.

"Wind to your back, Lark."

29

When you're far from home, it's not the big differences that surprise you most. It's the little things that stay the same.

Crouched and shivering behind a rain barrel to the back of the barracks, I looked up at the moon. It was the same moon I'd blinked at through my window in the orchard a little over a week gone. What was I expecting? A moon that was square instead of round? One that was purple instead of white? It just didn't seem possible that this world—the one where I was about to try to loose six Ordish men and my brother from the king's own jail— could share the same moon with the drowsy quiet of the orchard, but there it was. At quarter on the wane, the crescent looked like my thumbnail—a curved sliver in the sky. Not much of its light fell on the castle grounds, for which I was sore grateful.

Lark's directions were easy to follow, even in the dark. *Left at the kitchens, out into the stable yard, about a hundred paces till you come to a crack in the wall that looks like a frog sitting on a man's head, and then straight ahead to the barracks.* I'd come upon the place in plenty of time, but waiting and freezing my backside off behind the rain barrel gave me too much time to chew over all that could go ill. What if the herb got too spread out in the stew to do anything? What if we ran into a troop of guard somewhere we weren't expecting them? What if . . .

My worrying was cut short when someone grabbed me from behind, fixing one hand over my mouth and the other tight round my middle. There was no River this time, but it didn't stop me fighting like a weasel. I brought my right foot down hard on my attacker's instep and was rewarded with a painful grunt. I threw my head back, my skull making a satisfying *thunk* against a cheekbone.

"Only!"

I froze, my elbow halfway to a meeting with a soft sack of guts. The hand round my mouth came away. I wriggled free and spun round to face the enemy that knew my name.

"Sweet All!" whispered Gareth, clutching his face. "You fight dirty."

"Are you soft in the head? Grabbing a body in the dark like that! Mother's milk! What'd you think was going to happen?"

"Next time, I'll announce myself with a parade of cavalry, shall I?"

"What are you doing here? I thought you were going to meet us outside the gate at third bell to take them through the smugglers' tunnels!"

Gareth leaned back against the wall, rubbing his freckled cheek where there would be a fierce shiner the next day. "I thought . . . I thought you might need some help. Didn't want you to go blundering into something I could have steered you clear of."

I didn't quite know what to say. "I mean it, Gareth," I answered, "I really do owe you."

"Yes, you really do." The steward peeked round the rain barrel. "Here comes dinner, at any rate. You trust the kitchen boy?"

Crunching up the gravel path was a burly fellow carrying a heavy iron pot. He looked like there were a bed he'd rather be sleeping in rather than hauling dinner to the nightwatch.

"Rowan? As sure as the sunrise. It would've been easy as apples to do, too. A handful here, a handful there while the cook wasn't looking."

The man with the pot disappeared through the front door. "You didn't say exactly what it was handfuls *of*," Gareth said uneasily. "It's not anything dangerous, is it?"

"Psht, no. It's just a pretty big helping of senarel. You think this is a good place to stop while we wait for it to kick in?"

"When you say 'kick in' . . . what does it do?"

City folk. "You ever had things . . . slow down?"

"What things?"

"Things below the belt."

His freckles disappeared beneath a blush in the shadow of the barrel. "What things?"

"Oh, for the love of All, your *bowels*!"

"All right!" he said, stopping me. "So, senarel . . . ?"

"Clears you right out," I finished. "And it don't take much.

The amount me and Lark collected to put in that stew should be enough to . . . well, it should be enough."

I poked my head above the rain barrel to take a quick peek into the watch house. The kitchen steward had hung the pot on a hook in the small hearth and was already surrounded by six hungry watchmen, clutching their bowls.

"Hope it's better than the stew last night, Hal," one of 'em grumbled.

"How many times?" Hal answered sullenly. "I lug it; I don't cook it. You don't like it, take it up with Ralby." Hal backed up as the soldiers descended on the pot and, shaking his head, clumped a graceless exit toward the castle.

As the last guard filled his bowl, he jerked a thumb at the youngest watchman. "Take the rest to Hugin and Neale if they've got stomach for it. If not, the wetcollars can choke it down while they're waiting for their slop."

Looking longingly at his own full bowl, the young man grabbed a piece of leather by the fire, wrapped it round the handle of the pot, and began to haul it toward a narrow stairway at the far end of the room.

"That's the only way down to the cells," Gareth murmured.

I frowned. Our escape route was a little more pinched than made me comfortable. "There's no way out down below?"

The steward shook his head. "It *is* a dungeon."

We hugged the window ledge, watching the guards shovel down sloppy spoonfuls of stew. Most of them were half done by the time their youngest member returned from below. "Those river rats were panting like dogs over the smell of supper," he told his mates with a mean smile. "I think Hugin and Neale are gonna make a show over eating it, even if it does taste like horsemeat."

"I'm not sure this isn't horsemeat," one of the others grumbled, picking a piece of gristle out of his teeth.

"Just last week you said you wanted to dine like one of the cavalrymen, Ingram. Looks like you got your wish," said the watchman at the head of the table, laughing.

Ingram flung the gristle at him while the rest of the table burst into guffaws. Gareth snuck a glance at me.

"How long do you think it'll take?"

I kept my eyes on the soldiers. "Not long, I hope. Non would only use just a pinch in some hot milk and then cut it with cinnamon to make it gentle like." The cruel words of the men inside made me feel wicked. "I don't reckon this is going to be gentle."

The first one with a grimace across his face was the leanest of the men—a tall, ginger-haired fellow with a sparse beard. He put a fist to his belly. "Damn that Ralby. He could ruin a bowl of porridge."

"Not sitting well with you, Everett?" asked Ingram, scraping the bottom of his bowl.

"Remember the gut-twist from the chicken and dumplings a few months back?" moaned Everett, clutching his side.

"Oh, don't even talk about it," complained another watchman. "I can almost feel it now."

A sweat broke out on Everett's forehead. "I think this might be worse. I—" The man sprung up from his seat at the table, his chair upending behind him. "Mother's teeth!" He broke into a doubled-over run, out the door, past the rain barrel, and into the darkness.

"How close are the nearest privies?" I whispered to Gareth, trying to contain my sinful glee.

"On the other side of the stable block," he answered, pointing to a building a comfortable distance from where we were sat.

Inside, three more men were on their feet, cursing Ralby, including Ingram. The youngest looked despairingly on his half-empty bowl and dropped his spoon to the table with a clatter as his fellow night watchmen went stumbling for the door. I could hear the squeaking and whining of their entrails as they stampeded past like a herd of spooked sheep, desperately clenching their backsides to avoid a shameful accident.

The remaining guard winced, the herb beginning to work on his insides. "Someone's got to stay at post! Quick, tell Hugin and Neale not to . . ."

But it was already too late. Two helmeted heads appeared above the stairway's walled banister, followed by the twisting, groaning bodies of the dungeon guards, who didn't stop to so much as look at their mates before bowling out the door. "Oh, hells," the older watchman groaned before he was forced to follow, his guts all in a wrench. The youth, left alone in the guardroom, looked around in horror. I thought for a terrible moment he'd not eaten enough for the herb to take hold, but then his face screwed up suddenly, and he pitched forward as if he'd been punched. His feet skidded on the stone floor at he stumbled out after the rest of the watch, a great trump of wind launching him across the wide lawn toward the stables.

"That's all of them, right?" I asked Gareth.

"There are always eight on night watch at the cells, so . . ."

The steward had hardly finished his sentence before I was out from behind the barrel, through the door of the watch house, and clattering down the long flight of stone steps.

The stink of unwashed bodies and waste hit me hard as a fist as I burst into the cells. I covered my mouth with my sleeve as I swung my head round, on the lookout for any guardsmen that might have missed the fateful dinner. Lucky there didn't seem to be anyone about except for me and the ragged men who'd gathered at the bars of their cells to jaw on their jailers' sudden attack of whistle belly.

"Only!"

Jon's lovely, dirty face pressed up against the iron between us. I didn't wait but a second before running and jamming my arms through the metal to wrap round his too-thin body.

"Sweet All, Pip!" His voice broke as he squeezed me back, pressing me into the bars. "How'd you . . ."

I waved his question aside. "We ain't got time. I reckon the watchmen'll be tied up good for a while, but they might send others."

One of Jon's cellmates joined us by the bars. "Beg pardon, miss, but I think one of them fellows had the cell keys on his belt!"

My heart dropped to my boots, but a voice broke into the middle of my vexation.

"I'm working on that."

I'd been so caught up greeting my brother, I hadn't even noticed Gareth arrive, but the steward picked up the spoons

Hugin and Neale had cast aside in their dash to the privy. From a dim corner, he found a chunk of crumbled stone and set to work bashing the spoon's handles.

"What're you doing?"

"Making do," he answered sternly, his hand curled tightly round the stone. When both the spoon's handles were pounded thin and sharp, he dodged past me, jamming both of them into the keyhole of Jon's cell. "Grab one of the torches, will you?"

Quick to do as I was bid, I lifted a guttering torch off the wall and brought it closer. Tucking his tongue between his teeth, Gareth peered into the tiny hole and began to twist and jimmy the spoons into the lock's tumblers.

"You got more skills than just napkin folding, then," I noted.

"You know how I know where the smugglers' tunnels are?"

"You told me your brother showed you, but you were too white-feathered to go in."

Gareth didn't take his eyes off his delicate work. "Well, that's true. It was always Gable that went in, not me."

"Your brother's a smuggler?"

"My father died when I was four, and we had nearly nothing. Mother and Pryn took jobs in the palace kitchens and tried to prentice Gable to the stables, but he was too willful. He was supposed to look after me, and I guess he *did* in a way, because he took me with him when he started housebreaking."

I could scarce imagine a tiny, freckled Gareth as a thief. "And he taught you how to lockpick?"

He gave the spoons another twist. "We were lucky we were never caught. And when I turned eight, I managed to get work as a steward, but Gable had gotten a taste for trouble. He's been running goods ever since."

"I have to say, master, I'm much obliged to you, your brother, and his trouble at the moment," Jon added. A chorus of agreement erupted from the men behind him.

Closing one eye, Gareth gave a last, deft flick of his wrist and was rewarded with the *clunk* of the lock springing free. He jumped back as the cell door swung open, loosing the thankful Ordish. Jon caught me up in his arms while the rest of the men clasped the steward's hand and kissed his cheeks.

"You ain't half brave, Pip," my brother muttered into the top of my head.

I didn't feel so brave. My guts were all twisted up as if I'd eaten the stew, too. Gareth was already charging up the stairs, so I grasped Jon's hand to follow.

The watch room was still blessed empty of watchmen. The abandoned bowls of stew sat on the table, a tempting sight for hungry men. Two of the Ordish made a lunge for the vittles.

"Don't!" I shouted. They stopped, spoons in hand. "Unless you want a dose of what your jailers got."

"Val, Bannor, unless you want riverguts, I wouldn't." My brother chuckled. "Senarel, was it? Non'd have your hide for that."

"I reckon if it meant getting you out of jail, she'd've used something a lot less pleasant."

Sorry for the lost meal, the two grudgingly put down the spoons. Across the room, Gareth flung open a closet and was throwing soldiers' tunics at waiting Ordish hands. "These won't fool anyone on the grounds of the palace, but once we get into the city, they should at least stop anyone poking their noses too far into our business."

The tunics swamped some of the group and turned others into overstuffed sausages. But Gareth wasn't wrong—in the dark streets of Bellskeep, it'd be hard to tell some ragged prisoners from a troop of royal guards out on patrol.

Jon shrugged his tunic over his head and went to peer over Gareth's shoulder in the closet. "Is there anything small enough for Only?"

And, oh, that went through my belly like a knife. "Jon, I . . . I can't go."

"What d'you mean? Of course you're going!" Jon answered as he nudged Gareth to one side and began to dig through the togs himself.

"Jon, I done this for you and for the orchard. I'm staying."

My brother turned to look at me as if I'd sprouted an extra head. "Have you gone soft? You can't stay!"

"I've got no choice! If I run, they'll go after Mama and Papa. But I might be able to do some good here, Jon, for you and Maura and Barrow! I can't say no more, so don't ask, but . . . just trust me, can you?"

Jon's face twisted. He wasn't a fool, but he didn't have to like the hand he was dealt. I thought I'd more fighting to do, but instead, he turned to Gareth. "I don't know you, master, and I know I already got a great debt of kindness to repay, but can you make sure she don't get into any more trouble?"

The steward nodded solemnly. "I know what it is to want to protect your family, Master Fallow. I'll do the best I can."

"We're losing the dark, lads!" called one of the men cautiously, peering out the window for any stirrings.

Gareth led the way outside into the night. The men's quick breaths plumed in the air, which was still, but for some faraway howling, I noted with a grin. It wasn't a long way between the barracks and the nearest gate, but that space of grass might as well have been a mile when I thought about trying to get all of us across it without being seen. I only had to hope that Hal hadn't been late on his rounds.

As if in response to my thinking, a clamor rose in the gate-house, not two hundred paces away. The Ordish startled and we all flattened ourselves against the barracks as six more soldiers stumbled out, groaning and clutching their bellies. The man Jon had called Val gave a low whistle. "Remind me never to get on your sister's poor side, Fallow."

"I hope Rowan don't catch any bother for this," I whispered to Gareth.

"Everyone knows you're playing dice with your insides if you eat what Linus Ralby makes. Nobody'll think twice about the kitchen boy." He poked his head round the barracks. "It's all clear!"

On feet lighter than fae, we flew across the open field, expecting the wrath of the king, or even the Mother herself, to fall down on us at any moment. But cross we did, and tumbled into the gatehouse like rabbits down a warren. Now possessed of the idea they might actually be free men with a journey ahead, the Ordish fanned out in the room, gathering bits and pieces in a thrown-away sack—hard bread, a hunk of cheese, a few short swords, and a hatchet.

The moment of their going was on me. I wished I could have a few more in the company of my brother, but time was trickling away. One of the men tapped me timidly on the shoulder.

It was none other than the thin villain who'd so frighted us in the coach. A goose egg stood out still from the back of his head where I'd cracked him with my nameday chest.

"I'm Wash Blackrudder, miss. I ain't sorry I came on this ill adventure, 'cause if there were a chance of getting my Ora back, there was nothing I wouldn't've dared. I don't deserve it, but I must beg your pardon and the pardon of this good master here for my behavior in the Wood." The man, close to tears, bowed his head in shame. "It's been near five turns of the wheel. She's almost a woman grown now . . . please forgive me."

"My non says anyone can look like a villain if you judge 'em on their worst day. I reckon the day in the Wood wasn't your best," I told him. "If I see your Ora . . . I'll tell her there's nothing her papa wouldn't do to bring her back."

Blackrudder couldn't speak, but nodded.

"Master Blackrudder, did the man at the Southmeet tell you I was in the coach?"

"Told me how to get in and all. Didn't want me to tell anyone else, though. I was supposed to bring you to a clearing not far from the battle where he said he'd meet us."

The man from the Southmeet was in the forest on the night of the battle. Waiting for me. Another thousand questions piled up on my tongue, but the wary look on Gareth's face told me I didn't have time to ask them.

Jon pulled me to him once again. Under all the dirt and stink was the smell of the orchard, and I squeezed him so hard, I could near feel his ribs crack.

"This ain't right, Pip. Me going and you staying behind."

I put on my most fearless face and thought on what needed to be said. "Jon, the fella at the meet . . . I think maybe he just wanted the Ordish to look bad. What with the grain stores being burnt and all, maybe the king's looking for an excuse to do something worse to the river folk. Maybe you can pass the word on not to do anything more foolish?"

"Grain stores?"

"The Ordish have been burning grain stores, and—"

"Says who?" Jonquin puffed up. "Why would we do that?"

Why would we *do that?* My brother was still my brother, but part of him belonged somewhere else now. "I don't know, but—"

"No, Pip, you don't understand. Food ain't taken for granted on the river. I mean, no one's starving, but everything's hard come by. There ain't a man, woman, or whelp of us who'd put a torch to a grain store, even for the satisfaction of striking at the king."

That made me feel even more unsettled. "Something ain't right, Jon."

My brother frowned. "I'll say. If we manage to make it back to Farrier's Bay, I'll ask round after the man from the meet."

"You sure you don't know anything else about him?"

"Oh, aye! I remembered something just after we met by the

fire." Jon pulled up his sleeve. "He's got a wine-stain mark on his forearm, just here. He kept his cuffs buttoned, but a water fly came and took a bite of him while we were jawing. He couldn't help pulling it up to scratch."

I bit my lip. It'd be near impossible to go round the court trying to find reasons to ask gentlemen to hoist their sleeves. But it was better to have one clue than none.

Gareth raised his voice. "Most about the city round third bell like to keep themselves to themselves, so if you look like you're meant to be out on patrol, people should give you a wide berth. If you follow and do what I say, I promise I'll get you out unharmed."

The men's faces set grim and determined as he lifted the hood of his cloak and heaved the iron bar before the door up in order to swing the latch.

I didn't want them to go. Not Jon. Not Gareth. It wasn't right I was staying behind. Tears spilled down my cheeks as the Ordish filed out into the cold street, leaving just the steward and my brother alone in the gatehouse.

"You . . . you take good care, now," I said, hiccuping at Gareth. "Find me . . . in the morning? To let me know you're safe?"

"I will, I promise," he answered, giving me a freckled smile before stepping out to let me and Jon say our fare-thee-wells.

"I'd worry for you more," Jon began, putting a hand to my cheek, "if I hadn't just seen you take out fourteen of the king's watchmen single-handed."

"It wasn't single-handed. Lark and Rowan and Gareth helped, too."

"Even better. You already got those around you willing to stick their necks out and you only been here a *day*!"

Gareth poked his head in through the door. "We need to move."

My brother, now with a foot in two worlds, caught me up in a last embrace and sang soft and sweet in my ear.

Look to the river
When we take our leave,
When round the sun we go once more.
We'll meet again,
We'll meet again.

30

When trials beset you, one following another, do not lose faith.
She will strengthen bone with iron.
She will fill spirit with resolve.
She will make in you a heart of fire.
Call loud unto your Mother and She will stand with you
in your hour of need.

—Fourth Lesson of Loren

It wasn't till I heard the nearby rumble of cart wheels did I realize I'd gotten lost.

The only thing holding me together had been the errand I still couldn't believe we'd pulled off. *It ain't over yet,* I chided myself, *they still gotta make it out of the city. And I still gotta make it back to my chamber without . . . wait, I didn't see this on the way out, did I?*

A small mountain of crates near as big as me stood in my path, just to the left of a cobbled yard. I was sure I'd've noticed such a thing if I passed it. For certain my nose would have twigged the smell, which was ripe with onion and garlic. I was near the kitchens, but not where I'd come out.

I didn't have much time to stew on that when the sound of an approaching wagon on the cobbles drifted into the courtyard.

I nearly didn't have it in me to do anything for my own sake. I didn't want to do any more running or hiding. Whatever keeping me going had been all used up.

But Jon and Gareth are out there, and you can't tell a lie to save your life! If you're taken, they're taken.

The grinning faces of the steward and my brother gave me the poke I needed. Next to the full crates, a few empty ones sat, discarded and waiting to be taken back to the fields. Without thinking, I scrambled into one, shutting the hinged lid behind me. Through the slats, I could still see the courtyard, but it was through a haze of tears. *Onions! Sweet All, why'd I have to pick an onion one?* It was the one thing I always picked out of stews and roasts, though Mama'd always tell me off. Now it felt like every one of those picked-out bits had come back to have their satisfaction.

As I blinked furiously against the whiff, the cart rounded the corner into the courtyard. It was hard to make out from between the tight boards of the crate, but it didn't look like an ordinary delivery. There were no boxes in the back of the wagon, no crates like the one I was squeezed into. No logs, no game, and no bricks for the new ovens. What there were, were people.

A single torch burned outside the kitchen door, so I could only half see the driver's face when she came forward to thump it with her fist. She was a solid older woman in hunting leathers and many days' journey written all over her. Cross that she wasn't answered directly, she pounded again.

"All's guts, open the door!"

There was a chink of bolts thrown to, a squeal of hinges, and a fed-up voice I recognized from the morning as Mistress Abbot, the head of the kitchens.

"What on earth are you doing here, Margot? At this hour?" she asked.

The cart's driver scowled. "We only just made curfew and then one of 'em got loose. Spent the last few hours tracking him down. Then when we finally got to the barracks gate, there was no one to let us in! I could've gone round the front, but All help me, any more time with these rats and I'm going to snap." She pointed back at the wagon. "Me and Lorde thought maybe since half of 'em'll end up in your tender care anyway, we could drop them here?"

Mistress Abbot took a few more steps out into the courtyard, pulling her shawl about her shoulders and squinting at the wagon's cargo. I still couldn't see proper for Margot's thick legs before the crate, but my ears were working just fine and what I heard chilled me through. The voices coming from the back of the wagon belonged to whelps. Scared whelps.

The kitchen mistress sighed. "All right, but I certainly don't need all twelve. You'll have to take them through."

Margot clapped her big hands together. "Bless you, mistress. It's been a long road from the south." She shouted over her shoulder to her wagon mate. "We can dump 'em here, Lorde!"

Lorde, a big man with nothing much to say, grunted and leapt from the seat. As Margot moved to help him, I got my first look at the wagon.

I had to jam my whole fist in my mouth to keep from screaming. Ordish whelps, from barely six to the biggest at maybe thirteen, sat huddled together against the cold, clutching threadbare blankets round their shivering bodies. The older ones were doing their best to quiet the younger, most of whom were in floods, but it was hard, due to their hands being bound.

I was sore afraid the crate I'd stashed myself in would catch light with the heat of my fury. I'd risked my neck—risked many necks—to loose those desperate men, and these villains brought more whelps like Lark and Rowan to serve at the king's pleasure?

Non's sensible voice sounded a warning in my head. *Now, Pip, don't go getting in an upset . . .*

Upset? Hens get upset when there's a snake in the coop. A *horseman* gets upset when his mount tosses him in a puddle. By the Mother, I was so far past upset that I could've pulled the stars right out from the sky. Splinters of wood worked their way under my nails as my hands curled in fists of rage, but I barely noticed. I only had eyes for the small bodies being roughly shucked from the wagon.

"Come on, then," Mistress Abbot snipped, eager to be back to her breakfast preparations. "Get yourselves indoors. You'll have a bowl of oat porridge before you start." She seized the shoulder of one of the captives as they made their way toward her. "You. You've got a bit of muscle. Can you turn a spit?"

I couldn't make out the whelp's face under the blanket wrapped round his ears, but his meaning was clear when he spat on the ground at her feet.

Mistress Abbot's hand flashed out and caught the boy a swat

across the cheek. He stumbled, the blanket falling to the ground, as the stern woman put her hands on her hips. "I think mucking out the stables might be more to your liking."

The oldest pushed forward in the queue to help, but got a boot in the back for her trouble from Margot. "Eager to begin, are you?" the woman scoffed.

Both the ragged whelps looked up from the cobbles, staring daggers at the kitchen mistress.

Lorde's beefy mitts slid under the boy's arm and hauled him up.

"Let go, you eel! You flatfish! You dirty kingsman!" he hollered, trying to kick the man any way he could. But Lorde cuffed him again, as if he were nowt but an annoying pup, nipping at his heels. The boy yelped and stopped his thrashing.

"Don't hurt him!" cried his sister, trying to get to her feet. "He ain't gonna be any more trouble, are you, Marsh?"

Her brother's body sagged in surrender, but his eyes were still speaking spite. Mistress Abbot clucked. "Take that one straight to Master Piers. I think a night getting acquainted with the horseboxes might take the edge off him."

Lorde grunted again, slung the furious boy over his shoulder, and set off in the direction of the stables. The girl tugged the kitchen mistress's skirts. "Please, ma'am, don't let no harm come to him, he's just—"

Mistress Abbot grabbed her sharply by the chin, jerking her to her feet. "We're not savages—not like your folk. He'll not come to any harm, unless by harm, you mean hard work, which you know nothing of. You'll be fed and watered, and if you're lucky, you'll come to know Mother All and her mercy. If not, you wait till whatever sloth you call kin bring the king his due to collect you. Have we an understanding, girl?"

Shaking with cold and ire, the girl said nothing in reply.

The kitchen mistress released her as the last of the whelps filed through the door. "In," she commanded.

With a last cold glare, the whelp trudged slowly into the kitchens. Mistress Abbot stuck her head in after, calling for Hal.

"Can you make a start with these crates before you go? There's room in the store next to the potatoes."

The *clump* of the porter's steps drew nearer to my hiding place and I knew then any chance of escape was about to be lost.

Please don't pick this crate first, please don't pick this crate first, please don't . . .

Being hoisted in the air while stuck in a crate isn't comfortable for a body, especially one as tired and shook as mine. But Hal was bound and determined to stack the crates as quick as he could so he could be abed, so it weren't a gentle ride. Bumping against his large belly, I tried to see anything in the kitchen before us that looked familiar—a cupboard, a staircase, a door—

A door! From between the slats of the crate, I spotted a point on the route Lark had given me—a giant arch with the winged bull chiseled in stone above it. But between me and it was a whole kitchen.

My teeth rattled as Hal tossed the angriest box of onions the palace had ever seen to the floor and set off for another. There were folk bustling about, lighting fires, and readying breakfast for the castle staff. There wasn't any way to make an exit without being twigged in a flash. I bit a nail down to the quick. If I was caught and questioned, a whole night's work would go up in smoke. Gareth and the Ordish might be apprehended before they'd the chance to get out of the city.

Thud went the crate being stacked on top of mine. I realized then I was to be on the bottom of that great pile.

The second Hal turned the corner for the next load, I tested the lid with my shoulder. It was heavy. Real heavy. Who would've believed onions could be so heavy? The next crate would trap me for good.

There was nothing for it. I gathered up every last drop of spirit I had left in my body and shoved.

The lid exploded open, scattering the onions above me like tiny, stinking bombs, but I wasn't sticking around to see where any of them landed. Pulling my hood as far down over my face as it could go, I sprinted through the kitchen, dodging cooks, spit boys, and porters. Shouts rose up all around.

"Who's that?"

"What's going on?"

"Catch that boy!"

Thanking the Mother and the stable lad in North Hallow for my breeches, I ran as if all the seven hells were trying to take a bite out of my seat. I ducked between the ovens, dove up the stairs, and plunged into the hallways of the castle above, no one in the kitchen the wiser that the king's Mayquin had just made a decision that would change Orstral forever.

Isa had three whelps who were constantly squabbling. There were many chores on the barge that needed three pairs of hand to finish, but since they could never agree, the chores went unfinished or had bad endings. They were supposed to clean the dovecote, but they fought over who was to hold the doves and some flew away. They were supposed to trim the sail, but they fought over who would tie off the boom and ripped a hole in the cloth. They were supposed to paint the barge's water-side, but they fought over who would hold the brush and they all ended up in the river.

Isa told them, "Go into the forest, whelps, and bring me back three sticks."

The whelps did as they were told, thinking they were in for a switching. When they returned, they laid the sticks before their mam. "I want each of you to try to break your stick," she said.

The whelps did as they were told and broke each stick over their knees.

"Now, gather the pieces all together," said Isa, "and try to break the bundle."

The whelps did as they were told, and although they all tried, none of them could break the bundle of sticks.

"You whelps are like those sticks," said their mother. "If you set to quarreling and holding grudges, the world will snap you in half. But if you join together, you'll find strength in what you have in common and, though the world may try, it'll never break your back."

The three whelps saw the error of their ways and were peaceable ever after.

—Ordish folktale

Lark was snoring in the great bed, but I let her be.

I should've been eaten up by my night's labors, but when I finally reached the safety of my chamber and stashed my breeches at the back of the wardrobe, I couldn't find it in me to lie down. Lark's gentle snuffling weren't the reason. I knew what I had to do and I didn't want to waste no more time.

Lady Mollier'd been true to her word. Atop the little writing desk next to the window sat several sheets of fine, heavy paper, ink, and a quill, already cut. I took a match from the silver dish and struck it to light the small oil lamp perched on the edge.

The drapes weren't drawn, so I looked out on the dark winter sky. The moon that looked down on Bellskeep and the orchard had set, making way for the coming dawn. Somewhere, out in the city, were seven men trying to make their way back home and one brave boy leading them. Somewhere, down in the kitchens, there were twelve whelps, stolen away, far from theirs. And somewhere, in the middle of the castle, there was me, scratching away by the light of the lamp. When the pale blue of morning finally began to creep over the city, there were two letters folded neat and orderly, ready to be sent.

The first was to my family.

Dearest Mama, Papa, Non, and Ether,

> *Lady Hawliss has promised to deliver this for me. She is the kind lady wife to Constance Mollier and I hope you'll receive her well.*
> *Lady Mollier has given me pen and ink so that I might let you know I've been delivered to Bellskeep safe. You know I can't lie, not even with my pen, so I can tell you there's danger here, but there's good folk, too, so I'm not afraid. Tell Non I still got my green apple skin.*
> *The orchard's been in my heart every second I been gone from it. Today, Master Iordan showed me a map of Orstral and I asked where Presston was. When he pointed it out, I felt sad at first, but then happy to know it were there and it's ours. I wish I could be there to look on your faces, but, All willing, we'll be together again soon.*

> *Your loving Only*

And the second was to Lamia Folque.

To Her Grace, Lady Folque,

My non once told me it ain't us that make choices, but choices that make us.
I choose what you choose. I choose Orstral.

Only, the Mayquin

ACKNOWLEDGMENTS

⟶※⟵

Writing's a little like mountain climbing—every piece of rope, every carabiner, every hand- and foothold on the way deserves blessings heaped upon it for its role in holding you up and helping you reach your goal.

To the amazing women of the magical Internet sorority I'm honored to be a part of: "thank you" is almost too small. I owe this entire experience to your talent, wisdom, expertise, unwavering support and sketchy GIFs. Thanks especially to Amber Tuscan-Clites and Heather Griffin for being the most stalwart of critique partners, road-trip buddies, and providers of stories that still make me laugh almost three years later whenever I think of them.

To my agent, Jen Linnan, and my editor at Putnam, Arianne Lewin, my crazy gratitude for taking up Only's story and helping me run with it. Also, for making this experience as friendly and stress-free as possible by being available to any and all first-timer questions!

To Marlene (and Tom!) England and the rest of the bookish mess at the Curious Iguana in Frederick, Maryland, for providing not only an important space for the community to appreciate books and share ideas, but for taking me on as part of the team and giving me ten to fifteen hours every week where I can live and breathe stories written by other people. Many thanks also to the PRH Westminster team for being amazing cheerleaders.

To my mom and dad, who are probably super glad that, after all that college they paid for, I've finally decided what I wanted to do when I grow up. Thanks for your unshakable love and encouragement.

To Nick, Wren, and Ellie, the housemates that I both chose and made myself, you are the best and the loveliest, the weirdest and the funniest. And occasionally, when I'm up against a deadline, the quietest.

To friends and family both near and far who have been with me on this journey in the form of excited texts and social media messages, thank you all so, so much.

And finally, to the canal boat *Galileo*: long may she sail, wherever she may be.